Cog Stone Dreams

Diane Schochet

Red Phoenix Books
www.redphoenixbooks.com

Cog Stone Dreams is a work of fiction.
Except where noted with historical persons
or events, the names, characters, locales, and
situations are products of the author's
imagination and/or are used fictitiously.

Cog Stone Dreams
Edition: 1
©2011 Diane Schochet

Cover design by GraphizxDesigns
eBook conversion by Legend Maker

FIC014000 FICTION / Historical
FIC039000 FICTION / Visionary & Metaphysical
FIC010000 FICTURE/Fairy Tales, Folk Tales, Legends
& Mythology
NAT045050 NATURE / Ecosystems & Habitats /
Coastal Regions and Shorelines
NAT01100 NATURE/Environmental Conservation &
Protection
SOC04900 SOCIAL SCIENCE/Jewish Studies

PDF ISBN: 978-1-9377819-9-6
MOBI (Kindle) ISBN: 978-1-937781-55-2
e-pub (Sony, Nook) ISBN: 978-1-937781-56-9
iBook (Apple) ISBN: 978-1-937781-20-0
on-demand (CreateSpace) ISBN: 978-1-937781-
57-6
smashwords ISBN: 978-1-937781-58-3

iii

Acknowledgements

Kathy Pratt, Kathy Sartori, Darlene
Glass, Susan Klaren-Hatzenbuhler,
Terrill Smith, Judy Cheek, Mary
Bremier, Doctor Deborah Glik, Joanne
Park, Lynn Schubert and Mary Terzian
 gave me suggestions, asked questions
and made me think. They also enriched
my life by letting me read their excellent
writing and becoming my friends.

The story of the Westbruk Wetlands in
COG STONE DREAMS is based on the
history of the Bolsa Chica Wetlands.
Bill Halpin and Marinka Horack, both
Bolsa Chica historical experts, read the
manuscript for accuracy. Bill Kettler,
another Bolsa Chica expert, not only
read COG STONE DREAMS, but also
allowed me to use a story he told me
about finding skeletons on the wetlands
and storing them in his closet.

To my friends, Allena Kaplan, Dorothy
Silverman, Naomi Gustafson, and
Carole Ann Checco, who have been
stuck reading and listening to whatever
and whenever, my gratitude and love
forever.

Anna Eisenberg, one of my two splendid
nieces in Texas, (Barry Eisenberg, my
talented artist-poet brother raised his
daughters Jasper and Anna so well and

his granddaughter Zoe is just as wonderful) talked long distance with me about our shared muses and what a book cover should look like.

Jo Ann Mapson, Elizabeth George, Caroline Leavitt, Jessica Barksdale Inclan, Leslie Lehr, Kris Neri, and Patricia Kay, great teachers and writers, l tried to learn their lessons, listen to their encouragement and kept writing.

I am so grateful to be published by Red Phoenix Books. I met Doctor Claudia Alexander, the CEO of Red Phoenix Books, in Jessica Barksdale Inclan's advanced novel writing class. At the time I fell in love with Maru, Doctor Alexander's most unique character. At that time, I didn't know about the doctorate attached to Ms. Alexander's name and nor that if I googled her name there would be more than 98 million entries about her scientific achievements.

To my sons, thank you for growing up to be good and kind men, pursuing your own worthwhile dreams. Stephen, I'm so glad your book Hollywood Stories is doing so well. Michael, I think your books will do well too and I'm delighted that you are a happy husband and father. I love you, Wendy. You've been

excellent at all your endeavors,
especially being wife to my son and
mother to my granddaughters.

To Jordan and Ryann, my
granddaughters, you are shining
examples of what nine and eleven year-
olds should be and I am so glad that
you're in my life.

Leo, you are last and first. Thanks for
being you. Thanks for marrying me
more than fifty-one years ago. Thanks
for supporting my literary endeavors and
being here whenever I've needed you
for the last fifty six years. Haven't we
had a splendid time, my love?

December 26, 2011.

1.

Dear Dessa Dreams,
My dad will kill me if I flunk my
estuarial wetlands ecology test.
What's the best way to cheat?
Afraid to die in Phoenix.

Dear Afraid,
You little twit. Just because I'm
old, experienced and don't always
have ordinary dreams about flying
backwards, tsunamis and upside
down coyotes, what makes you think
I know the best way to cheat? I
don't.
Before I substituted living for
dreaming, I used to dream about the
Westbruk Estuarial Wetlands and, as
I always say, you can learn a great
deal from dreaming. If you're not
prone to dreaming, read a book and
study. Start now. Estuarial wetlands
are important and you're probably
too young to die.
Sincerely, Dessa Dreams.

This *Dear Dessa Dream* Advice
Column was published on January
23rd this year and appeared in all of
the sixty-five *Bulletin-Gazettes*. I
first dreamt about the Westbruk
Estuarial Wetlands on September 14,
1947, when I was ten.

That day my father, mother,
Bubby (that's what I called my
favorite grandmother) and I were
driving to our rented house in Los
Angeles in my dad's beat up old
Dodge after too much sun in San
Diego. A heavy rope secured the
front passenger door. Two other
ropes held a lumpy mattress and a
beach umbrella to the roof of the car.
We drank tepid cokes from five cent
green glass bottles and I wasn't
allowed to sing my favorite 1947
popular song, "Smoke, Smoke,
Smoke Your Cigarette" because Dad
had just tossed my parents' last
packs of Kools and Lucky Strikes.
Nobody sang. Nobody talked.

My mother didn't talk because
she didn't have anything to say. My
dad and Bubby were sunburned and
believed in suffering in silence. I
didn't dare open my mouth because
Dad said my voice made sunburns

unbearable. "Here!" He handed me a map of Southern California. "Instead of talking, you chart our course."

Before I could examine the map, the car belched, coughed, and died on the coast road in Westbruk, California between the Westbruk Wetlands and Cardboard Beach. My dad got out of the car and looked under the hood. I got out of the car, took the map, and smelled the situation. Yccch! It stank!

Westbruk Wetlands, two mesas and the low-lying swamp the mesas flanked, was a gigantic oil field with rusted derricks that spat smoke and noxious fumes.

Holding the map, I crossed the street to Cardboard Beach where people lived in cardboard boxes. Trash, mainly torn cardboard boxes and jagged open tin cans, was piled high. So were the shells of old cars. I carefully skirted the garbage, fish bones and feces left by people and other animals on the sand. Keeping clear of mangy dogs and feral cats, I noticed a dark, curly haired, extremely dirty boy watching me. He sat next to a rusted shell of a car on the only clean spot of sand. "Are you going to sleep in your car?" he asked after I plopped down beside him.

"I don't think so." I pretended to look at my map.

"If you're hungry," he said. "You can fish."

"I don't eat fish."

The boy laughed, showing me his crooked, dirty teeth. There was something about his looks that I really liked. "You look like Abraham Lincoln," I said.

"Who is Abraham Lincoln?"

I didn't have time to wonder at his answer because a Gull, flying low, startled me and an arrow shot skyward from the shell of a brown, rusted car and hit it. The bird fell and splattered blood right in front of me.

"Don't be scared," the boy said. "Grandpa just shot our dinner. Gulls taste good."

I nodded, hoping I wouldn't throw up.

A broom shot out of the car shell, then, and swept the gull toward it. A dirty hand, that sported a tattoo outlined in purple and looking like a cogwheel, reached for the dead gull. The broom, the hand, and the gull disappeared.

"Whatchya name?" the boy asked.

My throat hurt and I swallowed before answering, "Dessa, Dessa Halom."

"Halom's a funny name," he said.

"Halom means dream," I said. "In Jewish. I'm Jewish. What's your name?"

"Leo."

"Oh." I turned to look at the ocean. It was a clear day and I could see Catalina Island. I'd been there with my Brownie troop and didn't plan future trips because I was seasick on the boat and kept throwing up on the island. Turning right and looking north I saw the flat line of buildings that hugged the Long Beach, California shore and, on the horizon, the low hill line of San Pedro. I took off my sandals, put them on my map and waded into the ocean.

The water was cold. When it was up to my knees, I heard Leo yell, "Don't take them!"

I turned to look at him and saw a dirty, barefoot teenage girl running away with my sandals. I waded toward shore as fast as I could and was hit by a wave. Then my coin filled pink handkerchief fell out of my shorts pocket.

My dad gave me his loose change every night. He always said the coins were slated for my college education. "Never, never to be used for anything else." We kept the money in a large bowl on our dining room table. There was no bowl in the unfurnished room where we'd spent the weekend, so I'd put my dad's spare change on top of my handkerchief, tied the pink cloth around the coins, and stuffed it into the right pocket of my shorts so I wouldn't jingle-jangle when I walked.

How was I going to tell my sun burnt dad that I lost my shoes and the college money? I picked myself up, waded out of the ocean and sat on the sand next to the map. *Think!*

Leo sat next to me. "Look at this." He opened his hand and showed me a gray stone.

"What is it?" I asked.

"A cog stone."

"It looks like a cog wheel," I said. It also looked like the tattoo I'd just seen on the hand that had swept the gull under the car.

"It's nine thousand years old," Leo said. "People use cog stones for wishing or dreaming."

"How does it work for wishing?" Before he could answer, I turned away from the ocean to face the oil field-wetlands and noticed a thread making its way down the slope of the north mesa and growing larger in diameter as it sidled across the street like a malleable wire. When it reached the beach, I realized it was a snake with a triangular, diamond-shaped head and it was slithering toward me. As it neared my map I could hear a rattle and knew the reptile could kill me but didn't know what to do about it.

An arrow whooshed by my head, then, and sliced the rattler in two. Snake blood drenched the map.

"Grandpa's a great shot, ain't he?" Leo said.

I threw up and the map now smelled as bad as anything else on

the beach and looked like a Jackson
Pollack painting.

When I looked up I saw
Grandpa. He wore dirty, faded
brown pants. A black headband held
down his filthy brown, hair. His skin
was caked grit. Probably hadn't
washed for years. He grinned at me,
revealing pink bare gums. The
toothless smile didn't put me off.
My Bubby didn't have teeth either.
What made me cringe was Grandpa
aiming his bow and arrow at me.

"Don't worry he only shoots
enemies and food," Leo said. "As
long as you don't do us wrong and
we can't eat you, you're safe."

Leo put his cog stone in my
hand. "Close your eyes and wish for
something," he said.

I didn't want to close my eyes. I
needed to watch Grandpa. He was
scary and I was scared.

"Close your eyes," Leo said.
"Grandpa won't hurt you."

Why did I trust Leo? To this day,
I still don't know, but I did.

I closed my eyes, forgot about
Grandpa and concentrated on
wishing. I needed to find the college
money. I wanted the girl to return

my sandals. I really wanted a new
two-wheeler. I knew I should wish
for my mother to get well. She had
almost died when she didn't have the
baby she was supposed to have last
year and she hadn't been the same
since. Maybe I'll wish for straight
hair, I thought. My curly blonde hair
had too many snarls and Bubby
wasn't gentle with the brush. Maybe
I should wish that my nose would
never look like Bubby's. She'd told
me that her nose used to be just as
nice as mine but she picked at it too
much. Picking makes your nose too
wide for your face, Bubby said.
Maybe I should wish that I wouldn't
end up fat like my dad or skinny like
my mother. Finally I wished that I
wouldn't get in trouble.

When I opened my eyes my pink
handkerchief rushed to shore with
the incoming tide and the sandals
were at my side.

After I retrieved the handkerchief
I asked Leo what he wanted for the
cog stone.

"What will you give me?" he
asked.

"A nickel."

"Not enough," he said.

I had to have it.   As soon as I
owned it, I'd wish for my parents to
like each other again and for the
return of my mother's health. After
that I'd get a new two-wheeler and
maybe learn how to do long division.
"I'll pay you a dollar," I said.

"Do you have a dollar?"

There were four quarters and
three pennies in the wet pink
handkerchief.

"If I do, will you give me the
stone?" I asked.

"Maybe," he said. "Show me the
money."

I was dropping quarters into
Leo's outstretched hands when my
dad yelled, "Come back! Dessa!"

"I gotta go." I stuffed the stone,
the three pennies and the wet
handkerchief into my pocket, picked
up my sandals, and ran, leaving the
map where it was.

"Wait!" Leo said. "It's a one
wish stone!"

I turned and ran back to him.
"What!?" I was livid. "How come
you didn't tell me?" I had never
been so angry. I thought Leo must
be the worst person on earth. Only
Hitler was more awful and he was

dead. My throat was killing me. I had used a perfectly good wish just to get out of trouble.

The teenage girl who'd taken my sandals ran toward us. She picked up a shell off the sand and threw it at Leo's face. "Damn you, Leo!" she said. "You took my sandals."

Leo didn't flinch. "Luna, they're not your—".

Before he could say more an arrow hit Luna's arm and she fell over, got up and ran across the street toward the north mesa of the wetlands.

"There are other cog stones over there." Leo pointed toward the top of the mesa where Luna was climbing.

Grandpa smiled his toothless smile, aimed his bow and let the arrow rip. The missile flew through the sky and hit Luna on the right wing of her shoulder. She fell.

"She's not hurt," Leo said.

"Dessa!" my dad yelled. "Dessa!"

An arrow flew past my head missing me by an inch. I couldn't breathe.

Leo grabbed Grandpa's arm. Grandpa knocked Leo into the sand, and then aimed the bow and arrow again.

Leo yelled, "Run!"

I thought he was yelling at me but Luna stood up and ran. Her long black hair rushed through a wind that wasn't there. From where I stood she looked more like a goddess in a comic book than a dirty, thieving, teenager. Another arrow whizzed by me, hit Luna again and she fell.

Dad yelled, "Dessa!"

I ran toward him faster than I'd ever run in my life. Arrows flew by me. By the time I made it to the car, I was gasping.

"Please," I said to my dad, "I have to tell you what happened."

"I know what happened, Dessa," my dad said, as he shifted the car into drive. "When I called, you didn't come. That's what happened. I don't need to hear any more words from you."

I had just seen Grandpa shoot Luna with his bow and arrow. I'd seen her fall and didn't know whether she was dead or alive. If I could have told my dad what happened, would it have made a difference?

When we got home I was so tired I put on my mismatched pajamas and went to bed without eating dinner. And though I planned to throw the cog stone into the backyard incinerator, I fell asleep holding it.

* * *

My dream starts with the voice of GOD. I hear HIM say, "Come back 9000 years with me."

"Okay," I say as I fly from the top of mountains with screeching birds and ducks over a river that rushes to the sea. I'm not afraid of these flying, noisy creatures. Yet there are so many of them that when I look up I can barely see the sky.

When I look down I see deer, rabbits, squirrels, field mice and coyotes run free on mesas and pockets of land in the river. Low-lying bushes, some flowered with yellow, purple and lilac blooms, others covered with red berries and larger red fruits shelter and perfume the land. Otters play on the sand where the beach meets the sea.

Even though, there is so much beauty here, and the place where our car died on the way home from San Diego was so ugly, I think I'm at the same location.

Now I'm dropping. I plop into the middle of a hot pool and see Leo. His skin is darker and cleaner than when I saw him last. My skin looks darker and redder than usual. "I am so angry at you!" I say.

"Um," he says as he takes my hand and leads me across the pool toward an old lady.

She smiles, baring toothless gums.

"Are we in Westbruk? Where is your awful grandpa?" I ask Leo. "Did he murder Luna? I want to know what happened."

Leo doesn't answer.

"Um. Um. Um." The old lady blows out air so sour I put my hand to my nose and step away.

She keeps smiling.

Putting my free hand in the warm water, I say, "What do you know about Grandpa and Luna?" But what comes out of my mouth sounds like "Ummmm."

"Tum," the old lady says. Leo and I, still holding hands, follow her to a cooler part of the pool. She pulls a fish out of the water. While it's still squirming, she eats it.

Leo lets go of my hand and catches his own fish.

"I don't eat fish," I say. Again what comes out of my mouth is "Ummmmmmm."

"Tum. Um. Um," says the old lady.

"Um," says Leo.

"I'm here to get a ten wish cog stone," I tell Leo. I know I'm angry at him but can't seem to remember why.

Leo takes my hand again. He leads me out of the pool and up a steep path to the north mesa of the Wetlands. The old lady comes with us. On top of the mesa we meet three other toothless, old women. I feel inside my mouth to see if I have teeth but can't tell whether I do.

The ladies carve cog stones with hard crystal rocks.

"I need a ten wish stone," I say in the Um language. I feel very smart. I may not be able to get the intricacies of long division but a few minutes into this dream I can speak Um fluently.

"You should give the cog stone back." The tiniest old lady puts her hand out as if she's waiting for me to return it.

"No!" I say. "I paid for it."

"It won't do you any good," the tiny old lady says. "You haven't had cog stone lessons."

"Um. Um. Um," the other women say in agreement as they continue to carve.

"I'm willing to take lessons," I say. *How powerful is a cog stone? I need to do a bunch of things. Like, maybe, restore Luna to life if she needs restoring.*

"Um," the tiny woman says and motions for me to sit in front of her. I lose my footing and drop to the ground. The earth shakes. A coyote jumps. A deer falls on its back. I count twenty-five men walking to where the women sit. The men turn east, drop to the ground and get into the fetal position. I know about the fetal position because I read about it in the book "*HOW BABIES GROW*" that my mother gave me before she lost her baby.

One old lady puts cog stones on top of the men's right and left

shoulders. Then the earth shakes
again. A tsunami washes over the
Wetlands. The Great River rises and
goes south. I grab Leo's fingers.
We both go under water.

When the water recedes, I'm
alone. The Wetlands are barren.
Plants and animals are gone. Only
the twenty-five men I counted are
still in the fetal position, facing east.
Cog stones are still on their
shoulders. They're dead. I close my
eyes and listen to the stillness. There
are no bird songs, insect hums, or
animal noises. I can't hear tides
slapping the shore. Then somebody
snores and breaks the silence.

* * *

I awoke to the reassuring sound
of Bubby snoring. When I was ten
we shared a bed.

2.

Dear Dessa Dreams,
*   My gramma's old and smells*
bad. I don't wanna visit her no more

*but I would like to know where she
hides her money. What should I do?
Mean Son of a Witch in Wainright,
Kentucky.*

*Dear Mean Son,
  I dreamt about a grandmother
who exhaled spoiled fish breath, told
good stories and let me in on some
secrets. If you want to learn your
grandmother's secrets, visit her, hold
your nose and listen.
Sincerely, Dessa Dreams.*

Two weeks after my first cog
stone induced dream I sat with my
family at our small banged up
kitchen table, drinking gorgle
morgle, a brew of hot milk, raw eggs
and sugar, stirred with a spoon. It
was Bubby's concoction for sore
throats. (We didn't know you could
get salmonella from raw eggs and
hot milk could cause throat-irritating
phlegm.)
  Between puffs on his cigarette
and slurps of the gorgle morgle, my
dad shouted that my mother wasn't
sick.

"Yes, I am!" my mother yelled, blowing out her Kool cigarette smoke. "I should know how I feel."

"We can't afford your doctor bills," my dad said.

"How will I get well if I don't go to the doctor?"

Dad stubbed out his cigarette, then lit another. My parents' ashes almost always missed the ugly green ashtray in the middle of the table and floated in the air. Bubby and I could hardly breathe.

"Dessa and I are going to the beach for a couple of weeks," Bubby told my parents.

My parents didn't offer any resistance to Bubby's plan. They didn't seem to care that I would be missing a big chunk of school. I'd missed most of the fourth grade due to my constant sore throats. Because I thought Leo's grandpa would find me if I left the house, I was missing the fifth grade, too.

I knew how to add, subtract, divide and multiply. I wasn't sure about long division, fractions or percentages but if I needed to know these things, I could ask my dad. He was pretty smart when he wasn't sunburned. Even without going to school much I got A's in every subject except physical education, art, and penmanship. The fourth grade teacher said she couldn't give a grade in physical education to somebody who was almost always too sick to play a game. My drawings weren't as good as some kindergarteners'. And nobody could read my handwriting. However, I knew all the capitols from Canada to South America. Ask me to read out loud, I was a regular actress. Ask me to remember what I read and explain it to you; I was a phenom.

Three days later my dad drove Bubby and me to a boarding house two blocks from the ocean in Venice Beach, California. Besides our room, Bubby and I had the use of the bath and kitchen that we shared with the other ladies, all old, all Jewish, and, like Bubby, all Yiddish speaking.

There wasn't a closet in our room. We put our hangers under our double bed and stuffed our clothes in the drawers of a dresser with blue peeling paint. Bubby and I didn't care if our clothes were wrinkled.

In the morning Bubby tumbled out of bed and prayed. She combined her prayers with stretching exercises. She touched her toes. She brought her knees to her chest and rolled out the kinks in her back.

"What are you praying for?" I asked.

"Good things."

After a breakfast of bananas and peanut butter eaten in the Boarding House's communal kitchen, Bubby and I set off for the nearest Synagogue, two blocks and an alley away. What should have been a five-minute walk took an hour and a half because Bubby's feet always hurt. The best thing to do for feet pain, Bubby told me was to put them in the ocean that fronted Venice Beach.

The only people we saw were bench sitters, old people who sat on benches and stared at the ocean. Bubby and I sat next to a skinny old man wearing a big hat. He was reading, but when we came, he closed the September issue of *HISTORY & GEOGRAPHY* magazine, looked at us, smiled, and finger combed his white beard. "It's a nice day," he said in English.

It was cold and overcast, but Bubby agreed with him in Yiddish.

"I haven't seen you two before," the old man said, switching to Yiddish.

I looked at his *HISTORY & GEOGRAPHY*. *My Gosh!* There was a picture of my cog stone on the lower right corner of the cover. "Mister," I said. "Could I borrow your magazine?" I had to find out what my cog stone was doing there.

The old man stared at me.

"I just want to see something," I said.

"Don't bother the man!" Bubby unlaced her ugly, black, old lady shoes.

The old man smiled and said, "Here."

I took the magazine and found the table of contents. An article on cog stones was on page 68. There was a picture of Luna, the teenager who Grandpa had shot with his bow and arrows on page 69. It was a painting, not a photograph. She was lying on her stomach, her pretty face toward the viewer, eyes closed, and an arrow in her back. "That's Luna," I blurted. *So she is dead.*

"What?" The old man looked at the picture.

I pointed to Luna. "I knew her," I said.

The old man smiled as if he thought I was crazy.

I read the first paragraph on page 68.

"Basalt cog stones look like stars, starfish, sea anemone and cogwheels with tooth like projections that protrude from their round rims. Many of them have been found in the wetlands near Westbruk, California. They're often buried with male skeletons. These skeletons are in the fetal position, facing east. Local archeologists believe that both the stones and the human bones are more than 9000 years old."

Despite the picture on the cover there wasn't any information about my particular cog stone. I looked at the picture of Luna again. "I know her," I said.

The old man pulled his fingers through his beard.

"I saw her fall when the arrow pierced her back," I said.

The man patted my shoulder. "This girl died hundreds of years ago. Somebody just discovered the grave. I read the article."

"I saw her," I repeated.

Bubby shook her head. "Crazy meshuganah!" She pulled me off the bench and we plodded across the wide expanse of sand and waded into the ocean. It was cold.

The Synagogue was a small building fronted by rotting brown shingles and a freshly painted white door. We went to the tiny house adjoining it, sat on the front porch concrete steps and put our shoes on before Bubby rang the doorbell.

The Rabbi's wife opened the door. She was short and plump like Bubby. But unlike Bubby, she had teeth, her skin wasn't wrinkled or pock marked and she obviously hadn't picked her nose because it wasn't too wide for her face. She wore a long dark brown skirt, a long sleeve beige blouse and a matching beige scarf on her head. She smiled as she ushered us into a small living room. Bubby and I sat on a thread worn, brown couch. The Rebbitzen excused herself. I got up to look at the books on the bookcases that made up two of the walls in the room. Not one was in English.

The Rabbi's wife returned with a tray of three glasses of hot tea and a bowl full of sugar cubes. I put a sugar cube in my mouth and drank the tea. When the cube dissolved I took another.

"I'm glad to see you," the Rebbitzen told my Bubby and me. "You're just in time for Simchas Torah."

"What's Simchas Torah?" I asked.

"See," Bubby said in Yiddish. "I told you last time. She knows nothing."

Bubby couldn't read or write. Why did she say that I didn't know anything? It was embarrassing.

"Do you have any new books to read?" I wanted to change the subject.

"I have a new alef beith book." The Rebbitzen took a skinny picture book off one of the book case shelves and handed it to me. It was the kind of book that would have been appropriate for a three-year old and it wasn't in English.

"But," I tried to protest.

"You're reading it backwards," the Rebbitzen said to me.

This was a picture book with letters that I couldn't read, and it was supposed to be read from end to beginning. When I finished my glass of tea, there wouldn't be much to do, so I took it. "Thanks!"

"Take the book outside, Dessa," Bubby said between tiny slurps of tea. "I need to talk to the Rebbitzen."

"Here." The Rebbitzen handed me a second backwards picture book.

I sat on the front porch steps looking at the pictures in the first book. Like the Dick and Jane books I'd read in first grade, there were a mother and father, and a sister and brother. But, instead of Spot the dog, there was a rather rascally cat that made a horrible mess. If you looked at the book from end to beginning, you could tell that the brother and sister were getting in trouble because of the cat. The brother told his parents that it was his sister's fault. The sister blamed the brother. Nobody seemed to know the cat was the bad guy. I opened the second book and heard somebody whistle "Yankee Doodle."

The old man who'd lent me his *HISTORY & GEOGRAPHY* magazine came around the corner.

"Hi!" I said. "Do you remember me? My name's Dessa Halom."

"Hello Dessa Halom. I'm Moish Solomon." He smiled at me, walked up the steps, and knocked on the door.

When Bubby and the Rebbitzen came, Mr. Solomon asked if the Rabbi had left anything to read.

"I don't think so," the Rabbi's wife said.

I couldn't believe this answer and blurted out, "They have plenty to read. There are two walls of books."

"Mr. Solomon translates Russian and Polish into Hebrew," the Rabbi's wife said. "The Rabbi didn't leave any books for you, Moish. But, he'll be back later."

"Then I'll be back later." Moish walked around the corner and we could hear him whistling "Yankee Doodle."

"Wait!" I tried to go after him. I wanted to look at his *HISTORY & GEOGRAPHY* magazine again and read the article about Luna. Bubby held on to my shoulder. For an old woman, she had strong fingers.

"Moish looks pretty good for eighty-seven, doesn't he?" the Rabbi's wife said.

"He's younger than Bubby?" Moish looked a lot older than my eighty-nine, year old grandmother.

Bubby and the Rabbi's wife laughed.

(I was funny when I was ten.)

That night Bubby and I peeked through the curtains in the wood partition that divided the small Synagogue into two parts, one for females the other for males.

Boys and men wearing yarmulkes on their heads carried large and tiny Torahs. Moish carried an enormous Torah. "Mr. Moish Solomon must be pretty important if he gets to carry that big Torah," Bubby whispered to me.

One of the men passed out paper flags with pictures of Torahs to the boys. A white candle stuck into a red apple topped the wood dowel of each flag. The Rabbi's wife handed out identical banners to the girls. Men lit the boys' candles. Women lit ours. Somebody turned the lights off. All those flags, whirling around, lit by candlelight looked so pretty.

I smelled something awful. The stink was worse than fresh elephant poop at the Los Angeles Zoo. The back of my neck was much too hot. Something crackled like Rice Krispies on the "snap, crackle and pop" radio ads. Someone screamed. *Probably me*. The lights went on. My hair was on fire. The Rabbi's wife threw a large glass of water at me and I started to shiver as if I were cold instead of burning up. Moish Solomon took off his jacket and threw it through the curtains. It landed on my head. The jacket was ruined, my hair was singed and the fire was out.

I wasn't bald but my hair was shorter than a boy's and I had no more curls. I felt like crying but didn't. Not until the middle of the night.

"Bubby! Wake up! My stomach hurts!" Something sticky was coming out of my private parts.

"Sha!" Bubby said. "I'm asleep."

I touched the sticky stuff, then, brought my fingers to my nose. I could smell blood. "Bubby, I'm dying! I'm bleeding to death. You have to do something!" I shook her.

Bubby switched on the lamp, pulled the feather bed off me, looked at the small spot of blood on the sheets and laughed.

"How can you laugh?" I cried. "I'm dying!"

"My shana maidele (pretty girl) is a woman tonight," Bubby said. "It is so wonderful."

My stomach cramped from my toes to the top of my shoulders. My throat had never hurt so much. I cried and my Bubby continued to laugh. I hated her.

She got out of bed, leaving me to cry alone, as she shuffled down the hall, laughing.

Returning with some clean rags, she told me to put a rag between my legs.

As I had never heard about menstruation, I assumed I was going to spend my whole life changing smelly, bloody, rags. And I couldn't understand why Bubby was so happy about it.

"You know what this means, don't you?" Bubby smiled.

"What does it mean?"

"It means you're a woman now. You can have a baby."

"I'm only ten," I moaned.

"I had my first child when I was fourteen," Bubby said.

I stayed in bed for the next three days. Between my singed hair, the onset of my period, the fact that I was probably going to have a baby any minute and an arrow shooting grandpa was out there somewhere, I thought it best to stay in bed for the rest of my life.

The first day of my period I wasn't hungry though Bubby brought in food. The second day I was hungry and ate the food Bubby gave me. The third day, Bubby said if I wanted food, I'd have to go into the kitchen to get it with the rest of the boarders. I didn't want the old ladies to see me without hair, so I starved. The fourth day I was ravenous and hardly bleeding.

In the kitchen all the old ladies, except Milke Schneider, stared but didn't say anything about my hair. Milke Schneider said, "At least she doesn't have scars on her face."

"Dessa is beautiful," Bubby said. "And always will be."

I looked in the bathroom mirror to see if I was beautiful. I had large blue eyes, a nice nose and pimples. *Where did the pimples come from?*

"Bubby, I have pimples," I said when we sat on our bench, looking out to sea. I wore a scarf to hide my missing hair so my ears felt quite cozy that cold October evening.

"Some people say that chocolate causes pimples," she said, kissing my cheek.

Moish Solomon sat next to us then. He wore the fire-ruined jacket.

"I haven't had any chocolate for a long time," I said.

"Neither have I," Moish Solomon said. "Chocolate takes away fatigue, you know."

"Nobody's tired," Bubby said. "What fatigue?"

"The kind you get sleeping on a bench at night," Moish said.

"Who sleeps on a bench?" Bubby asked.

"A man who doesn't have a bed," Moish said.

"You don't have a bed?" Bubby asked.

"Nope."

Bubby laughed. "He's teasing us, Dessa."

"Your Bubby's right. It's a nice night." He pulled his fingers through his beard.

I put my hand out to feel the air and was hit with a raindrop. "It's raining," I said.

"Come on," Bubby said. "We have to get inside."

"Bye Mr. Solomon."

Bubby hooked her arm in mine and we walked as fast as we could toward our boardinghouse. At the corner, we turned and saw Moish lying on the sidewalk under the bench.

Bubby dragged me back to him. "What are you doing?" she asked Moish.

"I like rain and sleeping outside," he said.

"Come on," Bubby said.
"You're too old for this, Mr.
Solomon."

The three of us were wending
our way toward the Synagogue when
the rain started to come down hard.
The wind blew and I felt as if
somebody was throwing wet pins at
me. Bubby wrapped the soaked
scarf around my face. Only my nose
and eyes weren't covered.

There were no lights at the
Rabbi's house or at the Synagogue.
A hand written, cardboard sign
nailed to the door of the Synagogue
said that the Rabbi and his wife had
to go to their sick daughter's house
and would be back in a week.
Meanwhile, if you had any problems
ask Mr. Moish Solomon who was
more learned than the Rabbi. If you
needed to get in the temple, Mr. Dan
Schlomo had the key and would be
back tomorrow afternoon.

"Come with us," Bubby said to
Moish after I read the sign to her.

We rushed to the boardinghouse.
I took my pajamas to the bathroom
and changed into them after I wiped
myself dry.

My grandmother took the clothes that we'd stuffed into the drawers and made a bed for Moish on the floor. He said he was very comfortable. I said Bubby and I were comfortable under our feather bed. Actually, I was the only cozy one because Bubby and Moish went to sleep in their wet clothes.

In the morning, Milke Schneider knocked on our door and walked into our room. She often came to see if Bubby would rub salve into her arthritic legs. And Bubby, always obliging, did. Milke looked at Moish, who was still on the floor, and screamed. Then she hightailed through the hall to the kitchen as fast as her arthritic old legs would go and told the rest of the boarders my Bubby was a "fallen woman."

Moish said to Bubby, "A woman of valor who can find? For her price is far above rubies."

"What do you mean?" I asked.

"Your Bubby stretcheth out her hand to the poor; Yea, she reacheth forth her hands to the needy. Strength and dignity are her clothing."

Moish left.

Bubby, who was sneezing a lot, and I went into the kitchen. Nobody talked to us. "Keep your head up, Dessa," Bubby whispered. "Don't let anybody or anything stop you from being kind."

"Kind that's what she calls it," said Milke, who had been partially deaf until that morning.

My dad drove us home that afternoon.

Four days later Bubby had pneumonia.

In the hospital she had a plastic tent over her head and tubes in her nose and right arm. "Be kind, Dessa," she whispered.

My stomach was in my throat.

Bubby looked at my mother. "Get out of bed and see to it she's Jewish."

"You too," she said to my Dad. "See to it that Dessa celebrates her religion."

Three days later Bubby was dead.

My parents promised to raise me in the Jewish faith before she died.

How do you raise a Jewish child?

3.

Dear Dessa Dreams,
Should I go into business with a
crook?
Have a chance to get rich in
Chinook.

Dear Have a Chance,
Some crooks reform. I dreamt
about one that did. Investigate first.
And if the get rich plan is as good as
you think it is, jump in. But, don't
forget to stay honest!
Sincerely, Dessa Dreams.

How do you raise a Jewish child?
Move to a Jewish neighborhood.
Mother got out of bed and
scouted. She found two areas in Los
Angeles populated with Jews,
synagogues, and Jewish Community
Centers. Boyle Heights on the east
side was a slum. And the whole
west side, Beverly Hills, Brentwood,
Beverlywood and Cheviot Hills, was

highly desirable, mostly Jewish and too expensive.

One night, in February of 1948, my parents screamed at each other because they couldn't afford to move to the west side. My dad said he had a way to fix things. My mother said his way was immoral. And what was wrong with moving to Boyle Heights?

My dad said, "I don't want to live in a slum."

My mother said, "You don't care if Dessa is Jewish, do you?"

My dad walked out of the house.

The next morning, Dad came back.

"We can't afford to gamble!" my mother yelled.

"If we don't take a chance, we'll always be stuck here!" my dad yelled back.

"It's not your money," my mother screamed. "You have no right!"

Oh my gosh! I knew what money they were talking about. Sticking my cog stone under my pillow, I jumped out of bed, sprinted down the small hallway into the dining room and started to cough.

My mother, wearing her oldest nightgown, was breathing in and breathing out her Kools cigarette smoke.

My dad, wearing his go to work clothes, puffed on the Lucky Strike he held between his teeth. His hand was in the dusty glass bowl that sat on top of the dusty, small mahogany dining table. That bowl held the money that was never, never to be used for anything but my college education. Dad looked at me, scooped out the last few coins in the bowl, put them in a pillowcase, walked through our tiny living room to the front door and left the house again.

My mother walked to their bedroom. It was the cleanest room in our house. The shiny mahogany, headboard, matching bed stands and chest of drawers were the only pieces of furniture in our house that were dusted daily. No smoking was allowed in the room because of the mattress fire that my dad had put out by sticking our garden hose through the orange curtains that draped the bedroom window. When my dad told the mattress story, my mother had forgotten to stub out her cigarette before she fell asleep; in my mother's version, my dad was the culprit.

I sat on the orange chenille bedspread wanting to discuss the college education money.

"Let me alone, Dessa," my mother said. "Leave the room and close the door behind you."

I walked out. My throat was sore but didn't hurt too much. After all, I didn't really have anything to discuss with my mother. I wasn't sure that I wanted to go to college. I wasn't sure what college was. There were other things to do with money. I still wanted a new two-wheeler.

Wondering what my dad was going to do with the college money, I ran out the front door to see if I could find him. It was dark but I could see his Dodge turning right at the corner.

I was a good runner, but never would have caught up if the car's right front tire hadn't bumped the curb, then, gone over it, smashing into a roller skate.

My dad jumped out of the Dodge, leaving his door open, and rushed around the car to investigate. Dad was fat, but moved fast.

"I can help," I panted, out of breath from running.

"Go home, Dessa!" my dad said. "It's still dark. You need your sleep."

"Do you think the skate ruined your tire?" I asked.

Dad lit a match and examined for damage. There didn't seem to be any. "Go home!"

I could tell he was mad at me. "Okay." I moved backwards because I was afraid of match flames.

Dad blew out the first match and lit another. While he examined the inside of the tire, I went around the car, climbed in through my dad's open door, scrambled into the back seat, put my head down and closed my eyes.

Dad's car screeched to a stop and I fell off the seat. "Ow!" I said, opening my eyes.

"What are you doing here, Dessa?" Dad was looking at me.

He was still angry. When I was ten, I could read my dad. "I came to watch the college money." I knew how to stick it to him.

Dad shrugged his shoulders and got out of the car, taking the pillowcase with him. I followed. It was still dark. My mismatched pajamas, the top short sleeved, pink cotton, the bottom faded purple flannel, and my bare-feet were no protection from the cold.

"Do you have something to comb your hair?"

I pulled my fingers through the hair that was growing fast.

Except for the occasional buzz of the telephone wires overhead, a bit of bird song, and the hum of other cars on nearby streets, there were no comforting sounds. I knew I shouldn't be there, standing on the sidewalk in front of MOM AND POP FRIENDLY FOOD STORE. The sign on the entrance read CLOSED. Dad pushed the door and entered. I followed. There was no light on but there was enough illumination to see that there wasn't any food in the friendly food store. The whole back wall was a bookcase. Dad lifted some magazines from one of the middle shelves and pushed a button that looked like a doorbell buzzer. The shelves turned into a door, swinging toward us on three hinges. We went through it into a well-lit small room with blackboards for walls. The names AINTREE, ARLINGTON, BAY MEADOWS, BELMONT, CHURCHILL DOWNS, DELMAR, DELAWARE PARK, FAIR GROUNDS, HAWTHORNE, HIALEAH, HOLLYWOOD PARK, SANTA ANITA, SARATOGA, SUFFOLK DOWNS and TAMPA BAY DOWNS were clearly printed in pastel colored chalk on the top of each blackboard section. Below these titles:

	WIN	PLACE	SHOW
No. 10	24.80	13.60	5.60
No. 7		7.60	3.90
No. 6			2.10

A young woman clad in a low-cut, black dress stood next to a man who sat on a high stool at a high rectangular table in the middle of the small floor. Sporting a visor on his head, the man's right arm was around the woman's shoulder. He held a phone receiver in his left hand. "Number 10 pays 24.80 to win. Number 6 is 2.10 to show so that means I owe you 26.90 and you owe me three thousand and thirty one twenty. Whaddya mean you're coming over to pick up your money? You owe me. I don't owe you nothing. Don't argue, Buddy Boy! I know my numbers."

The numbers were behind the man talking on the phone. "Can he see behind his head?" I asked my dad.

The man slammed down the phone. "What's she doing here?" He asked, looking at me.

"This is Dessa, the naughty girl who snuck into my car," my dad said, pushing me in front of him.

Why does he have to tell them how bad I am?

"I like naughty girls. Don't I, Janey?" The man winked at the woman next to him.

"I ain't naughty," Janey said. "I love you, Mugs. What I do, I do for love."

The phone rang. "Hello. Schuster Enterprises. What can I do for you?" Mugs said to the phone receiver. "Speak of the devil; I was just thinking about you. Of course you're not the devil. You are the most beautiful woman I've ever saw. Especially since you had the nose job."

Tears ran down Janey's face. *Why?*

"Schuster Enterprises ain't into betting anymore," Mugs continued. "I told you we're going legit. Yeah. Yeah. Everybody has their own money. I'm not financing nothing. We're going legit, babe. Love ya."

Janey was sobbing. Why? I couldn't figure it out.

"Quit the bawling, Janey. You know I love the wife," Mugs said. "I adore you and love her. That's the way it is."

Janey kept crying and Mugs turned to look at me. "Your daughter needs someone to dress her better and comb her hair, Willie," he told my dad. "She could be a real beauty."

The phone rang again. "Schuster Enterprises… Yeah… Okay. We're on our way." Mugs put the phone down and told Janie to erase the black boards. "We gotta go," he told my dad. "Ben and the moron are already there."

Two men waited for us in an alley behind a large brick building. "This is Mr. Serlop and Mr. Blamberg," my dad said. "She's Dessa."

"I bet you're an Odessa." Mr. Blamberg was tall and dressed in a gray suit and white shirt. His black shoes were shiny.

"No," I said. "I'm just Dessa."

The sun was up, but the alley's dirty macadam was still cold. My toes were icy. I had a sore throat that I knew was going to be horrible soon.

"Odessa is a city in the Ukraine," Mr. Blamberg continued.

"Who cares, Robert?" Mr. Serlop said. "The kid says her name is Dessa." Mr. Serlop was also dressed in gray. His suit was rumpled and looked old. He smelled like a mothball.

"Odessa's a beautiful place on the Black Sea," Robert Blamberg said.

"Look around," Mugs Schuster ordered.

I looked around and saw a bunch of enormous wooden crates.

A man holding a bullhorn stood on the largest box and looked straight at Mugs. "Do you have my marker?" he asked.

Mugs nodded. "I have your I.O.U."

"Do you know why Odessa is important?" Robert Blamberg asked me.

"I'll have to deal in a few minutes if you wanna have a chance before the big guys get here," the man with the bullhorn said.

"Who are the big guys?" I asked. My dad looked pretty big to me. He was the fattest man there.

"The guys that know what's in these crates," Mr. Serlop said as he made his own cigarette by rolling white paper around bits of brown tobacco.

"Ben, ya don't need to do that anymore. You're outta jail now," Mugs said. "Halom, give him one of your cigarettes."

My dad handed Ben Serlop a Lucky Strike.

"Give him the pack, Willie," Mugs told my dad. "I can't stand skimps."

"The reason Odessa is important is because it has the second most beautiful and second most important opera house in the world," Robert Blamberg said.

"I don't have a whole pack," my dad said.

"La Scala is the best opera house," Robert Blamberg said.

"Do you know what's in the crates?" Mugs asked the man with the bullhorn.

"All I know is they're valuable."

"How valuable?" Ben asked. He examined a crate while puffing on my dad's next to last Lucky Strike. "None of these are labeled."

I looked at the bottom of the closest box and read the word "TIT". "This one's labeled," I said.

"Where?" my dad asked.

I pointed.

"I love tits," Mugs Schuster said. "A whole box of tits, guys."

"I haven't seen a good tit in five years," Ben Serlop said.

Robert Blamberg said, "I wish I was inside the Odessa Opera House listening to Tosca."

Mugs walked toward the man with the bullhorn. The rest of us followed. "We want that one." Mugs pointed to the box labeled "TIT"

"Five hundred dollars and my marker," said the man with the bullhorn.

"Your marker will have to do," Mugs said.

The man with the bullhorn grimaced. "Get it outta here in five minutes and you can have it."

Dad and Ben tried to push the box marked "TIT". It wouldn't budge. "It's too heavy," my dad said.

"It will kill our car," I said.

Three men dressed in brown suits walked into the alley.

"Give me the five hundred," the man with the bullhorn said. "This has to look legit."

Robert took crisp bills out of a new black, leather wallet. Ben took money that looked like it had been buried in a vacant lot for ten years out of his faded beige burlap tobacco pouch. And my dad took my college education out of the pillowcase. They handed the money to Mugs who counted it faster than I'd ever seen money counted. "Three hundred dollars and twenty-three cents," Mugs said.

The man with the bullhorn shouted, "Lot 71 has been sold to Schuster Enterprises."

"Now what are we going to do with it?" Mugs said to nobody at all.

"The big box will kill our car," I repeated.

One of the brown suited men came by and asked which one us represented Schuster Enterprises.

"I'm Mugs Schuster," Mugs said.

Another brown suited man told the first brown suited man, "Schuster Enterprises is a Jew bookie joint. Don't get involved."

"But they have ti—"said the first man before he was interrupted.

"There has to be other boxes of ti-," the second man said before my dad cut him off.

"I'm William Halom, president of Universal Container Ware," my dad said. "I can deal with you."

"Are you a Jew?"

"How much will you give us for the container?" My dad ignored the man's question.

"How much do you want?" the man asked.

"How much are you offering?"

"Five thousand."

"Great," Robert Blamberg said. "Odessa here I come."

"I am the President of Universal and its certified dealer. Mr. Blamberg's my leg man," my dad said with an authority in his voice that I'd never heard before.

"How much do you want?" the first brown suited man asked.

"Twenty-five thousand," my dad said.

"Cash," Ben Serlop said.

"Ten thousand," Second brown suit said.

They settled at twelve thousand.

That night, as we sat at the dining room table, Dad replaced the money he took in the morning. Then he added two new one hundred dollar bills. "This is for Dessa's college education," he said. "Never, never to be used for anything else."

I was so elated. I had been happy all day. Then my mother told my dad, "You sold yourself to the devil." She walked through the hall to their bedroom.

When I was older, my dad explained that "tit" was titanium. And a box of titanium was worth more than a box of gold.

A week after he sold the box of "tit" to the "brown suits," Dad quit his job and spent his days buying and selling. We were out of debt and getting rich, he said. "Wasn't that great!"

"No," my mother said. "No person with any kind of morals would go into business with Mr. Schuster, Mr. Serlop or Mr. Blamberg."

"We can afford to move to a good Jewish neighborhood," my dad said.

Mother closed her mouth.

Mr. Serlop died of natural causes in 1949. Mugs Schuster was arrested for income tax evasion and died in jail. Mr. Blamberg took his family every year to attend the operas at La

Scala in Milan and the Met in New York.

And we moved.

4.

Dear Dessa Dreams,

I need to make a living. I tried to write a book, but couldn't spell so I quit. I wanted to be a baker and tried to bake a cake; it exploded in my oven. I wanted to be a running coach and tried to run a marathon. I twisted my ankle before the end of the first mile. How do I fake a resume?
Failing in Fontana.

Dear Failing,

Make it don't fake it. I dreamt about a man who started as a bus boy. Now he owns a chain of dog food restaurants. There is a spell check on your computer so you can write a book. Use a better cake recipe and you'll learn to bake. Your ankle will get better and you'll run again. If one thing is impossible,

attempt something else. Anything is
possible if you keep trying.
Sincerely, Dessa Dreams.

We moved to the west side of
Los Angeles in the summer of 1949.
As soon as I crammed my books into
my new maple bookcase and stuffed
my new and old clothes into my new
maple dresser, I took off to explore
the neighborhood that my dad said
was full of people just like us, newly
rich and Jewish. Every one of them,
he said, wanted the very best for
their children. Every one of them
wanted their children to be raised
with good Jewish values.

In the old neighborhood our
house was a two-bedroom, one bath
bungalow that needed painting.
Weeds grew to my dad's waist in the
front yard, an incinerator for burning
garbage was in the back and a
termite-infested fence surrounded the
whole sorry lot. Most of the other
houses looked just as bad as ours.
Though some were a little bit neater
and two doors down there was a
spectacular dahlia garden that
everybody in the neighborhood
treated with reverence.

All the houses in the new neighborhood were freshly painted and neatly manicured. There were no spectacular gardens and hardly any weeds. After an hour of scouting the streets, I knew the old neighborhood was the better place. The new area was too quiet. There were no visible twelve year olds playing in the streets. I went home and asked my parents why we'd moved to such a horrible place.

My mother said, "Take your clothes out of the dresser and hang them in your closet. Your dresser is only for your pajamas, underwear and folded sweaters."

Who is this mother? Doesn't she realize the severity of the situation? "What am I going to do?" I said. "Everybody needs friends."

"Hang your clothes in your closet and organize your books," my dad said. "Then we'll discuss it."

My dad's solution was to find the playgrounds, the parks, the schools and the library. "That's where you'll find other kids," he said.

I searched for days. There were no playgrounds, parks, schools, or library in the ten by six block tract of houses we now called home. I was so angry; I moped in my room for three days. The weather was conducive to moping. The first two days combined June gloom and gray smog. The third day it rained.

The fourth day was clear sky gorgeous. Nothing smells fresher than a June day in Southern California after it rains. Not being able to stay inside, I jumped on my new bike.

Two blocks from my house I spotted a girl wearing a wool plaid skirt, a silk blouse and a cashmere sweater. Her brown and white saddle shoes retained a shine while sinking in mud. She sat on a cardboard box in the one vacant lot in the neighborhood and wrote in a large red notebook. Thinking she was my age, I fell off my bike, dumped it on the sidewalk, walked right into the muddy lot and sat on the box next to her. The box collapsed and she laughed. I liked her immediately.

"I'm busy," she said when she stopped laughing.

"I'm Dessa," I said.

"I'm Jean," she said. "I'm very busy."

"What are you doing?"

"I'm writing a poem." Jean waved a number two yellow pencil in the air as if it were a magic wand.

"What about?" I asked, wishing that I'd brought a pencil and tablet. I'd never written a poem but it seemed like a good enterprise.

"I'm writing about mud," she said.

"Oh, I can help," I said. "There is a bud in the mud." I pointed at a dandelion.

"There's a thud in the mud. We can chew our cud in the mud. The mud is a dud. What about suds in the muds?"

"Put your fingers in the mud," Jean said.

I thought this was silly but so wanted companionship I would have pet a lion if she'd asked. I touched the mud and quickly drew my fingers away.

"Keep your hands there," Jean ordered.

I pressed my fingers into the mud and didn't like the sensation.

"What do you feel?"

"Wet mud," I said.

"What's another word?" she asked.

"Another word?" *What is she talking about?*

"Another word for wet," she said. "Another word to describe the mud."

"Moist?"

"What about sodden?" she said.

"The sodden mud came down with a thud," I said.

"After the rain, I walked in the mud, sinking into the sodden---. Sodden what?" she asked.

"Sinking into the sodden soil," I said.

"Sinking into the sodden soil of the only vacant lot," she said.

"The lot with a pot," I said rubbing my dirty hand across the cardboard box.

"Oh Dessa!"

I could tell she was disappointed with me but had no idea why.

"Why did you ruin it with the pot lot rhyme?" she said. "I thought you had something with the sodden soil."

"Did you think I was a kindred spirit?" I asked.

"So you've read *ANNE OF GREEN GABLES,*" she said.

I nodded. I liked sitting on a flattened cardboard box, thinking about words to describe mud.

After that, I saw Jean Sturmss almost every day, and when I started seventh grade, I started with a friend.

On the third week of school Jean and I sat in the school cafeteria picking at our meatloaf, mashed potatoes, and canned string beans.

"My parents think if I hang around Jewish people, I'll get to be Jewish by osmosis," I said, hoping I wouldn't gag on the gray looking string beans.

"Being Jewish is great," she said. "My mom says it's a practical religion."

"Why?"

"My mom converted to Judaism. She says every Jewish rule has a reason." Jean formed flowers with her string beans and mashed potatoes.

"What do you mean?"

"I'm going to Paris." She took a tiny bite of meatloaf.

"What are you going to do in Paris?" I asked.

"Same as here," she said. "Go to school. We have an apartment in Paris."

"You can't go," I said. "You have to speak French in Paris."

"Je parle francais," she said. "Don't worry. I'll be back."

Jean left the following day and I didn't hear from her, not by letter or western union, until she returned three months later.

I was so angry. How could she leave without giving me enough warning to get used to the idea? I didn't talk to anybody at school. Afternoons and evenings I moped in my room.

After enduring my unpleasant behavior for three weeks, my parents enrolled me in the Hadin-Blass School of Dramatic Arts. My parents loved theater. Before my mother lost the baby, they used to invite their friends over to read plays out loud. I had watched them use lampshades as hats, rulers as swords, and doilies as blankets. My parents were hams; they over acted but I thought they had lots of talent.

The Hadin-Blass School was a
100-seat theater with a small
proscenium stage. Dad signed me
up, paid my tuition and introduced
me to Dan Blass and his wife Marie
Hadin in the small foyer that served
as the theater entrance.

Marie, a slim, beautifully dressed
blonde lady, sported more makeup
than any woman I'd ever seen. Her
eyelashes were so weighed down
with mascara; I wondered how she
kept her eyes open. When she said I
would be perfect for the role they
had in mind for me; my dad left.

Dan Blass agreed with his wife.
He was the kind of bald man you
probably wouldn't notice unless you
listened to "MY PAL RICHIE"
every week on the radio. Dan Blass
was Richie's kind but gruff
grandfather. After one hour in
drama school, I discovered Mr. Blass
was not an actor. He was kind and
gruff in real life.

Marie and Dan gave me the part
of the teenage daughter in PORTIA
WON'T RETURN. If I hadn't
enrolled, I don't know what Marie
and Dan would have done. There
were no other kids in the drama

school to play the part of the young teenager who interfered with everything and everybody. For the first two acts, I was considered a pest. But, luckily for me, I caught leukemia and died in the middle of Act III. My parents, grandparents and uncle and aunt spent the rest of the play wishing I would return to life.

I got to see the real Marie Hadin in my second week of acting school. Why in the hell hadn't I memorized my lines, she wanted to know.

Was I supposed to memorize lines? Had anybody mentioned it? My parents put on plays. They never memorized lines.

Was I an idiot? How was Marie supposed to work with an idiot? The play was opening in less than a month. I didn't know my lines and hadn't been blocked.

"Start blocking her now," Dan said. He was moving a couch from stage left to stage right.

"Stage right", "stage left", "up stage" and "down stage" were the only words I'd memorized during the week between classes.

"She can learn the lines as she goes," Dan said.

A week later I lost my script. Afraid of getting in trouble, I didn't mention the loss to anybody and arrived at the theater with no lines memorized again.

Marie employed her fail-safe method for dealing with stupid actors; she whispered my lines to me. "I've lost the pumpkin," Marie whispered.

"I've lost the pumpkin," I said.

"With feeling," Marie whispered.

"I've lost the pumpkin with feeling."

"Say that you lost the pumpkin and look behind the couch," Marie whispered.

I could tell her teeth were clenched and I wasn't sure which couch I was to look behind. There were two on stage. Marie shoved me to stage right.

Pasted on the back of the couch were two pages of my lines with instructions on what to do as I said them. Marie and Dan were resourceful. My problem: If I stood, I couldn't see the lines. If I knelt the audience wouldn't see me.

Dan stood in the back row. "I can't hear you, Dessa," he said.

"Enunciate the words, Dessa."

"Pumpkin, Dessa."

"Project, Dessa."

"Project!"

"Use your diaphragm."

"Project!"

"Don't yell!"

"Project!"

Three weeks later I was exhausted, still didn't know my lines and Dan explained "hell" week. As soon as school was over, I was to rush to the theater and bring my dinner in a brown paper sack. We'd be rehearsing until ten; some nights we'd probably go to midnight or later.

"My parents won't let me stay till midnight." I wasn't sure whether they would or wouldn't. Both of them would have loved to be actors. Maybe they would think that staying up late wasn't too much to suffer for art.

We stumbled through the rehearsal the next day. I knew how bad I was. I knew that people of integrity would not charge money to see me in a play.

The following day I still didn't know my lines but I knew where to find them posted and I managed, though not very well. Dan and the other actors said they couldn't hear me; that I must learn to project. I had three days to perfect the technique.

The Thursday afternoon before the play opened, Dan called me into the box office. He sat on a tall wooden stool in the glass cubicle with the small pass through window and told me I was a great actress and he believed in me. "Theater is definitely in your future," he said. Rarely had he met anybody with such shiny talent. However, with my voice, that wouldn't project no matter how much training he gave me, he thought I should go into television not theater. So he had asked a friend to replace me.

I didn't want to be replaced and started to cry.

"Don't worry," Dan said, patting me on the shoulder. "I have a better part for you. I've written it just for you, to display your talents."

"What's the part?" I stopped crying.

"You're going to be the slut."

"What's a slut?"

A twenty-year old professional actress came to rehearsal and memorized the lines of the teenager in four hours.

As a slut I had only one line: "Come on over and see what you've been missing."

Marie and Dan taught me how to move my hips when I walked but I was twelve and looked eleven.

We opened on Friday night and had the final run through with lights, costumes and make up on Friday afternoon because the twenty-year old teenage replacement had a prior engagement Thursday night.

I loved what happened. I was wrapped in a costume with padded rear and breasts. Marie used a curling iron to fluff my hair. At that time curling irons could be a fire hazard and, at the least, could singe and dry out your hair. But I didn't know about the perils and felt, when I looked in the mirror, that I had the best hairstyle I'd ever seen. Dan and Marie didn't think I looked enough like a slut. So Marie found a musty smelling blonde wig and stuck it on my head. Now I looked like a tart, she said. What I liked best was the pancake makeup that clogged pores and encouraged acne, because it also covered blemishes and enhanced eyes and lips. There was a pretty face looking back at me from the dressing room mirror; a pretty face that didn't look like me; a pretty face that could disguise me, so if I ever met grandpa and his arrows again, he wouldn't recognize me.

By the time Jean got back to school, I was hooked on theater, happy to see her, friendly to everybody and enjoying myself.

I kept having a good time during the two years it took my radiating-good-health mother to pick out furniture, find a gardener, hire a housekeeper, join a reform Synagogue, enter me into after school classes at that Synagogue, and convince my dad to join a Jewish Country Club. As soon as these tasks were completed she asked my dad for a job.

"No," he said. "My wife doesn't need to work."

I heard my mother ask for a job nine more times. The tenth time my

dad said, "No," my mother went to
bed in her French Provincial
designed bedroom, stayed there and I
began to worry about Grandpa and
his arrows again. Two weeks later I
took my cog stone to bed with me.

5.

Dear Dessa Dreams,
    The judge says I have to decide.
Poppa is a rich, bad guy about to
marry a new woman. Momma
doesn't want me. Who should I
choose?
Thirteen in Santa Fe.

Dear Thirteen,
    If Momma doesn't want you,
choose Poppa. I dreamt about a bad
father who reformed. Maybe your
father will reform. If not, he's rich.
And it's better to be rich than poor.
Sincerely, Dessa Dreams.

I only dreamt part of my reply.
My dad always said that it was better
to be rich than poor. The rest of the

answer was based on cog stone induced dreams I had when I was in the ninth grade. My parents' marriage was disintegrating then. If their arguments were too big for me to handle, I went to sleep with my cog stone, dreamt about the Westbruk Wetlands, heard the voice of God and tried to find a Cog Stone good for wishing.

* * *

GOD says, "It is the year 1542. Do you see how beautiful the Westbruk Wetlands are, Dessa?"

GOD is right. The wetlands are beautiful.

Leo and I tread water in a warm pool. We're both naked. I'm fourteen. I'm not sure how old Leo is. I don't think he's changed much since I saw him last. I have. My breasts are bigger. Maybe Leo can't see them in the water. Lots of people bathe with us. Everybody is very clean.

I know I should be looking for Grandpa and asking about Luna but I'm too sleepy. "Wowump," I say. The people that live on the Westbruk Wetlands in 1542 don't speak Um,

English or Yiddish but I understand them. I am an extremely good linguist in my dreams.

Women are grinding acorns with pestles and mortars. "Where do they get acorns?" I ask. "I can't see any oak trees on the wetlands."

"Dessa, we walked all day to get the acorns," Leo says.

"Hmmmn!"

I watch men and children drink worm soup and notice how kind these people are to each other. No one yells. No one insults. Everybody helps. I remember Bubby told me to be kind. *How do you learn to be kind?* "I need to talk to an old woman," I tell Leo. "I need to learn some stuff. And I need a cog stone for wishing. I've gotta get my mother out of her bedroom." *And do something about Luna. How odd! I haven't thought about Luna since I was ten.*

We walk out of the pool, shake off the water, climb to the mesa and look out to sea. "My goodness," I say. Three big, old-fashioned looking galleons sail near shore. People on the bow of the first ship seem to be watching us.

An old lady with missing front teeth hands Leo a cog stone.

"Is that for me?" I ask.

I guess it isn't because Leo throws the stone toward the first ship. My eyesight is very good. I can see the woman who catches the stone as well as if I were looking through high-powered binoculars. She looks like an older version of Luna. *Is Luna alive?* Her hair is dark and long, her face beautiful. She stands next to a young girl who also looks like Luna. Maybe they are mother and daughter, I think.

A man, dressed like an officer from another time, probably the ship's captain, takes the stone away from the woman and throws it back to Leo.

I put my hands out, but before I can grasp the cog stone GOD says, "The man who threw the stone to Leo is Juan Sebastian Cabrillo. Senor Cabrillo and some people he knows are going to tell you some stories, Dessa."

"Dessa hasn't had any cog stone lessons," the old woman with the missing teeth says.

"That's true," God says.

"How is Dessa going to remember the stories when she wakes up? She's smart but not that smart?"

"Easy," God says, "I'll have a scribe write the stories. Dessa will find them on her bed stand when she wakes. For now, Dessa will listen."

I sit on the beach. Juan Sebastian Cabrillo stands on the deck of his boat and starts to speak. Even though he's more than a mile away, I can hear his every word.

6.

JUAN SEBASTIAN CABRILLO

My name is Juan Sebastian Cabrillo. I don't remember my parents or if I was born in Portugal or Espana. As a child, I begged for food on the winding streets of Sevila, Espana. When I was nine or ten, Alonso Sanchez de Ortega, a rich merchant, found me sleeping in the doorway of his business and took me home to be a companion to his son, Diego. The family lived in a big house on a hill just out side the Jewish Quarter. I got to sleep in a room for the first time (it doesn't rain in a room) and decided I wanted to join Senor Alonzo's family. They ate food every day.

I listened to them speak and learned to lisp like they did. I watched them walk and soon I was strutting the same way. I asked Diego's cousin, also Diego, what I needed to do to become part of their family.

"There's nothing you can do," he said. "You'll never be part of our family."

"Oh, Diego, there must be something." I touched my new shirt. It was clean and soft.

"You can marry Beatriz." Diego, the cousin, laughed.

Senor Alonso's daughter Beatriz was eight years old.

Later, the same year, Alonso Sanchez de Ortega sent his son Diego to Jamaica for a military education and possible wealth attaining opportunities. I went along as Diego's companion. Before boarding our ship, I told Beatriz I was going to marry her.

"I'm going to marry you, too, Juan Sebastian," she said. Then she ran behind her father and hid from me.

It was a gray, cold day but I felt warm as I looked up into the eyes of my benefactor.

"So you want to marry my daughter?" Senor Alfonso smiled.

"I am going to marry her."

Senor Alonso lifted his daughter so that her bonneted face was so close I could smell her. She had the scent of security.

"If you're going to marry this girl," Senor Alonso said, "you will have to work very hard. Only a rich man will marry my daughter."

I waved at Beatriz when I boarded the ship. She waved back. When we set sail, she was still waving.

I loved the sea. While Diego and most of the other passengers shitted loose stools and threw up, I spent my time asking questions. I wanted to know how the boat was caulked, how to repair a sail, what was the best kind of wood to use for the new

carvel planking, were the sundials
we were transporting to the new
world reliable?

In Jamaica I discovered that the
military was the best place for a boy
with no money or family to help him
get ahead. I went with Diego every
day and participated in his training.
I was scrawny so everybody knocked
me down in hand-to-hand combat. I
trained with the harquebus and never
hit a target. But I was talented with a
crossbow. On the second day I
picked it up, my aim was truer and I
was faster than any other trainee.

I was still a boy when I went to
Cuba and marched with other
crossbowmen and Jamaican slaves.
When we stopped to rest in a
clearing surrounded by trees, Cuban
natives gave us food and water.
After we were sated, one of our men
picked up a sword. Others picked up
their swords, crossbows and
harquebuses. The Cubans had no
chance. I stood and watched as our
army murdered 2000 men, women
and children. Then I threw up on the
blood stained ground.

LUNAONE

My name is Lunaone. I am the first wife of Juan Sebastian Cabrillo. He doesn't know his people or where he was born. I know who my people are. I know where I am from.

Juan told me he participated in the massacre of two thousand Cubans. He also told me about his part in the destruction of the Aztecs. "Nobody liked the Aztecs," he said. "The rotters killed twenty-thousand people each year."

Then Juan repeated and repeated the story about the Aztec called Nantilan.

Nantilan, who had a pretty wife and three children, was standing outside his stone house, drinking bitter chocolate, when two warriors came to get him.

"We have a gift for you," the first warrior said.

"A gift?" Nantilan said. "You don't need to give me anything." He was enjoying the chocolate.

"Come on!" The second warrior said. "It's behind the new pyramid. You will never guess what it is."

But Nantilan did guess. Before he could run away the two warriors grabbed his arms and dragged him across the ground and up the stairs of the new pyramid. They strapped him to a flat stone altar. The high Aztec Priest called Montauka stood on the altar and smiled down at Nantilan.

"Why me?" Nantilan was so frightened he wet himself.

"Why not you?" Montauka chanted a prayer, and then carefully removed Nantilan's beating heart with a sharp piece of volcanic glass at the end of his macuahuitl.

The two warriors tossed the rest of Nantilan down the stairs.

Later that evening Montezuma, the Emperor of the Aztecs, ate Nantilan's cooked thighs covered with chili peppers. He said the meal was "very tasty!"

When Juan first came to Mexico, he was put in charge of boat building. The plan was to attack Tenochtitlan, the island Aztec stronghold, by boat. There was plenty of cloth from old ships to make sails. There was ample wood for building the boats in the Mexican highlands. Juan had his men bore holes in trees and build fires under the holes to suck out resin for the pitch needed for waterproofing. In

Espana, he said, the fat to make pitch
was taken from animals called cows.
In Mexico, there weren't any cows,
so as soon as an Indian was killed
Juan had him butchered for his fat.
When he told me that he only
butchered hostile Indians and that it
was necessary, I wanted to spit in his
face.

After Juan's boats crashed into
the Aztec canoes, the Spaniards
bombarded the Aztec city with
cannon fire. Juan told me 100,000
people died. How many are
100,000? I don't know this number.

Juan won a horse for his
participation in the massacre. A
horse was rare, he said, but it didn't
make you rich. He wanted to be
rich. So he left Mexico and followed
a man called Pedro de Alvarado to
my home in Guatemala, hoping to
find his fortune.

When Alvarado and Cabrillo first
came to my country, Guatemala was
a land of peaceful towns, well-
cultivated fields and streams with
clear water for drinking. There were
also high, volcanically active,
mountains, bottomless ravines,

impassable jungles and steaming marshlands.

Alvarado and his followers fought fierce battles with my people, vanquishing one village after another.

When the Spaniards got tired of fighting, Alvarado sent emissaries to talk to the Chief of each tribe that hadn't yet proclaimed Espana as their country.

Juan came to speak to the Chief of my tribe. When I first saw him I thought he was ugly. All Spaniards looked ugly to me. How could they not? They're evil.

Juan asked to talk to the headman and an interpreter. I was the interpreter. I have good ears for understanding.

"I am here representing Pedro de Alvarado," Juan told me to tell the Chief. "He is Emperor of the World. He is not God. But he wants to give you a God-like gift."

"How nice!" my tall, good-looking, dumb brother, the Chief said.

"Alvarado, the Emperor of the World, will tell you how to get on

the Road to Paradise," Juan
continued.

I thought the message was the
funniest thing I'd ever heard and bit
my bottom lip so I wouldn't laugh.
Before translating this drivel to my
brother, I asked Cabrillo, "What do
we need to do to get on the Paradise
Road?"

"It's simple," he said. "All you
have to do is vow your allegiance to
the Emperor."

I told my brother what Cabrillo
said.

"What should we do?" My
brother, the Chief, always asked me
what to do.

JUAN SEBASTIAN
CABRILLO

The place I stood seemed to be
more prosperous than the Aztec
capitol. It was surrounded by a
ravine and only accessible by a
drawbridge and a dangerous, very
steep path.

The interpreter, the most
beautiful woman I'd ever seen, said,
"We are the last of our tribes and
know our people have been
surrendering to you. We want to

surrender, too. First we will feed you a great feast. Then you will show us the Road to Paradise."

"Yes," I said, then, made my way down the steep path to the bottom of the ravine where Alvarado and the rest of our men waited for me.

LUNAONE

My plan was to get the Spaniards drunk on Quetzalteca. Then we would burn our city, leave our homes and cut down the drawbridge after we crossed it.

"We'll lose everything," my brother said.

"We'll rebuild in a better place," I told him. "Where the Spaniards can't find us."

JUAN SEBASTIAN CABRILLO

Alvarado surveyed the situation. "This could be a trap," he told me.

Just in case Alvarado was right and there was an ambush waiting, I scaled the steep path by myself. A great smelling feast was already on the ground. I hadn't tasted good food for a long time, but, even so, I was able to keep a clear head. I told the beautiful interpreter to tell the Chief that we had many presents to give him. "Would you let some of your men help us carry them?"

"Of course." She smiled at me. She had the best of all smiles.

LUNAONE

I told my brother what Juan had said. As usual, he asked me what I thought. I couldn't foresee any harm. My brother told fifteen of our men to follow Cabrillo down the hill.

"Will they be enough?" I smiled at Juan.

"A few more would be perfect," he said, returning my smile.

My brother ordered ten more men to go with Cabrillo.

"Could you come, too?" Juan asked. "We might need an interpreter."

I agreed. Used to the steep path, I descended easily as did the twenty-five men of my tribe who accompanied us. Cabrillo kept tripping and, on the most treacherous part of the path, slid on his rear end. I didn't laugh and signaled our men not to either which was difficult because the men kept making bawdy remarks about how Cabrillo's rear end and maybe other parts of him would be ruined by our descent.

When we reached the bottom of the ravine, a soldier grabbed one of our men. Then the rest of the soldiers grabbed the rest of our men, holding them in place with knives to their throats. Alvarado took a rope, wrapped it around the neck of my childhood friend, Lanop, and pulled on it till his neck broke. Our men tried to get away, but couldn't. The men that weren't strangled to death were thrown into a big fire. I will hear their yells in my head for the rest of my life. Our women screamed as they ran down the hill. My brother ran after them. Other men followed.

"Don't hurt my sister!" my brother yelled.

None of the Spaniards understood him. Alvarado stabbed my brother. More murders. More killings. Any man that survived became a slave.

Alvarado told his men to look at our women and choose a wife if they wanted.

Juan chose me. He took me to Santiago de Guatemala, a town located in an ancient cornfield where he became a rich ecomendero, the owner of a large estate. All the natives working and living on his land had to give part of their produce and earnings to him, as well as do what ever he asked. He said this good life was part of the spoils of conquest. I took advantage and lived well.

Now and then Juan followed Alvarado to Honduras and El Salvador. I didn't run away when he was gone because after our first coupling I got pregnant. Every time Juan came back from his travels we coupled. I had three daughters that I loved and would have done anything for. If I didn't love Juan, I grew not to hate him. Everything went on the same good and easy way until Juan sailed back to Espana. While he was gone I was the rich wife of an ecomendero. When he returned he brought a new wife.

BEATRIZ

I am Beatriz Sanchez Ortega de Cabrillo, the only woman Juan

Sebastian Cabrillo married in the Church, so therefore, his only true wife. I met Juan and promised to marry him when I was eight years old. When he left Espana he was a poor boy. When he came back he was a rich landowner.

I heard Lunaone's voice before I saw her. She and her daughter, Lunatwo, were talking about me. Hidden between the house and my trunks, I listened to the women I planned to evict from my household, wanting to know what they had to say about me.

While we were in Espana and on our voyage to the New World Juan didn't mention Lunaone and her daughters. But last night at dinner I asked Juan why Lunatwo, a girl of about thirteen, was sitting at our table.

"She's my daughter," he said.

I patted the girl on her hand and smiled. "Then she'll be my daughter, too."

She pulled her hand away from me.

"Lunatwo has a mother," Juan said.

I watched him sip his wine. I sipped mine. I'll have to do something about this, I thought.

"She's not as beautiful as you are, Mama," Lunatwo said of me. "Her nose has a bump on it. Her ears stick out and her eyes are large and shifty looking. Besides she lisps when she talks."

Then I heard the most beautifully modulated speaking voice I'd ever heard say, "High class Spaniards lisp."

"You must get out of bed, Mama," Lunatwo said.

LUNAONE

Before I married Juan, I never had a bed. Now I had one and loved it. If I left it, Beatriz might take it, I thought. So I stayed in my bed all day.

BEATRIZ

I wasn't interested in Lunaone's bed. I'd brought my own. As soon as I found out about Lunaone and her daughters, I ordered the workers to build me a bigger house. I didn't want to live in her house.

LUNAONE

Juan smiled at everything Beatriz did. But at night he came to see me. He loved Beatriz, he told me, but she was too delicate. Even so, she was pregnant before spring. In the late fall, she had a baby boy. She called him Juan Sebastian and I'd never seen my husband so happy.

Soon Beatriz was in charge and I wasn't welcome. Neither were my daughters. Beatriz arranged for my two oldest girls to marry Spanish men. They moved to the men's estates and I never saw them again. Only my daughter, Lunatwo, was left to me.

Juan was away from home, tending his new ship building business, on September 11, 1541, the day we call "The Upheaval." A pounding rainstorm drenched us. Then the earth shook. Mud sloshed down from the volcano at the edge of our town and fell on my head. Then it seemed to rise from my feet slowly up to my neck. I stood, not being able to move, and shouted, "Lunatwo! Lunatwo!"

Beatriz screamed, "Juan Sebastian! Juan Sebastian!"

By the time Lunatwo pulled me out of the mud, our houses were ruined. Our fields were devastated. Our crops were spoiled.

Juan came back the next day. I followed him as he surveyed the damage. Inert, unidentifiable legs and arms reached out from the mud.

Beatriz told everybody what to do and how to do it. "Clear the mud," she ordered.

"We don't have tools," her chief worker said.

"Use your hands," she said.

I dug. So did Juan and Beatriz. We dug until we were blacker than the mud. We breathed mud. "Help us!" I told Lunatwo.

She dug and didn't complain. But, nine months later, when Juan was ready to leave again, she begged him to take her with him. "I don't want to live here any more," she said. "I can't stand the mud."

We already had other houses. But everything was still dirty. Food was hard to come by. The farmers who used to give us part of their food didn't have anything to give. We were all skinny, even Beatriz's baby.

"It may be years before I come back," Juan told Lunatwo. "You don't want to come with me."

"Yes, I do!" Lunatwo said.

"Take her!" I said. "This mud is not my daughter's destiny."

"I will be sailing soon," Juan said. "The only women that come on my ships are whores."

"I've been your whore," I said. "It hasn't been a bad life."

"Take her!" Beatriz said. "I'm going to have another baby. Only your legal children belong here."

I smiled. My daughter had the choice to be a whore or stay where she was unwanted. *What are my choices?*

Juan, Lunatwo and I rode horses to the coast. When we reached Juan's ship, he walked the gangway to the forecastle. Lunatwo and I went aboard with other sorry looking women who would whore like we would for the men on the voyage.

We stood on the deck while the men looked us over. My heart was in my throat but I didn't cry. I am a Chief's daughter. I am a Chief's sister. I can do anything, I told myself.

One man put his hand on my wrist. He was younger than most and not as ugly. He smelled but I've smelled worse. Then Juan yelled from the top deck, "She's not to be touched."

The man dropped my wrist as if it were a hot pot. Then he touched my daughter's wrist and looked up at Juan. My husband nodded.

LUNATWO

We put out to sea on gentle waters on June 27, 1542 and that night I coupled with the young man and he told me to call him Antonio.

LUNAONE

There were three galleons in our fleet. Our ship, the San Salvador, was the biggest, about one hundred feet long and twenty-five feet wide. One of the men on the ship was a priest. *Would he be willing to marry Lunatwo and the young man?* I knew that if a priest married them, the young man would not be able to bring a Beatriz, second wife, into my daughter's life.

"You don't have to tell the Priest that you've already coupled," I told Lunatwo.

LUNATWO

I told Antonio about my mother's idea while we ate. The hard biscuits and salted meat weren't so easy to cut. I forgot about wedding plans for a minute and thought instead of the fresh fruit I'd eaten every day in Santiago de Guatemala. "I wish I had some fruit," I said.

Antonio poured wine. "There is no fresh fruit here," he said. "And, just so you know, I'm never going to marry a whore."

I drank four glasses of wine and fell asleep while coupling. Antonio slapped my face to wake me up.

LUNAONE

After Lunatwo told me what happened, I told Juan. "We must save her from him," I said.

"He's from a good family." My man put my hand on his groin. "Touch me, Lunaone. Stroke me."

"He slapped her," I said.

When Juan's hand moved to my core, touching, probing, I stopped thinking. I couldn't ask for anything except, "continue, continue, continue. . ."

For the next 129 days Antonio never hit my daughter. I think Juan told him not to.

On the one hundred thirtieth day we sailed into a very good closed harbor and I heard the voice of GOD for the first time. HE said, "This beautiful land will some day be called San Diego, California."

I'd read a romance novel written in the early 1500's about a mythical place called California. Yes, I read. Juan taught me. I taught my daughters. I wonder if Beatriz knows how to read.

The novel about California mentioned pearls that were supposed to fall out of oysters and beautiful black women who owned gold weapons. I didn't see oysters, pearls, the black women or their gold weapons.

Cabrillo went ashore and claimed the land for Espana. I watched from my deck as three of the California natives gave him gifts. That night Antonio and two of his friends went ashore. The natives shot them with their bows and arrows and Antonio came back to the ship moaning in pain. Juan came to watch as I cleaned the surface wound on Antonio's right shoulder.

"Kill them! Capitain!" Antonio yelled.

"No!" I said. "It will just be another war."

"You're right," Juan didn't retaliate. Instead he captured two little boys, loaded them with presents and let them go. After that is was easy for my husband to make friends with the natives.

LUNATWO

Antonio asked me who my mother was. "Why does Capitain Cabrillo listen to her?"

I didn't answer. He spent his time lying on the deck, watching me. I brought him food but didn't talk. I didn't feel like it.

LUNAONE

Two weeks later our ship skirted a beautiful piece of land where a small stream rushed between two mesas to meet the sea. This time

GOD said, "This is my place. Someday I will call it Westbruk."

A young man stood on shore and smiled at us. When he tossed a stone in my direction, I caught it. It was flat with small teeth like protrusions sticking out of its round rim. I handed the stone to Juan. "It's good luck," I said.

"We'll leave the luck where we found it." Juan threw the stone back to the young man on the beach.

Other people standing near the young man smiled at us. "They seem so friendly," I said.

Every few days we explored a new port. GOD called these places Long Beach, Santa Monica, Ventura, and Santa Barbara. There was so much smoke in Long Beach I found it difficult to breathe. The people living there were burning brush and grasses in preparation for a rabbit hunt. That night I ate rabbit for the first time. It was delicious!

Because of the smoke we encountered, Juan did not call the long beach, Long Beach. Not hearing the voice of GOD, he called the place where the beach is very long, Bay of Smokes. I thought it a fitting name but didn't argue the point with GOD.

When we went ashore, Juan took a sword, stuck it into the ground and said, "This land and all the surrounding land belongs to Espana."

By that time Antonio had recovered completely thanks to Lunatwo's good nursing. He and a few other men cut down trees and put them around the sword. Then Juan read el requerimento to the natives in both Spanish and Latin. This document said the people that lived on the land just taken for Espana were now Spanish and must adopt the Christian religion. Of course the people didn't understand. But they were nice and shared their provisions with us. I particularly liked eating something they called acorn mush.

Sailing north again, winter grew fierce. I'd never been so cold. My clothing wasn't adequate but I kept my mouth shut and didn't complain. Lunatwo didn't either. Winds whipped the cargo across our ship, tearing most of the sails. The other two ships looked as if they were floundering.

"It's too dangerous to sail further north," Juan said. He turned the ships south.

ANTONIO

My name is Antonio.

We were exhausted and sailed toward the nearest island seeking fresh water. I went on shore with some of our men. The natives attacked us with large sticks. I sat on the sand too tired to fight. My back hurt where they hit me. My head was bleeding. My arms were so sore; I couldn't lift them so I closed my eyes and prepared to die. When I opened them my Capitain walked ashore with another contingent of our men. I watched as Capitain Cabrillo hit his right foot on a rocky ridge. It looked to me as if he broke something and was suffering horrible pain. But he shouted orders and didn't leave the island until all of us were safe.

LUNAONE

Juan summoned Lunatwo and me to his cabin. Blood and green pus oozed from his right leg. Antonio and the Priest were with him.

"Antonio wants to marry you, my daughter," Juan told Lunatwo.

"No!" Lunatwo said.

"Marriage is your only protection," Juan said. "I'm dying. Do what I say."

Lunatwo looked at me. I didn't like Antonio but I agreed with my husband. Marriage was Lunatwo's only protection. *What will my protection be when my husband dies?*

Juan died a few minutes after the Priest married Lunatwo to Antonio.

Antonio slapped Lunatwo eight times that night. I heard the slaps. I heard her screams. I heard his moans when he finally bedded her. Each night she took more slaps before he got his way. By the time they were up to nineteen slaps, we neared the place GOD had called Westbruk. I took my daughter's hand. We jumped in the water and landed on top of a whale that took us to shore. The man that had thrown me the lucky stone was waiting. He handed me the stone. It slipped out of my hand and disappeared into the sand. He smiled at my daughter.

I was old. Soon my teeth would fall. Soon my skin would wrinkle. But I was free.

* * *

I found the pages with the Cabrillo stories on my bed stand the morning after Lunaone finished recounting her tale in my cog stone induced dream.

* * *

"GOD, what should I do with the stories?

"Go to the library. Find out all you can about Cabrillo. If you find that these stories could be true, use them any way you want."

* * *

I went to the library, spent long hours researching the explorer Juan Sebastian Cabrillo, retyped the pages and handed them to Mrs. Hopkins, my third period, 11th Grade, advanced English teacher, and was awarded an "A."

* * *

"Thank you, GOD!"

"You're welcome, Dessa."

* * *

An easy 'A', I thought. I'll probably breeze through my senior year and then on to UCLA.

Wrong!

7.

Dear Dessa Dreams,
    My girlfriend says the only way to prove my love is to change my religion. I don't want to. So what should I do?
In a quandary in Quantico.

Dear In A Quandary,
    I dreamt about some people who changed their religion. They lost their culture and disappeared. Even so, my advice is to study the situation. Read about your girlfriend's religion. Then make up your mind.
 Sincerely, Dessa Dreams.

In September of 1954, when I was seventeen, my Dad laid down an ultimatum. My mother had to get out of bed and participate in what could be a very nice life or he was going to leave her. They were invited everywhere. Dad went. Mother stayed home. They could afford vacations anywhere in the world. Dad went. Mother stayed home. Dad said they were "haves" and should get involved in charitable events and help the "have-nots. Dad said they could afford to go to the latest plays and check out nightclubs featuring the newest singers and comedians. They should go to the Synagogue services on Friday night. My dad went. My mother stayed home.

One Friday night, my mother called me into their bedroom. "Look in the closet, Dessa."

I opened the door and looked in their enormous walk-in-closet. My dad's clothes were gone. "Where are his things?" My throat hurt. I wondered if I was coming down with something.

"Your dad left," my mother said. "He took his belongings with him."

"I thought he was going to the Synagogue." I touched the empty wooden rod where my dad's clothes used to hang and then turned to face my mother.

"It isn't right," she said. "If he were sick, I wouldn't be running around. I'd be by his side helping him find the right doctor."

For me, life seemed just the same. Dad was always gone before. He was always gone now. Mother was always in bed before. She was always in bed now.

In October my high school counselor, Mrs. Lemon, called me to her office.

I sat across the small blue desk from the overweight lady with fading brown hair. We called her "Lemonade" because she was nice and we liked her. When "Lemonade" was serious she had a drab look, when she smiled she was beautiful. She was perfect for her job. She made us want to try harder. She knew our problems before we stated them. And she knew how to get us to solve them ourselves. When I'm stymied on a Dear Dessa Dreams question, I think of Lemonade and ask myself how she would have solved the problem.

"Dessa," she said. "Have you made up your mind?" She sat still, not wiggling or writing with her freshly sharpened #2 pencil on the tablet that rested next to the folder labeled "DESSA HALOM". "Do you really want to go to UCLA?"

I nodded. "My mother went there." The lady that stayed in bed all day had a college education.

"There are other schools," she said.

"Not for me." I put my hand in my lap. My crinoline half-slip itched.

"What if you don't get in?"

UCLA wasn't easy to get in. I had flunked chemistry. Mrs. Nelson, the chemistry teacher, had struck a deal with me. She'd give me a "C" if I promised to take chemistry in college. I felt I was Faust dealing with the devil, but I wanted to get into UCLA. "Don't you think I'll get in?"

"I think you should keep your options open." Lemonade took a package of lemon drops out of her top drawer and handed me one. I put the little yellow candy smothered in white sugar in my mouth and sucked.

"Now you do well enough in school, but you don't have any extracurricular activities," she said.

Both of us made candy-sucking sounds.

"I write the *Dear Dessa Dreams* column," I said.

"What's that?"

In the eleventh grade my father helped me get an after school job answering the phone in the one room office at the *WEEK SAVER*. People paid to get their ads in the 12 to 36 pages, door-to-door handout. If you wanted to sell a used bike or announce a charity event you bought an ad. It was a great job because there weren't many phone calls and I had plenty of time to read my favorite best sellers and "*TRUE LOVE &REAL ROMANCE*" magazines.

One day Mr. Johnson, my cigar chewing, tobacco spitting boss, called a meeting of all his employees, the nine delivery guys and me. We sat on folding chairs and bundles of *WEEK SAVERS* strewn over the cement floor behind the counter. That day, although he held the cigar at ready, Mr. Johnson didn't chew or spit. He told us *DOLLAR SAVERS,* a new company, was selling their ads cheaper than ours. Mr. Johnson couldn't afford to cut the price of an ad. He wanted to know if any of us had any ideas.

Personally, I didn't care. It wasn't an interesting job. The pay wasn't good. There wasn't one of the delivery guys that I would have been caught dead with. But that day Mr. Johnson looked so sad I wanted to help him. I looked down at my latest issue of "*TRUE LOVE & REAL ROMANCE.*" It was opened to the advice column. "We can give advice," I blurted.

Mr. Johnson moved the cigar toward his mouth. "Advice about what?" he said.

"About anything," I said.

"Who will give this advice?" The cigar was almost to his lips.

"I will," I said.

"You have to be an expert to give advice," he said. "What are you an expert in?"

"Life, dreams," I said.

Mr. Johnson bit the cigar, chewed, then, spat the remains on the floor.

The following morning I wrote both the question and answer letters for the first *Dear Dessa Dreams* column. Mr. Johnson published it. Within a week all sorts of letters were sent to the WEEK SAVER asking Dear Dessa Dreams for advice and business improved so much, Mr. Johnson opened three more offices. By the time I was seventeen, my *Dear Dessa Dreams* columns were appearing in *WEEK SAVERS* in San Diego, Bakersfield and Fresno as well as L.A.

After telling this to Lemonade, she said, I should still "hedge my bets". She showed me a list of activities I could participate in. Since I was in the 12th grade, I didn't have time to be bad in something and improve. I looked at the list. Art. I couldn't draw. Student government. You had to be elected. People that were elected had started running in the tenth grade. Theater. I had been in four plays at the Hadin-Blass Theater and would have done more if the theater hadn't closed because of the rat infestation behind the back wall of the dressing room. That was when Marie said, "Enough is enough. I can't stand shepherding these untalented nincompoops through another play."

I knew she wasn't talking about me. Dan Blass had told me over and over how talented I was or would be if I ever got the hang of projecting.

"I'll do theater." Maybe I can be a movie star, I thought.

Lemonade smiled. "I have a better idea. You can be a reporter on the Madison High Journal." Lemonade's dimples were quivering. She'd solved another problem.

Mr. Angelinas, the journalism teacher and Madison Journal faculty advisor, did not want me to give advice.

"I'm good at giving advice," I said. "Lemonade, I mean Mrs. Lemon, wants me to do something that I'm good at."

"The Madison Journal doesn't give advice." The tall thin man fingered his red, white and blue striped tie and stared at me. "Close your eyes," he said.

I complied.

"What am I wearing?" he asked.

"A suit, a shirt, a tie."

"What colors?" Mr. Angelinas asked.

I knew the tie was red, white and blue. I didn't know the color of the suit or shirt. I wasn't sure if he was wearing a jacket. I shrugged.

"Open your eyes," he said.

I did.

"Now tell me what you see," he said.

"Your jacket is sort of brownish, grayish, tannish, and yellowish."

"Would you like to read brownish, grayish, tannish, yellowish in the Madison Journal?" He raised his right arm each time he spoke as if to punctuate the colors or lead a band.

Then I saw it. "You're wearing your turquoise stoned, silver watch on your right wrist," I said. "Not on your left."

He smiled. "You're ready for your first assignment, Halom."

"Thanks, Angelinas. Mister Angelinas."

My assignment was to interview Darla Preston, the new physical education teacher at our school and the 1952 World Field Archery Champion.

Miss Preston was tall and serious. She had short blonde hair. I thought she could be pretty if she applied make up. Lipstick wouldn't be enough. Her blonde eyelashes needed mascara. Her blonde eyebrows wanted penciling. Her very pale cheeks demanded rouge. Since I was a blonde I decided I probably needed the same kind of cosmetics and planned to check myself in the mirror as soon as I got home.

We sat on the banged up bleachers in the gym. Darla looked at me. I looked at her. Finally she said, "Aren't you going to ask me some questions?"

"I'm going to ask you some questions as soon as I think of them," I said. *Why can't the questions come spilling out? Maybe journalism isn't going to be the easy extracurricular activity to stick on my college applications if I don't get into UCLA.*

"How about we meet at the archery field?" she said. "Saturday at Motor Park. There's a nice field just a little south of Pico Ave. You can watch me shoot."

I got to the park early. The sun was barely up in the pink eastern sky. The ten-target archery field was empty. I thought I could hear the grass grow or the wind blow or something whizzing in the air. It was the sound of an archer shooting. The man was so far away from the field, I hadn't noticed him. One arrow after another came out of his quiver and with remarkable speed, he aimed, shot and hit every bull's eye.

The archer seemed familiar. He looked like the Grandpa who had shot Luna with his bow and arrows on Cardboard Beach across from the Westbruk Wetlands. But this man was too clean. He had a barbershop short haircut and didn't sport a hair band. He smiled at me, revealing teeth that looked real. Then he picked up the bow, aimed the arrow and I saw the cog stone tattoo on the back of his hand. It was Grandpa. I screamed, "Leo's Grandpa!"

He turned to look at me. *Does he recognize me? I must've changed since I was ten.* I hoped I had.

"Who are you?" he yelled. "What's your name?"

I could feel my heart beating in my throat and started to run. Three arrows darted after me and missed. I ran as fast as I could by the tennis courts, the pool, and the building that housed the basketball courts and other indoor recreational activities. Wedding receptions were sometimes held there and that morning the trashcans overflowed with wedding leftovers. The flowers in the trash looked better than the ones growing on the ground. Why was I thinking about flowers? I had to get away. I could hardly breathe when I ran into Darla Preston's arms. Crying and trying to catch my breath, I told Miss Preston about the man who shot his arrows at me and missed by quarter inches. I told her how he hit every bull's eye. But I didn't mention that he was "Grandpa."

"Somebody that good wouldn't have missed you, even if you were running," she said when she drove me home.

I got in bed and stayed there the rest of the weekend.

My mother stood in my bedroom doorway and watched me. I heard her use the phone in the hallway and tell my dad that I needed to see a doctor. "If you don't want her to end up as sick as I am," she said, "You better do something."

On Monday my dad took me to the doctor.

I sat on a brown medical table while Doctor Singer touched my forehead with his wrinkled, brown spotted fingers, listened to my chest with his stethoscope and thrust his tiny flashlight into my ears. Then he stuck his Popsicle stick into my throat while I said, "Ahhh."

"She has viral pneumonia," the gray haired doctor told my dad. "You don't have to worry," he continued. "We have a new miracle drug. I administer it in the morning. People recover in the afternoon."

Doctor Singer gave me the shot. By afternoon I was throwing up. Within the week I was in the hospital with an ulcerated colon. The antibiotic was taken off the market before the year was out but not before most of the people that took it spent some time in the hospital.

The stomach ache was awful. More than awful. I don't remember the pain of childbirth anymore, but I still recall my ulcerated colon. There was a fire in my abdomen and I spent hours sitting on the toilet, if I could get there quick enough. I didn't have enough clean under pants or pajamas to cover my emergencies. I smelled of toilet day and night. Thin before the illness, I was concentration camp skinny afterwards and spent months recuperating.

My mother got out of bed to take care of me. My dad came home. We spent our evenings in my bedroom. My parents smoked their cigarettes. Ashes flew. I slept in the smoked filled room.

When the bouts of diarrhea stopped and the pain receded, I was still very weak and had to have a home teacher.

Decrepit Mrs. Spencer loved teaching sick kids. Same pay. Less work. She gave me lessons in elementary school addition, subtraction, multiplication and division. I had already passed

algebra and geometry. For English I
handed Spence, as I called her, my
DEAR DESSA DREAMS column.
She corrected the few mistakes I
purposely made and gave me an "A."
She decided I should study
California history because she had
some old, out of date California
history textbooks. That these books
had been written for fifth graders and
I was in the twelfth grade didn't
seem important to Spence. It was
okay with me because as soon as I
read about Father Junipero Serra, the
Franciscan Missionary that claimed
California for Spain, I was hooked
and had some cog stone induced
dreams about the man.

8.

GOD says, "It is the year 1775,
Dessa. The people who live on the
wetlands call me CHINCHINCH.
They think I look like a coyote,
know my rules and treat each other

and my land well. I walk with them."

I'm in a kiicha, a willow stick and cord grass shelter. Leo holds me in his arms. "I must go to see," he says, but doesn't go.

While luxuriating in his closeness and warmth, I notice something humming. "Do you hear it?" I ask.

"Fleas," he says. "You'll have to burn the kiicha when I'm gone."

I can't burn anything. I'm afraid of fire in and out of dreams.

"Where did Leo go?" Luna asks me. We're outside looking at the kiicha. *What is she doing here? Is she alive?*

Luna hands me two willow sticks. I hand them back to her. She rubs the sticks together and starts a fire. I'm scared and can't breathe until the kiicha is ash.

We put willow sticks into the soft, marsh-mud and weave cord grass around them. I seem to know what I'm doing and am enjoying the task when GOD says, "Look at this."

A book drops from the sky. I catch it and take it into the new kiicha to examine. It's too dark to see.

Outside Luna is gone and it's quiet. The people must be in their kiichas, I think. The animals must be visiting the south mesa. I sit next to my kiicha and lean against it. It doesn't look sturdy, but it doesn't fall from my weight.

I look at the book that fell from the sky. Reading is my favorite activity. I wonder if Luna and Leo like to read.

The book is leather bound. The gold lettered title reads, "*Palous's Diario*."

"I've translated the book into English for you," GOD says. "It's a lost book. Only you get to see it."

"You didn't need to translate it," I tell GOD. "I'm a regular linguist in my dreams. I can learn any language in a few minutes."

"Sometimes it is difficult to *read* a new language," GOD says.

"Right," I agree.

Palous's Diario

Today I write about the most holy man I've ever met. I believe my writing may be instrumental in his nomination for sainthood. I know that only a miracle can make you a saint. So before time passes and I forget, I'm recording one of his miracles.

The holy man, Father Junipero Serra, was born on the island of Majorca, in the kingdom of Espana on November 24, 1713. His parents called him Miguel Jose. Serra changed his name to Junipero at the age of sixteen when he became a Monk in the order of St. Francis.

I, too, am from the island of Majorca and a Monk in the order of St. Francis. My name is Palou.

In 1749, when Junipero was thirty-six and I was thirty-two, we sailed to Mexico and landed in Vera Cruz. From there we walked to Mexico City. Two days into our trek, a mosquito bit Junipero on his right thigh. Some nights, Junipero sticks wires in his skirt. He believes in suffering for God. I think the wires scratched the mosquito bite because it festered and became infected. Each day the bloody sore enlarged. Junipero suffered hot fevers and cold sweats. The pain must have been unbearable. But he bore it without complaining. We, the four other missionaries and I, told him to stop and rest. Padre Serra wouldn't do it. God was giving him a chance to prove himself, he said. "How wonderful God is!" The man looked upon pain with joy. I saw him beat himself with stones. I saw him wear the wires. One time, when he was preaching in front of a large crowd, he urged the sinners to repent their sins. Then he took off his top clothes, nakeding himself to the waist, picked up a chain and beat his back with it. He said, "I am a sinner." He hit himself harder and harder.

A man in the congregation, named Victorio, rushed to the Padre and grabbed the chain away. Victorio nakeded himself to the waist and beat himself. Over and over again. The last words I heard Victorio say were, "I am the sinner. I will never be able to atone. What should I do?"

Padre Serra administered the last unction and sanction before Victorio died. Junipero told me it was a good thing. "Victorio is now a soul enjoying the presence of God."

Of course, none of these things are what make a man a saint.

But, I believe what I am about to write could and should be enough for sainthood consideration.

One day when we walked through the province of Huasteca, we stopped at a small village to preach the word of God. Usually when we stopped in a village, the people ceased their labors to listen to what we had to say. When Padre Serra spoke, because he was the best and most charismatic speaker, they not only discontinued what they were doing, they changed their ways and became men and women of God. That day only five people came to hear us. I could tell Junipero was disappointed, but he didn't say so.

Two days later somebody brought the message to us that sixty people in that village had been visited by a great scourge and died. None of the sixty had attended our service. After that, in the villages we preached in Huasteca, all the people attended our Mass. They were punctual. They listened to every word. They converted to Christianity.

But as we walked on, the rumors, as to what happened, changed. It was said that where we preached, people fell sick and died. Soon people wouldn't let us into their villages.

At the time, Junipero's leg was giving him great problems. One evening when the sun was about to set, we saw storm clouds in the sky. Not only would it rain, the wind would blow. We couldn't find a tree for shelter and kept walking.

Seeing lightening and hearing thunder, it still hadn't started to rain when we came upon a little adobe house. I rapped on the wood door. A smiling, middle-aged man greeted us. "Come in," he said. "My name is Jerardo. Mi casa es su casa. My house is your house." He was dressed in the plain clothes of a simple peasant. A rope around his waist held up his pants. He wore no shoes. "My wife, Rosita, will have dinner ready soon," he said. "Meanwhile, my son Jerardito will get you anything you want."

The house had one room. Tempting smells of food wafted through it. Rosita tended the fire in the large fireplace. She was dressed in a long brown dress that looked as if it could have been white once. A child of about five stood in the corner and grinned at us. What a handsome child! In the priesthood we give up earthly pleasures and that is all right with me. But when I looked at that obviously special child I wondered for a moment if I'd made the right choice. Maybe I would have liked to be married and have a son.

In the morning after a very good breakfast made of corn meal mush, all kinds of spices and tiny bits of meat, we left.

We had walked up and then down one hill when we met some muleteers herding scrawny, loud braying mules. "Padres, you look well rested," the tallest muleteer said. "Why aren't you wet? It rained last night."

"We slept well last night," I said. "We were inside."

"Oh?" The tall muleteer stopped petting his mule and looked directly into Padre Serra's eyes. "Where did you stay?"

"At Jerardo's house," Padre Serra said.

"Who is Jerardo?" the muleteer asked.

"The man who lives in the adobe house on the other side of the hill," I said.

"There's no house on the other side of the hill," the muleteer said.

Junipero smiled. He never argued with anyone or said anything to cause pain. My friend never joked. He was always serious. We had been in the house. We knew it was there. If the Muleteer had said that there was no God, would Junipero give argument? I heard a man say such a thing to him. And Junipero said, "You will find God, my friend. I would like you to find Him today because then I can rest, knowing that you will live forever."

The Muleteers led their mules to the top of the hill. "Come, look!" called the tallest Muleteer. "There is no house."

Junipero limped up the hill. His leg must have given him great pain. We followed. Looking down, there was only a leafless tree where Jerardo's house should have stood,

"Our hosts were Joseph, Mary and Jesus," Junipero said.

"That's impossible," the shortest muleteer said.

"It's possible," the tallest muleteer said. "They aren't wet and it rained last night."

Suddenly I knew what I'd always suspected. I was traveling with a saint.

Luna pulls Palou's diario away from me. "Leo is in trouble," she says. "We must go and help him."

"First you've got to tell me whether you're dead or alive," I say and take back the diario.

Luna doesn't answer so I follow her and traipse south. We cross low pockets of land, climb the south mesa, skip over wet sand near the ocean, jump over low hills that hug the shore, and fly with the birds to a grove of oaks. Through the trees I see bits of ocean. GOD says, "Welcome to San Juan Capistrano."

Leo stands near three soldiers wearing broad brimmed hats, cowboy like chaps and thick leather jackets, and two priests dressed in coarse, gray cloth habits and pointed hoods made of the same material.

One soldier says "Adios" and walks away. He must be Spanish, I think. I study Spanish at school. It is my language of choice to get into UCLA.

The soldiers shoulder holsters of ammunition as well as swords, lances and pistols. Dark braided long hair grows from the top of their head to the middle of their spines. One of the soldiers is older than the other. His skin is darker.

The lighter skinned, younger soldier says to the older, darker one, "You want this land, too, Mulatto?"

"My name is Manuel Nieto." The older soldier wrinkles his already wrinkled brow. "Call me Corporal Nieto," he says. "Not mulatto."

"I don't laugh at you because you're mulatto," the younger soldier says. "I laugh because you always say I want this land and that land. I laugh because I know ordinary soldiers like us don't get to own land."

"This soldier will have land," Corporal Nieto says. "This ordinary soldier will die a rich man."

The other soldier laughs and his clothes shake. I count nine layers of leather in his jacket. All that leather would protect the soldiers from Grandpa's arrows, I think.

Men, women and children circle Leo, the priests and the soldiers. The children are naked. The women wear rabbit-skin skirts, hemmed with grasses that reach to their knees. I look down and see that I'm wearing the same outfit. So is Luna. Bright colored beads decorate our outfits. Our breasts are bare. Leo and the other males wear animal skins on their shoulders. At first, I try not to stare at their bare genitals. But, then I remember I'm dreaming and look full force.

Some people stoop to the ground and pick up acorns. They hand them to the Priests and soldiers.

"What a wonderful present," I hear the soldier nearest to me say. I can tell he's being sarcastic and doesn't think something you pick up off the ground is much of a gift.

I walk toward the soldier. "These people gave you their most important food," I say. "How could any gift be better?"

The soldier pushes me away from him with his gun.

"Leave her alone," one of the Priests orders.

It's too late. The soldier's gun goes off. The cartridge misses me but tears a hole in the ground. All of us jump at the bang and I fall down even though I'm not hurt. I'm not even scared.

The Priests carry on as if nothing has happened. One of them hands bright colored ribbons to the people that gave him acorns.

"Act like you love the worthless pieces of cloth," Luna orders. "Otherwise the awful noise will sound again."

Everybody smiles at the priest handing out the ribbons.

"My name is Father Lausen," he says.

Men and boys help Father Lausen and another priest raise a tall cross of rough-hewn wood and plant it into the ground. Father Lausen says, "I proclaim this to be holy ground and claim it and all the surrounding land to be now part of the Spanish Kingdom."

The soldiers and priests hit the bottom of the oaks with their swords and lances. When the trees fall, they pull them to a flat clearing. Leo, the other men and boys help them haul.

Now a new soldier rushes into the oak glade. "Indians are attacking the San Diego Mission," he yells. "A priest has been killed. The buildings have been burnt to the ground."

"Does Father Serra know?" Padre Lausen asks the soldier.

The soldier nods. "Father Serra says it is a good thing because now we have the blood of a martyr to bless our mission."

For a few moments Padre Lausen doesn't speak or move. Then he looks at the sky, mouths some words upward and, then, orders the men to cease working.

The two priests bury some silver bells in the ground and take off walking fast.

GOD says, "Blink your eyes, Dessa."

I blink my eyes.

GOD says, "A year has passed. It is now October 31, 1776."

1776 looks just like 1775. We're still in the same arbor of oaks in San Juan Capistrano. The people, including me, are still dressed the same. The women grind acorns. The men hunt and fish.

Three priests walk into the glade followed by ten soldiers. "I am Father Junipero Serra," says the gauntest priest who walks with a limp. He is quiet and stares at us for a long time before he says, "I'm here to share God's word with you. If you listen to me, you will thrive. If you don't, you'll go to hell."

"These are happy people," I tell Father Serra. I wish I had something to cover my breasts but Serra doesn't look at them. He looks directly into my eyes and I realize he doesn't understand my words. But I continue. "They live the best of lives. They're nice to each other."

Father Serra turns to look at one of the other priests. He tells him, "These poor people look happy, but their time on earth is temporary. They must learn now, not later, that everlasting life is theirs or eternal hell. Life is short. Death is forever."

"What is he saying?" Leo asks me.

"He wants you to believe in his God," I say.

"What about Chinchinch?" Leo asks.

I shrug.

Leo stoops to pick up an acorn off the ground and hands it to the Father.

"Thank you," Padre Serra says. "You already know that it is better to give than to receive. It will be easy for you to go the rest of the way."

I tell Leo what Padre Serra said.

"Tell him, we always give. When I made my first hunt, I didn't partake of my deer but gave it to the other people. Tell him we already know about giving."

"I don't know how to tell him," I say.

"If you will take Jesus as your savior, you will live in light," Padre Serra says.

"Chinchinch says we have to be good," Leo says in our language. "If we are good, people will know us because good people have enough to eat. Good people are strong and sturdy. They are fat with good health."

"If you don't believe in Jesus, you will go to hell," Father Serra says in Spanish. He's very serious. No smile lights up his face. He is skinnier than any man I've ever seen. "Do you know about hell, my son? People burn in hell. The fires in hell go on forever."

"If you are bad a snake or a scorpion will bite you," Leo tells the priest who can't understand him.

"Hell is forever," Father Serra says.

I translate. Leo runs. A soldier aims his gun and shoots. Leo falls over.

Then my dream jumps and flashes like a movie in fast-forward. The soldiers shoot other people as the San Juan Capistrano Mission is erected.

All these fast moving images hurt my head. I close my eyes. When I open them, I'm leaning against my kiicha on the north mesa of the Westbruk Wetlands, reading the last few pages of Palous's Diario.

Palous's Diario

My friend, Junipero Serra, is dead. The man, who I know will be proclaimed saint someday, had one grand passion, to baptize Indians and save their souls. To draw people to his beliefs, this man burnt his flesh with a lit torch. He worked with his own hands to build the missions. He walked from mission to mission in spite of his never healing leg. He slept with wires scratching his skin so he wouldn't forget his duties. He starved himself and suffered bouts of scurvy. Since morning the people waited for us to toll the death bell. When we rang it, the crowds wept. The soldiers had to guard the sacred dead man so that people wouldn't tear his habit into pieces. They wanted the shreds for holy souvenirs.

Before he died, Junipero ordered his own plain coffin.

When he was placed in the casket, there was a 101-gun salute. Then there was another 101-gun salute echoing the first volley. Nobody but a general merits such honor.

The Indians cried. They crowded in, pushing and shoving to touch

anything that was part of the man.
And if some of them died because of
illness, we Spanish brought with us;
if some of them were forced to do
our bidding; if some of them suffered
because we chose their husbands and
wives for them; if some endured
great pain because we broke up their
families and changed their way of
life; if the brown jacket soldiers that
accompanied us sometimes lassoed
their women and raped them, it had
nothing to do with the man I firmly
believe will be elevated to sainthood.
Today I see by their tears, these
people know Junipero Serra brought
them everlasting life through the
introduction of Jesus Christ. No man
could have done more.

I close the book. Somebody
says, "You need to have your tonsils
out, Dessa. Somebody shakes my
shoulder. I'm leaving my dream.

9.

Dear Dessa Dreams,

Father left all his money to Aunt Tillie. She's a nasty old pig who never did nothing for him. Should I kill her or go to court?
Done Wrong in Dedham.

Dear Done Wrong,
I dreamt about an ordinary soldier who was given the largest land grant in California. He died. So will Aunt Tillie. Wait around and every once in a while do something nice for her.
Sincerely, Dessa Dreams

"Dessa, you have to get up," my dad said.

"I don't want to."

I'd had a lifetime of sore throats before Doctor Singer decided I needed an immediate tonsillectomy. What do you wear to have your tonsils out? Did I have to take a shower? I didn't want to brush my teeth or wash my face. I was too enervated by my colon problems and felt like I'd been tired forever.

School wasn't over. I wouldn't be well enough to go to the prom. Nobody had asked me, but somebody might. I'd heard people say that I was nice and pretty. Of course, they said it before I had viral pneumonia, an ulcerated colon and tonsillitis. I wondered if I would be able to go to grad night or, even more important, graduation. If you didn't go to graduation, could you graduate? If you didn't graduate, I knew you couldn't go to UCLA.

I had asked Doctor Singer how long it took to recuperate after a tonsillectomy.

Before he could answer my dad had said, "I walked home a half hour after I had my tonsils out." *Of course, he did.*

According to my dad he learned to swim when he was three. One of his mother's boy friends threw him into the deep end of the pool. My aunt Freddy taught Dad to read when he was four and a half. Freddy and Dad went to the Carnegie Library to get the books for these reading lessons. The library was near the flophouse hotel where they lived. Dad learned to drive a manual shift car when he was eleven. His mother got out of the car, told my dad to drive home and left him there to figure out how the car worked. He figured it out.

Dad was too strong to comprehend how weak I was. He certainly couldn't understand my mother's hypochondria.

But, I had Doctor Singer in my corner. He looked straight at my Dad and said, "She's not going to recover as fast as you did. She's anemic."

Why didn't he stick up for my mother? He was her doctor, too.

The anesthesiologist tried to take my cog stone way. "You might hurt yourself," he said.

"I need it. It's my dream stone."

"Let her keep it." Doctor Singer washed his hands.

"Start counting to one hundred," the anesthesiologist said.

I didn't have to count. Holding on to my stone, I started to dream.

10.

GOD says, "It is 1783."

I'm flying over a map of
Southern California that is bounded
in the south by the Westbruk
Wetlands and the Santa Ana River
and in the north by the Los Angeles
River.

Corporal Manuel Nieto, who, in
another one of my cog stone induced
dreams, said he was going to own
lots of property and die a rich man,
rides his brown horse over the map.
When he gets to the Westbruk
Wetlands, he jumps off the steed,
takes a feather quill from a leather
pouch tied to his saddle, dips it into a
small container of ink and writes a
letter. I hover over him, read his
Spanish words and instantly
translate.

My Dearest Governor Fages,

I am aware that I'm an ordinary,
old, mulatto soldier. Nobody has
remarked on my bravery. I have no
right to the spoils of war because I
have not participated in any wars.
When the uprising took place at the
San Diego Mission, I wasn't there.
There have been no other skirmishes
while I have marched with the
"leather jackets" as we call
ourselves.

However, I believe in JESUS, as do my wife and children. I've asked HIM for the land that spans the foothills to the ocean bounded by the Los Angeles River in the north and the Santa Ana River in the south. HE has told me that if it is all right with you, it would be all right with HIM for me to own this land.

Furthermore, HE has pointed out that I am in my late forties and cannot stay in the army forever.

I would greatly appreciate if you would look into this matter.

Your eternal servant, Manuel Nieto, Lowly Corporal in the Kingdom of Espana Army.

GOD says, "Blink your eyes, Dessa."

I blink my eyes.

GOD says, "It is 1784."

Manuel Nieto is running, dancing and jumping on the north mesa of the Westbruk Wetlands. "It's mine! It's all mine!" He seems so happy.

"What is Corporal Nieto talking about?" I ask GOD.

"The King of Spain has granted Manuel Nieto's wish. The corporal owns the Westbruk Wetlands and all the earth from the Los Angeles River to the Santa Ana River, from the foothills to the sea."

My throat hurts.

"You're alright, Dessa," my mother says. "The surgery went fine."

* * *

My parents looked down at me and smiled.

Tonsils out hurt more than tonsils in.

11.

Dear Dessa Dreams,
I'm forty-four and in love with a fourteen year old. What should I do?
Old Man from Astoria Falls,
Wyoming.

Dear Old Man,
If you don't want to go to jail, forget her.
Sincerely, Dessa Dreams.

Because of a regimen that included lots of rest and weekly Vitamin B12 shots, I recuperated and, in September of 1955, started my first term at UCLA, majoring in Theater Arts, specializing in television.

"Guess what?" I said to Jean Sturmss on the phone.

"What?" she asked.

Whenever Jean, who I'd met when I was twelve, was in Los Angeles and not residing in Paris, Rome, London or New York, we talked on the phone every day and took lunch or dinner together every week.

"We're going to analyze the DBC network mini-series *Cabel Sturmss* in my Introduction to Television class. Aren't you related to him?" I was in my pajamas, sitting at the kitchen table taking sips of my favorite concoction, half a cup coffee, half a cup heavy cream, and two tablespoons of sugar.

"He was my great, great grandfather," she said. "I wrote my second novel about him. He is sooo interesting; you'll have to read my book."

Jean and I were both eighteen, both freshmen at UCLA and she'd already had written two books.

"I want to read it," I said.

"I'll give you a copy."

"What's the name of the book?"

"Cabel Sturmss," she said. "You're going to like it better than the TVseries."

"Why?" I took another sip of coffee.

"I tell the truth about his sex life," she said. "It was very interesting."

"You sound funny," I said.

"Do you sound funny?" she asked.

"What?"

"I'm trying to imitate you," she said.

"Why?"

"I want to sound like you," she said.

"Why?"

"Imitation is the sincerest form of flattery." She hung up.

So did I.

12.

For the next eighteen weeks I analyzed the kinescope of the television mini-series "CABEL STURMSS" in my Introduction to Television Class and perused Jean's novel. The three witches from Shakespeare's play MACBETH danced around dead bodies, shouted explanations and complained about injustices in the miniseries. The witches were absent in Jean's novel but the plot lines, as well as the title, were the same. Here's the story:

It snowed in Lunenburg, Massachusetts on Friday evening, February 9, 1810. Inside a cozy saltbox house, twelve-year old Cabel Sturmss sat with his seven siblings around the dining table. Cabel's Papa, Levi, a sickly, skinny man, lit the Shabbos candles. Candle light and the fire in the fireplace provided the only illumination in the room. Papa Levi coughed and wheezed as he chanted the Sabbath prayers.

Cabel's Mama, Elizabeth, looked almost as pale and weak as her husband. She put soup and freshly made bread on the table.

For a moment nobody ate or spoke, then, Cabel's ten-year old brother Jacob tasted his soup. "Are you going to tell us a story, Papa?" he asked.

Papa Levi stirred his soup but didn't taste it. He smelled his bread but didn't eat it. "Of course, I'll tell you a story." Between coughs and wheezes he said, "A long time ago there were two intelligent rabbis."

"All rabbis are intelligent," Mama said before coughing yellow phlegm into her plain linen handkerchief.

"Yes," Papa said. "All are intelligent, but not all are wise." Trying to stop coughing, he took a sip of soup. "Once upon a time there was a non-Jew who wanted to find out about the Jewish religion. He went to Rabbi Shamai and said, 'Rabbi please teach me your religion.'

"Rabbi Shamai said, 'It would take me years to teach you my religion. There are 613 laws. And besides the laws there are special intricacies to be learned about these laws. I don't have time to teach you all these things.'

"The non-Jew still wanted to learn about the Jewish religion, so he visited Rabbi Hillel.

"'What can I do for you?' Rabbi Hillel asked with a welcoming smile.

"'I want to learn about the Jewish religion,' the non-Jew said.

"'I will teach you,' Rabbi Hillel said. 'It is easy.'

"'Really?' asked the non-Jew.

"'What is hateful to you, do not do to your neighbor,' Rabbi Hillel said. 'That is the whole Jewish religion. Everything else is commentary.'"

"That's why we can't have slaves," Cabel said. "Because it would be hateful to be a slave and awful to own one."

Papa Levi nodded, coughed, gasped and fell forward. His head plopped into the soup and he died.

Mama screamed, "What should we do?"

"I will do what needs to be done, Mama," Cabel said. But, he didn't know what needed to be done.

In the mini-series, the three witches from *MACBETH* danced around Papa, chanting, "Fire burn and cauldron bubble. Toil and trouble. Toil and Trouble. Three months later death will double."

Three months later, Cabel added some wood to the fire and went to find his mother. She was dead in her bed.

"What should we do?" Ruth, the four year old, asked.

Cabel was scared and his wrists hurt so much he thought he would never lift them again. *I will do what needs to be done.* "Follow me," he told his brothers and sisters.

He led them to the closest neighbor. "Our parents died," he told the neighbor who lived in a salt box house similar to the Sturmss' dwelling. "What should we do?"

"I haven't the slightest idea," the man said before he slammed his door.

Cabel wanted to cry but didn't. His wrists felt as if iron bracelets were tightened around them. "Our parents died," he told the second closest neighbor.

144

"Bury them," the second neighbor said before he closed his door.

The children dragged Papa Levi from the table and Mama Elizabeth from her bed to some hard looking dirt just outside their house. Cabel handed the one shovel they owned to Jacob and said, "The rest of us will use our hands to dig."

"Papa and Mama smell horrible," Benjamin, the ten year old, said. "I'm going to gag."

"Hurry up!" Cabel instructed his siblings. "The sooner we bury them the better off we'll be." He prayed that he would do what must be done without gagging or crying.

Ruth threw up on her dead mother, then, sobbed.

"Stop crying!" Cabel hugged his little sister.

"I'm hungry," Ruth said.

Cabel laughed.

"What's so funny?" Ruth asked.

"You just threw up and you want to eat." Cabel kissed his sister's smelly cheek.

"Is that funny?" she asked.

The children ate raw potatoes in the cellar.

"Potatoes are supposed to be soft," Benjamin said.

"And hot," Jacob said.

"We need to get back to the neighbors before dark," Cabel told the children as he chomped on a tasteless, crisp, raw potato.

"We buried them," Cabel told the neighbor. "What do we do now?"

"Get ye to a Jewish orphanage," the man said. "No Christians will take ye in."

"What's an orphanage?" Jacob asked.

The man closed the door on the children. Cabel felt the bands on his wrists extend to circle his ankles. But, he told himself; I will do what needs be done. He turned, lifted his feet and walked down the dirt path. The children followed him.

The neighbor came after them. "Wait," he said. "I'll take the little one."

Cabel nodded. "Please don't let me cry," he whispered to God.

The neighbor lifted Ruth.

"No! You can't take my sister," six-year old Esther cried. "We're the only girls. We have to stay together."

"Please, sir," Cabel said.

The neighbor squinted. "If I take her, I'm raising them both to be Christians."

Cabel went from house to house unloading his siblings on people who told him the children would be raised in the Christian religion.

The man at the last house said he would take Jacob and Cabel.

"I can't stay, sir," Cabel told the benefactor.

"Why not?" Jacob asked. "You can't leave me!"

"I'm too old to change my religion," Cabel said. "I like what Papa told us about Judaism."

"I'm too old, too." Tears ran down Jacob's face.

"Stop crying!" Cabel pushed his brother into the small house.

"I'll take good care of him," the man told Cabel. "And if you change your mind, you'll be welcome too."

Cabel walked forty-two miles from Lunenburg to the Boston harbor. He surveyed the situation, stopped in front of the biggest ship and looked up at the captain. "Do you have a job for me?" Cabel asked.

The captain put his index finger to his neat brown beard. "How old are you?" he asked.

"How old do you need to be to get a job?" Cabel couldn't stop trembling. His wrists were still very sore. Every time Cabel didn't know what to do the imaginary bands on his wrists grew tighter.

The captain tapped his fingers on the ship's rail before he answered, "You have to be sixteen to work on my ship."

"I'm sixteen." Cabel stood on his tiptoes and hoped that he looked older than his twelve years.

The captain laughed. "What is your name?"

"Cabel Sturmss."

"Why should I hire you, Cabel Sturmss?"

"I'm smart, sir."

"What are you smart in? Lifting cargo? Hoisting sails?"

"I can do arithmetic, sir. I've been doing my papa's business since I was twelve."

"You look like you're ten," the Captain said.

"Ask me some numbers, sir,"
Cabel said.

"Can I read your handwriting?"
the Captain asked.

"I'm a scribe, sir." Cabel prayed
his handwriting was as good as his
papa had always said it was.

In the mini-series, fast-forward,
montage, Cabel traveled by ship to
ports in the East Indies, China, West
Indies and Mexico. Constantly
promoted, he started by entering
numbers into a ledger and eventually
became the ship's super cargo (chief
purchasing agent).

Cabel married a woman called
Persis and made slow, passionate
love to her in a small bed covered by
a feather comforter. One of the
feathers stuck out of the duvet and
caught Persis in her right nostril.
Cabel laughed.

"How can you laugh?" Persis
asked, pulling the feather out.

Cabel kissed her.

"I think I'm pregnant," Persis
said.

"How wonderful!"

"I'm afraid," Persis said. "Babies
die. What if our baby dies?"

"Our baby isn't going to die." Cabel kissed his wife on her pink lips.

"Just in case." Persis sat up. "I'm going to do something about it."

"What are you talking about?" Cabel asked, gently fingering his wife's right cheek.

Cabel's wrists hurt as he stood outside the brick Park Street Church with its two hundred seventeen foot white steeple which could be seen from any place in Boston. He waited for Persis, while listening to abolitionists spout antislavery doctrine. He decided the speakers made sense and he agreed with them.

Persis walked out of the church, carrying their new baby. "He is now John Jacob Sturmss," she said, smiling at her husband.

Cabel felt his heart pound. His wrists were too heavy to lift. "I'm leaving," he told his wife. "I left you a packet of money. It should be enough for your life and his education."

"What are you saying, Cabel?" The baby cried. Persis lifted him to her shoulder.

"I'm a Jew, Persis. I told you I didn't want my son to be baptized."

Persis moved the baby to her other shoulder. "And I told you, Cabel. I can't take such a risk. The baptism gives John Jacob a chance whether he lives or dies."

Cabel kissed his baby and sailed south the next day.

In the main plaza of the dusty town of Vera Cruz, Mexico, Cabel and an old lady sat on wooden rocking chairs and rocked.

"You will sell me the property?" Cabel asked the woman.

"I'm only a woman." She touched the ivory comb that fastened a black lace mantilla to her hair. "Only my husband can deal with you."

Cabel patted the woman's heavily ringed, wrinkled with brown age spots, hands. "Your husband is dead. You own the property now."

"No body will sell to you. You're not Mexican."

"I'll become a Mexican citizen."

"It doesn't matter." She sneezed.

Cabel took a crisp white handkerchief out of his pocket and handed it to her.

She rubbed her nose with it. "Gracias, Don Sturmss."

"Don Cabel Sturmss. I like the sound of it."

"People may call you that to your face," the old lady said. "But they won't deal with you."

"Why not?"

"Mexicanos don't do business with Jews."

"I'm going to have to lose myself to get ahead." Cabel could feel his heart pound. His wrists hurt as if he were lifting a heavy weight.

"Maybe you should change your religion." The old lady spat in Cabel's handkerchief, then handed it back to him.

He looked at the phlegm on the square of white linen. "Yes," he said. "I will do what needs to be done."

From Mexico, Don Cabel Sturmss sailed to California and got rich, by selling goods that were legally traded and illegally smuggled at his warehouse in San Pedro, California.

William Knight owned a liquor store down the road from Cabel's warehouse. On the morning of September 20, 1835, William sampled his own wares. In an hour he was drunk. In two hours he was drunk and angry. Cabel Sturmss had sold him a barrel of sour wine and wouldn't give the money back. William took a sharp knife, sheathed it and sauntered down the street in a drunken stupor. When he arrived at the open door of Cabel's warehouse, Knight drawled, "Cabel Sturmss! I wanna see ya! Now!"

Cabel was in his office writing numbers in a ledger book. He heard Mister Knight but kept writing.

"I wan' my money, Mr. Sturmss," William Knight said when he entered Cabel's office. "You cheated and sold me *saer* wine. There's not nothing sa bad as *saer* wine."

"I sell as is, Mr. Knight, everybody knows that." Cabel put his ledger down and stood up. "I can't be sampling every wine barrel I sell like some people I know."

William stuck his elbow into Cabel's chest. "Whatchu inferrin'?"

"Don't poke me, Mr. Knight. I'm the wrong man to elbow."

"Are ya now? Well, I'm the wrong man to cheat." William took his knife out of its sheath and cut Cabel's face from eyebrow to chin.

Cabel tried to fight back but the tight bands he felt around his wrists wouldn't allow him to lift his hands. Losing blood, he fell backwards and hit his head. Still conscious, he told himself, "I will do what needs be done." But he couldn't do anything.

Mr. Knight opened Cabel's mouth and said, "You're never going to talk down to me again." He cut off part of Cabel's tongue and was about to make another slash, when he heard voices and ran out of the office, passing two men coming toward him in the warehouse. Arrested that afternoon, Knight spent five years in jail.

Cabel's wrists never hurt again. All his pain was concentrated in the permanent purple gash that went from the top of his forehead to the bottom of his chin and the gouged out part of his tongue. For the rest of his life, he drooled constantly and had a horrible speech impediment.

Five months later, soldiers caught Cabel and his cohorts lifting contraband off a sailing ship on to a lonely dock.

In a small courtroom, bare of the architectural embellishments courts had in the east, Cabel's lawyer pleaded the case while the judge, jury and a room full of spectators watched. The lawyer didn't say Cabel was innocent. "In fact, he isn't innocent, your honor. But he's not guilty. And if he's not guilty or even if he is, look what this man has had done to him."

Cabel told himself, "I must do what needs be done." He turned so that every person in the courtroom could see his mutilated face and hoped he could withstand the pain of showing off his ugliness.

The lawyer took two steps toward the jury box. He rested his hand on the wood railing and looked at an elderly juror. "I ask you now and I ask you to answer me good and truly. Have you never smuggled?" The lawyer turned his head and looked at another juror. "I have heard about your smuggling days. You cannot lie to me."

"What kind of defense is this?" the judge asked.

"The usage defense." The lawyer was a young, thin man wearing a brown suit that was too large for him. "If everybody breaks the law then the law is no longer a law."

"What do you mean?" the judge asked.

The lawyer walked to the judge's bench. "I have heard that even people who sit in high places have dabbled in smuggling when they were younger," the lawyer said.

"Are you threatening me?" the judge asked the lawyer.

"Of course not," the lawyer said. "I'm just repeating rumors that I've heard."

"Let me testify," Cabel lifted his hand to his face. His purple scar throbbed. The hole in his tongue smarted.

"I can't let you testify, Cabel," the lawyer said. "Nobody can understand you and you look like a horse. Everybody calls you 'horse face'."

"The judge is dishonest." Cabel slurred his words as if he were drunk which he wasn't or if part of his tongue had been cut off, which it had.

"What if the judge isn't dishonest? We really don't know if

anyone on the jury has ever smuggled anything." The lawyer shook his head. "We don't have a good defense, Cabel."

The judge asked the jury foreman, "Guilty or not?"

"Guilty!" shouted the skinny, old foreman who sneezed twice after he announced the verdict.

Cabel held his ugly head high. *I will be all right because I will do what needs to be done.* He was right. Instead of going to jail he was appointed the custom's officer for the Port of Los Angeles.

Did he bribe someone to get this position? If so, Jean didn't say anything about it in her novel and it wasn't mentioned in the mini-series.

This wasn't the only time Cabel was caught smuggling. The first time was in 1831. At that time, Manuel Victorio, the Mexican appointed Governor, tried to oust Sturmss from California.

Cabel didn't leave. He told himself that he would do what needs to be done and joined forces with Jose Bandino, a man who led a successful uprising against Governor

Victorio. The governor fled to
Mexico. Cabel stayed in California.

Jose Bandino was a big spender.
He spent money on uprisings and on
the upkeep of the large tracts of land
he owned. He spent money so he
wouldn't feel bored. His sons helped
him spend money. They were
gamblers good at losing. Jose and
his wife were socialite trendsetters in
California. They constantly hosted
big money eating fiestas. Jose
Bandino was very handsome. He
taught Californios to dance.

"I don't know how to dance," one
pretty senorita told Jose.

"Relax," he told the woman. "I
will move you. The music will
move you. We will be perfect."
And they were.

Jose spent so much money he had
to borrow from his married
daughters' husbands. At first the
men seemed glad to help. But Jose's
money problems never ended; and
the sons-in-law stopped lending.

One day Jose asked Cabel to help
him.

"You need money?" Cabel,
slurring his words, put his right
index finger on his scar.

"Yes, I do. I owe a lot."

"I am a lonely man," Cabel said.

The two men were sitting on the porch of Jose's heavily mortgaged hacienda, drinking cool water.

"You'll always have me for a friend," Jose Bandino told Cabel.

"I would like to marry your daughter, Adelita," Cabel slurred. His tongue burned as if a lemon had been rubbed into the wound.

Jose jumped up. "My daughter is so beautiful. She's so young."

"How badly do you need the money?" Cabel asked.

"I'm going to lose everything." Jose sat back down on his wood chair and put his face in his hands. "Adelita is only fourteen. How old are you?"

"Forty-four. I'm very lonely, Jose."

"How much will you loan me?" Jose's face was still in his hands.

"I won't lend you any money. I'll give it to you. As long as you are my father-in-law, you and yours will never want."

There were tears in Jose's eyes when he agreed to the marriage.

Isabella Bandino, an old duenna-chaperone, sat in the middle of the large room, embroidering a red and yellow flower on a white cloth. She didn't look up from her stitches and if she heard the conversation taking place, she made no sign.

Don Cabel Sturmss sat on a faded red velvet chair on one side of the large room. His intended, Adelita Bandino, sat on a faded green velvet chair on the other side. They looked at each other. It was almost as if they were alone. But, of course, they weren't. Isabella kept stitching.

"Do you want to get married?" Don Cabel fingered his scar.

Adelita clapped. "Of course."

"Why?" Cabel's tongue hurt.

"Every girl wants to be married. To be the mistress. To not have to listen to her mother, her married sisters, her duenna."

Isabella coughed but didn't look up. Her tiny stitches were almost a work of art.

"What will be different when we marry?" Cabel asked.

"We'll have parties. We'll invite the best people."

"Will that make you happy?"

"So happy!" she answered. "So happy!"

On the day they were married at the San Gabriel Mission, Cabel went into the confessional for the first time.

"Do you want to confess, my son?" the Priest asked.

"Confess what?" Cabel wondered if the Priest could see how ugly he was.

"Confess your sins, my son."

Why would he confess his sins to a stranger? He certainly wasn't going to tell this priest that he'd left a wife and son in Boston.

"Isn't there anything?" the Priest prodded.

Cabel felt the hole in his tongue getting larger. He closed his eyes and could see his own purple scar. He could see his little baby son. He couldn't remember what Persis looked like. Then he thought about his papa. "I haven't stayed true to my religion, Padre."

"What do you mean, my son?"

"My papa said that I should not do to someone else what is hateful to me."

"Your father sounds like a wise man. Now do you want to confess?"

"I think I've said what needs be said. I'll try to be a good husband."

On their wedding night, Cabel and Adelita sat side by side, leaning against ivory pillows that the duenna, Isabella, had stitched especially for the occasion. Their legs were stretched out under an ivory duvet covered feather-bed. Their sheets were ivory silk.

Cabel felt his hardness and wanting under his silk nightshirt. "Would you take your night gown off?" he asked, looking straight ahead. "I would like to look at you."

Adelita lifted her ivory silk nightgown over her head. "You can look now," she said.

The duvet covered Adelita to her waist. Cabel looked at the young woman who was his new wife. Her breasts were small and perked up. Cabel touched her. He was as gentle as he could be.

"Feels nice," she said.

He kissed her forehead, her cheeks, her neck and then her lips. He wanted to stick his tongue between her lips but feared to do so. He put his hand on her smooth stomach, then lowered it and met no resistance.

"Palo!" she yelled.

Cabel sat up.

"Why do you stop?" she demanded.

"Who is Palo?"

"My horse," she said.

He smiled then lowered himself on to her. At first, he was gentle, up and down. Up and down. Then he couldn't hold back. Up and down, faster and faster until there was an explosion in his head.

Adelita screamed, "Better than Palo! You're better than Palo, Cabel!" She reached for Cabel's hand and placed it on her breast.

"Palo can't do this," she said as his hand caressed her.

"What can Palo do?" Cabel felt his hardness returning.

"When I ride Palo, my privates tingle and tingle and tingle until I scream. I have to go alone when I ride Palo. It is the best feeling, Cabel. Except for what happened between us tonight, it is the best feeling I ever had.

Later she told him, "I knew it would be good with you. I knew I wanted to marry you as soon as I heard about the man they call 'Horse Face.' I knew that a man who looked like a horse would please me."

Cabel kissed his wife on her lips and stuck his mutilated tongue into her mouth.

The Sturmss lived in a grande ranchero they called El Palacio. They hosted informal dances, formal balls and bullfights. Only the crème de la crème of California were invited.

In the mini-series the first witch said, "How dare they not invite me?"

"I have been Adelita's friend all her life," the second witch said.

The three witches donned fancy ball clothes, walked to the Palacio and were turned away from the party. They picked stones and mud chunks from the ground and threw them at the Palacio windows. Other people joined the witches and also threw stones at the magnificent Sturmss' abode.

Because the Palacio had three feet
thick adobe walls, the people inside
didn't notice the stone-throwing
outsiders. They danced on top of
expensive, colorful carpets that
covered a hard packed dirt floor in
the one hundred feet long ballroom.
Women wore silk and satin dresses
with long trains. Men wore thousand
dollar suits embroidered with silver
threads. When they weren't dancing
the men broke eggs filled with
confetti, cologne or gold dust over
each other's heads.

Cabel looked at the party-goers
and wondered why he was living
such a shallow life. What would his
father have thought? His tongue hurt.

"I am so happy, Cabel." Adelita
reached up to kiss his scar.

He forgot his pain.

Outside, the Witches and their
men friends dragged cannon to the
front of El Palacio and fired a
cannon ball into the front door.

The male party-goers dropped
their eggs, picked up their guns and
shot into the air. The outsiders fled.

On a cool Monday in 1849, when
California was already an American

state, Abelardo Ruiz, a middle-aged man dressed like an ordinary vaquero ranch hand, walked into Cabel's office. "I don't have the money to register my land," he told Cabel.

Senor Ruiz, a distant relative of Manuel Nieto and one of the many heirs to his estate, owned the land that would someday be known as the town of Westbruk and the Westbruk Wetlands. All Spanish land grants had to be registered when the United States took California from Mexico. Registration cost more money than Ruiz could afford. "My Rancho is worthless." Abelardo was sweating and kept wiping his face with a large red handkerchief. "But still and all, I want to pass it on to my children."

On horseback, Abelardo Ruiz and Cabel surveyed the Westbruk Wetlands at the end of March. The mesas were green. The water was clear. A few stray cattle grazed. "This place isn't good for nothing," Abelardo said. "But it's mine. I don't want to lose it."

In the miniseries Cabel looked up from the lower wetlands toward the Westbruk Mesa. That's when I spotted Grandpa and Luna sitting on two golden Palominos.

Grandpa took an arrow out of his quiver. There was a close up of his hand. To me the cog stone tattoo seemed to jump out of the television monitor. Grandpa aimed his bow at Cabel. Luna yelled, "Ahhh!" and galloped toward Cabel and Abelardo. Grandpa turned, aimed his arrow and let it fly. The arrow hit Luna in her back and she fell off her horse.

"Let's see that part over again," I yelled out in class.

Everybody looked at me. Sam Mackeroy, my teacher, turned off the kinescope and said, "Quiet! We're watching a program." He turned the TV back on.

I couldn't concentrate. *Is Luna alive?*

I stayed after class and asked Mr. Mackeroy, "How can I find out about those actors?"

"Which actors?" He chomped on a Baby Ruth Bar and talked with his mouth full of chocolate.

"Those people on the horses. You know the man with the cog stone tattoo on his hand."

Mackeroy didn't know what I was talking about. I didn't explain.

In the last episode of the mini-series Sturmss loaned Ruiz fifty calves to pay for the registration fees on his Rancho. But though he loaned him animals, he told Ruiz, "I expect to be paid back in money. The interest will be 5% and compounded monthly."

Ruiz couldn't afford to pay. In February of 1861, Sturmss bought the wetlands and the rest of what would be known as the city of Westbruk at a public auction.

Snow clouded the kinescope. Mackeroy turned it off and told us to stretch.

When he turned the TV on again, cows in Westbruk changed from thriving to dying. Torrents of rain flooded the land, then, disappeared into dry holes. Green grass turned yellow, then brown, and then died. Crickets devoured the small plots of grass still growing.

"There has never been so many crickets in California," the first witch said.   "Streams, ponds and springs disappear. There is no fresh water."

"Cabel and Adelita didn't invite us to the party," the second witch said. "Now they'll suffer."

There was another storm. The three witches danced in the rain while the water washed away the land.

Cabel stood on the porch of the Palacio, telling himself that he would do what needed to be done. He told Adelita, who stood next to him, with her heavily ringed hand on his shoulder, "I'll sell the hides. All is not lost."

"All is lost," said the second witch. "Cabel is done for."

A hideous picture of starving cows, their bones puncturing their hides was on the TV screen.

"Not only cows are suffering," the first witch said. "Cabel's servants are dying of small pox."

Grandpa, reappearing on the screen, died of small pox. He was such a good actor; I could feel his death throes.

Cabel had been one of the richest men in California. Now he wasn't

able to pay $150.00 in back taxes.
"I'm losing everything," Cabel told
his wealthy friend Percival Robinson
as the two men cantered their horses
across the north mesa. The drought
resistant native plants that grew on
the wetlands were thriving again.
The wild flowers were blooming.
The prickly pears were ready for
picking if you wore gloves to protect
yourself from the thorns.

"I wish I could help you, my
friend," Percival said. The actor that
played Percival in the TV series was
overweight and didn't sit his horse
well.

Cabel had a good seat but looked
uglier than ever. Probably the
makeup man added more purple to
his scar in each frame.

"You can help me, Percival,"
Cabel said. "I have an idea." His
speech was more slurred than ever.

"What's your idea?" Percival
wanted to know.

"You pay my debts. The two of
us will sell this land. People in the
east and Europe don't know about
the floods and droughts. They'll
want to buy."

Percival put his finger on his nose. "What will we call this company?"

Cabel trotted his horse toward the sea. His tongue and face hurt but he told himself he would do what needs to be done. He rode back to Percival. "We'll call it the Percival Robinson Trust."

Percival smiled.

Very attractive maps and brochures were folded and stuffed in envelopes that were crammed into mailbags and sent to distant places.

The Percival Robinson Trust sold more than 20,000 acres in its first year of business.*

*I went to the Westbruk Public Library and found out that Hans Westbruk bought most of those 20,000 acres which included what is now a large part of Westbruk town proper and a tiny bit of the Westbruk Wetlands. Hans Westbruk was originally from somewhere in Germany, but was residing in Quentin, Illinois at the time of the purchase.

According to what I read, Mr. Westbruk owned a thriving tavern in Quentin and was a married man. One rainy night, he saw his wife fornicating with an ironmonger in back of his tavern. The following morning, the town blacksmith found Westbruk's wife dead in the hay in the ironmonger's barn. The ironmonger had disappeared. Within a week, Mr. Westbruk sold his tavern and bought land in Southern California from the Percival Robinson Trust with the proceeds of the sale. In 1870 he moved to California and established the town of Westbruk, granting life time use of acre and half acre land plots to any man who would sign a paper promising to follow Mr. Westbruk's rules.

Rules of Westbruk
1. Attend the Westbruk Presbyterian Church.
2. Abstain from drinking liquor and join the Westbruk Christian Temperance Society.
3. Don't grow grapes.
4. Commit no crimes against God or Man.
5. Help your neighbor if he needs help.
Copies of these rules can still be found all over Westbruk, eg. The Police

Station, City Hall, Municipal Court House, Historical Society. Etc.

According to the history books, in the late eighteen hundreds and the early nineteen hundreds the rules seemed to work and everybody who lived in Westbruk thrived. That is everybody except Hans Westbruk. He didn't charge rent. He didn't farm. And he donated so much money to the church and charities of Westbruk, he depleted his savings.

Don Cabel Sturmss didn't fare much better than Westbruk. When he died on August 23, 1871 at the Grand Hotel in San Francisco at the age of seventy-three he hadn't recaptured his wealth.

"Cabel Sturmss is dead," said the first witch.

"Nobody's mourning," the second witch said.

"Somebody is," said the third witch.

Adelita Bandino Sturmss, Cabel's wife, was devastated. "There will never be another party without Cabel," she said. It wasn't true. Adelita married two more times and

kept having parties until she died in
1912, leaving an enormous estate.
Thirty-two lawsuits were filed for
eighty-six hopeful heirs. Forty-one
of the hopeful claimed they were part
of the Sturmss family.

The three witches cackled at the
end of the mini-series.

I called Jean. "Hi!"

"Hi!" she said. Her "Hi!"
sounded just like my "Hi!"

"Stop imitating me!" I ordered.

"Can't help it," she said.

"Did any of your Sturmss'
relatives get something from Adelita
Bandino's estate?"

"My grandfather did."

She sounded just like me. "Stop
mimicking me!

"I can't help it," Jean said.
"Don't get mad."

But I was mad. *What is wrong
with her?*

Other students in my Introduction
to Television class gave cogent
critiques as to why it was a good or
bad idea to use the three witches
from *MACBETH* in the mini-series.
They also spoke to whether the scene

changes were adequate to keep our attention and would it have been better to make "CABEL STURMSS" into a movie. I was the only person in the class interested in learning about the extras.

While the other students wrote their analyses, I contacted the Walmarin Studio who produced the miniseries and asked if there was a way to get the names and addresses of the extras that appeared in "CABEL STURMSS."

"We don't keep names and addresses of extras," the Walmarin operator told me. "Extras come and go."

"Well yes," I said. "But is there a possibility? I'd be. . ."

"No!" She hung up on me.

13.

Dear Dessa Dreams,
I have a chance for a new job out west. My fiancé wants to stay in Wisconsin. She's not adventurous

*and doesn't want us to risk. Should I
kidnap her or leave without her?
Ready for adventure in Racine.*

*Dear Ready,
    I dreamt about a man who
wanted to go west. When he asked
his love to come with him, she turned
him down. He married another
woman. It wasn't a happy marriage.
So I think you should kidnap her.
Only kidding. Maybe give your
fiancé the final choice: come with
you or be left behind. If she says
she's not going, then you have a
choice to go without her or stay
where you are. Write me another
letter if you need more information.
Sincerely, Dessa Dreams.*

On the first Wednesday night in
November of 1955, my dad yelled,
"You're a hypochondriac!"

"I'm sick," my mother moaned.
"Every bone in my body hurts."

"Get out of bed!"

"It's the middle of the night,
Willie."

Then a glass broke and I could
feel the shards cut my ears. My

mother had broken a glass every night for the last four nights. I got the broom and dustpan out of the kitchen utility closet.

"Don't sweep!" My dad said. "She can sweep her own Goddamn mess."

I didn't want to look at them. I was so angry. *Am I the only grownup here?* Concentrate, I told myself. Get up every piece of glass.

"I'm too weak to sweep!" My mother cowered on her side of the bed.

My dad pretended to read a metallurgy book. "Well, then, when you need to use the toilet, you can cut your feet," he said.

"He wants to kill me, Dessa." While rolling and unrolling the sheet, my mother looked straight ahead as if I were some place fixed on the wall like a family portrait.

I kept sweeping till I cut my foot. "Oww!" It hurt.

My mother stopped fiddling with the sheet. "I'm sorry, Dessa," she said. "I didn't do it on purpose."

"Yeah!" My dad got out of bed, put on his slippers, went into their bathroom and came back with a bottle of Mercurochrome and a large bandage.

I bandaged my foot, went to my room, got in bed and reached for my cog stone.

* * *

GOD says, "It is 1898."

Leo is naked.

"Put your clothes on," I say. "You're too old to run around naked."

Ignoring me, he walks a fast pace toward a distinguished, well-dressed man sitting on a buckboard and looking old fashioned like an actor in the movie *Meet Me in Saint Louis*. "You can't build a gun club, Count Von Baumschlager," Leo tells the man.

Is Leo going to introduce me to the Count? What is a gun club?

"No!" my dad yells. "I won't!"

* * *

"I told you," my dad screamed.

I turned on the lamp that rested on my maple side table. It was 2:30 in the morning.

"Clothes, food, entertainment, books, anything you want, but I won't pay your doctor bills anymore," my dad said.

"You're sentencing me to death," my mother said.

In the morning my dad left my mother again.

Mother got out of bed, took art classes, swimming lessons and shopped. She offered to buy me some new clothes, but I wasn't interested. I was a theater arts major specializing in TV and theater arts majors at UCLA dressed like Bohemians. I wore my dirty paint clothes even on the days I didn't paint sets. I didn't wear make up. I hardly remembered to wash my face or brush my teeth.

Was I going through some kind of depression? No. Because, though my parents were occupied with their incipient divorce, I was in love for the first time. At least, I thought I was.

The day I met Micah at Hillwood Country Club I looked clean because I had just gotten out of the club's almost Olympic sized pool.

"Hello gorgeous," were the first two words he said to me.

Who is he talking to? I was the only one there.

Micah, wearing a bright red bathing suit, sat on the chaise lounge next to the chair where I'd put my towel. He kept talking. I didn't hear what he said because I was too busy wondering why he was talking to me. He said "gorgeous" again. But I didn't know what the context was. *Should I sit in the chair?* I sat. "My name is Dessa," I said, wrapping my towel around my wet bathing suit and wishing I had some lipstick.

"I'm Micah Silverberg," he said, reaching his dry hand out to grasp my wet one.

I had seen him at the club before and knew his name. I also knew that he was in his last year in law school and his parents were both lawyers. My dad frequented the same charitable events, and attended the same reform Synagogue on high holidays as the Silverberg's. He'd played golf with Micah's father at least three times.

Micah was twenty-three. At eighteen I regarded him as an older man. He'd graduated college summa cum laude and had his own Phi Beta Kappa key. *How smart is he?*

In 1955 I spent a lot of time playing hearts and was the best shoot-the-mooner at Hillwood until Micah showed up.

My best friend, Jean Sturmss, and I spent one Saturday morning rigging the deck. Our mission: To wipe out Micah. "I've already dealt the cards," I told him.

"I already dealt the cards," Jean said.

She's imitating me again. What is wrong with her?

Micah smiled, looked at his cards and shot the moon.

Jean smiled at Micah as if he had performed a miracle. I was mad at both of them. Then I turned toward Micah. He was looking at me and smiling. Perfect teeth! Shiny warm eyes! This is the guy for me, I thought.

Both my parents agreed. My dad said Micah's future looked good. His lawyer parents owned the law firm that represented the Oliver Drugstores. "Ollies" was one of the largest drug store chains in the western United States in 1955 and in the process of expanding.

Micah wasn't only rich, handsome and smart; he was nice. We went out to dinner, to the movies, and to summer concerts at the Hollywood Bowl. "It's too loud," I said when I first heard the *1812 Overture.*

"It's just right." He put his hands over my ears and kissed me. "You're just right, too, Dessa."

We went for hikes in Griffith Park, played miniature golf and went to the beach.

One day, after we walked miles in the sand, I showed Micah the bench Bubbie and I used to sit on to watch the tidal phosphorescence at Venice Beach. "She told me to be kind," I told him.

"You are kind," he said. Then he took my hands and kissed me softly on the lips. "You're beautiful, Dessa."

"You arc too," I said.

"Did you read the *ART OF LOVING*?" Micah asked.

I'd heard about it. It was a new book.

"I like what it says about loving," he said. "The main thing is to concentrate on the here and now. Do you concentrate?" he asked.

"No," I said. "I dream."

When we got back to his car he presented me with a copy of the *ART OF LOVING*. It was inscribed: "*To Dessa, the person who inspires my concentration.*"

In October of 1956, Micah called to tell me that he was in a phone booth at the airport on his way to New York and after thinking and thinking and pondering and pondering; he decided we should get married.

"Yes," I said, meaning for him to go on with the conversation.

"I knew you'd say yes," he said. "We are beshert."

"What does beshert mean?" The phone receiver was sweating in my hand.

"It means we're meant for each other," he said. "I'll see you when I get back from New York."

"But, wait." *Am I engaged?*

I heard a voice that I couldn't make out. Then I heard Micah say, "She said yes, Mom."

But I hadn't said yes. Had I?

"Gotta go, Dessa." Micah hung up.

The man that had just proposed marriage hadn't mentioned that he loved me. And I didn't know if I loved him.

14.

Dear Dessa,
I'm engaged to marry Charles. But I'd like to marry Jim. Is there a way to marry both of them?
Indecisive in Gary, Indiana

Dear Indecisive,
I dreamt about a girl who was engaged to the perfect man but fell in love with somebody else. The somebody else wasn't perfect but she married him and lived a not so perfect life.

Don't marry anybody if you're indecisive.
Sincerely, Dessa Dreams.

In September of 1959, when Jean Sturmss and I were twenty-one, she joined the Phi Sigs and was one of the new pledges presented to the world on Sorority Presents Night. She invited Micah, me and everybody else she knew to the "propitious occasion," as she dubbed it.

Jean told me she'd decided to join a sorority in her senior year because she wasn't meeting any good guys. Her mother told her good men could be found at sororities and sorority girls always got married. Even though, Jean was very smart and very talented, her main ambition was to marry. One day before the semester started, she told me that she would really like to marry somebody like Micah. If somebody like Micah wanted to marry her, she wouldn't be as indecisive as I was. That conversation made me appreciate Micah. Jean and I both agreed he was probably the best thing that ever happened to me.

So there we were, Micah and I, sitting on metal folding chairs in the large front room of the Phi Sig House to give Jean our moral support when Micah excused himself. He needed to go to the restroom.

I sat on my uncomfortable chair thinking that I would never join a sorority. Theater arts bohemians didn't go out for sororities. Then, again, though Jean wasn't a theater arts bohemian, she was a writer. How could a talented writer join a sorority?

My right foot fell asleep. I stretched it to stamp out the tingles and kicked a white sock inside of a large brown, scuffed, loafer. "I'm sorry," I said to the sock and shoe, then looked up to the face the shoe and sock belonged to and jumped. I was looking at Leo, the boy I had met on Cardboard Beach when I was ten. The Leo who'd sold me my dream inducing cog stone. The Leo I dreamt about. "Leo?" I said.

"Do I know you?" He smiled the same crooked teeth smile.

"We met when we were ten," I said. "I was ten. I don't know how old you were. How old are you now?"

"Twenty-two."

"I was ten and you were eleven," I said.

"Vas it in the orphanage or the school?" He seemed to have an accent or speech impairment.

"It was on the beach," I said.

"When I was eleven I never went to the beach," he said.

"You're a liar," I said.

Instead of arguing the point, he asked me to dance. A Strauss waltz was playing on the record player and I walked into the arms of a man who knew how to waltz. He had on cologne or after-shave lotion, I'm not sure which, and his breath smelled minty.

At the end of the dance, people clapped for us, we bowed and Micah walked across the floor and took my hand.

"Come on, Micah," I said. "I want to dance some more."

Micah danced slow and close. I kept moving away, not wanting to feel his hardness. *Why?*

Leo tried to cut in. Micah stuck his hand out and shook Leo's hand.

"I'm Micah Silverberg," he said. "Dessa and I are engaged."

"I'm Leonard Lechmann," Leo said. "What is your last name, Dessa?"

"Halom," I said. "Dessa Halom. Why do you ask? I told you Halom means dream. Don't you remember? I was ten and you were eleven."

What is your phone number, Dessa Halom?"

I liked his accent.

"Are you nuts?" Micah told Leonard. "I just told you we're engaged."

"I've known him since I was ten," I told Micah. Then I recited my phone number.

Micah turned and walked out of the sorority house.

Leonard/Leo put his arms out.

"Put Your Hand On My Shoulder" by Paul Soleman was on the record player.

"Put your hand on my shoulder
Hold my hand in your hand.
Move a little closer,
Dance with me, my love,
tonight. "

Leonard/Leo pulled me closer. I put my hand on his shoulder. I held his hand. We were back on the dance floor.

"Put your cheek next to mine, dear.

Let your heart hear my heart.
Move a little bit closer.
Dance with me, my love, tonight."

Leonard tried to kiss me. Suddenly I thought about Micah and felt guilty. I turned my head and his kiss landed on my right cheek.

"When we hear the music play, that's when we'll begin to sway.
So move a little bit closer.
And dance with me, my love, tonight."

Leonard pulled me closer. My chest was against his chest, my stomach against his stomach, my privates against his hardness. We didn't dance; we swayed. I could hear him breathe.

When the music stopped, it hurt to move away from the man who dominated my dreams.

The next song was "Good night Irene."

Jean Sturmss' father drove Jean and me home.

By the time Micah called to apologize, (what had gotten in to him? he said, of course, I could give my phone number to a friend that I'd known since I was ten), I had already promised to see Leonard.

Leonard said he would pick me up at seven. At nine my mother told me to go to bed. I was being stood up.

Of course, Leonard couldn't be counted on. He'd sold me a cog stone under false pretenses when I was ten. He had a grandpa who shot arrows and killed people. He was a liar from a bad family. Well, I wasn't hurt. That guy didn't have the power to hurt me, not even in my dreams.

At nine thirty, I tossed the cog stone out the window. At nine forty-five I retrieved it by crawling on my hands and knees in our muddy rose garden.

Leonard rang the doorbell at ten and laughed when he saw my dirty skirt. "I'm sorry, Dessa," he said. "I got lost and didn't have your phone number with me."

I didn't believe him. He was still that eleven year old who lied to me. But, even so I changed my skirt and went.

Leonard held my hand as we walked down steep stairs surrounded by tall sunflowers and taller palms that led to the entry of a tri-level, triangular looking house in the fancy Los Feliz area of Los Angeles.

When we entered the house, Jean was standing on a Persian rug in the entry with our host Joshua Aesenberg, one of Leonard's frat brothers. Joshua was shorter than Jean. He sported old fashioned, frameless glasses, and didn't look anything like the person Jean had often described to me as her tall, dark and handsome dream man. *Micah?*

In the mirrored restroom, even the ceiling reflected our images, Jean told me Joshua was quite wonderful, but she cared for somebody else.

"Who?" I asked.

"You must be blind," she said.

"I'm not blind!"

"I'm not blind," Jean aped me.

"Why do you keep mimicking me?" I asked. "It's not nice."

"Imitation is the sincerest form of flattery," she said.

I didn't feel flattered, but, instead of delving into it, I told her that Leonard had been three hours late.

She said I was the dumbest person she'd ever met. "Leonard's not even cute. He looks like Abraham Lincoln."

"Isn't that good?" I asked.

Jean stared at me. "Isn't that good?" she mimicked.

I walked out of the bathroom.

Joshua put the record "Put Your Hand On My Shoulder" by Paul Soleman on the record player. *Did Leonard tell him to?* The rugs in the enormous living room had been rolled back to the walls. The four couches hugged the rugs, leaving lots of wood floor to dance on. Leonard asked me to dance. Boy, he could dance. We did a fox trot. We were so good, people stopped to watch us.

"Put your hand on my shoulder"

Leonard whispered, "I like you, Dessa."

"Hold my hand in your hand."

Leonard kissed my hand.

I could see Jean squinting at us. Were her eyes shooting venom?

"Move a little closer."

We moved closer. Our hearts beat together. My breasts were warm. The inner core between my thighs was damp.

"Dance with me, my love, tonight."

"I really like you, Dessa."

We decided to leave the party.

The cold air outside woke me up. I was engaged to another man and knew nothing about Leonard. I hadn't seen him since we were children.

We sat in his two-toned, bright red and splotchy brown rust convertible. The bumper was dented and the top was missing. There was a large beach umbrella in the back seat in case of an emergency, like a light rain.

"Are you hungry?" he asked.

I was.

"What do you feel like eating?"

"Salad with lots of thousand island dressing," I said. "I still don't like fish."

Leonard didn't start the car. He took a cigarette out of a package in his shirt pocket and lit it. "Why do you think you know me?" he asked.

By then, I'd figured out that my parents' cigarette smoke had caused a lot of my sore throats. Ever since my hair caught fire in the Orthodox Shul on Simchas Torah, I was afraid of flames, uneasy around matches and lit cigarettes. But I didn't say anything about my discomfort because I wanted to know more about Leonard. "Tell me something about yourself," I said.

"I was born in Subotica, Yugoslavia," he said. "I spent World War II in Bucharest, Rumania. After the war, we escaped the Communists and went to Vienna." Leonard blew his smoke over the topless window. "There is no way we could have met before."

He's lying.

He threw the cigarette into the street and started the car.

I asked him to drive me home.

I took my cog stone to bed with me.

* * *

GOD says, "It is 1901."

Leo sits on a small wooden chair at a small wooden table in a small room. He's writing a letter. I stand behind him and read it.

To Mr. Theodore Roosevelt
President of the United States of
America.

Dear Your Honor the President
Roosevelt,
I am a citizen of the United
States and own a small piece of
farmland near the north mesa of the
Westbruk Wetlands, in southern
California. This is a swampland, not
easy to work. I hand dug the
irrigation ditches to drain water. My
horses used to sink in the mud. But
now I've attached wooden plates to
my horses' feet and they don't sink
anymore. In the last few years I
have been able to grow potatoes,
lima beans and celery and was
enjoying a nice life until the
members of the local fancy-
schmancy Gun Club dammed my
navigable stream. I believe this is a
violation of our national navigation
laws and because of the damming

*people of the area now suffer from
Typhoid and Malaria.*

Somebody moans and Leo stands
and walks to a small trundle bed in
the corner of the room where Luna,
covered with a pile of blankets,
shivers. He takes a cloth, puts it in a
water basin, and wipes her face.

"Water," she says. "I'm so
thirsty."

"I'll get you some water," I say.

The phone rings. Do we have
telephones in 1901? The phone rings
again.

* * *

It was morning and Micah was
on the phone. He wanted to know if
I would like to drive with him to
Santa Barbara.

"Too much homework," I said.
"Can I have a rain check?"

That evening Micah called again.
He wanted to talk wedding plans.

"When you get back," I said.

"Dessa, do you want to get
married?"

"Of course." Every young
woman wanted to get married in
1959.

"Do you want to marry <u>me,</u>
Dessa?"

I took a breath before I answered. "You've the best thing that ever happened to me, Micah." I told the truth but hadn't answered his question. *Did he notice?*

I heard him take a deep breath and let it out before he said, "You are the best thing that ever happened, Dessa."

I called Jean to discuss the situation. But instead of talking about Micah I asked her about Teddy Roosevelt.

"Teddy Roosevelt?" Jean asked, sounding so much like me we could have been twins.

Why did she copy my voice? It doesn't matter, I told myself. "Remember that paper you wrote about Teddy Roosevelt in Eleventh Grade Advanced English? I want to read it."

"It wasn't about Teddy Roosevelt," she said. "It was about a Gun Club, the people who started it and the people who lived around it."

"That's the paper I want to read," I said. "Do you still have it?" I knew she did. She kept everything she wrote.

15.

April 11, 1954
Dear Mrs. Hopkins,

Thanks for letting me stray from Teddy Roosevelt so I can explore my family background instead. As I told you, both of my parents are descended from very rich, old California families. My great, great, grandfather, Cabel Sturmss, was one of the biggest landowners in California at one time. He died in 1871. Adelita Bandino Sturmss, his widow, married two more men, and died in 1912 intestate, leaving one of the largest estates in California at that time. Thirty-five Bandinos, and forty-one Sturmss went to court to fight over her seven and a half million dollars. My grandfather, "Stoney" Sturmss, was one of the litigants.

So here goes my paper from a lot of points of view just as you assigned.
Sincerely, Jean Sturmss

ESSAY BY JEAN AUTEN
STURMSS FOR THIRD PERIOD

11th GRADE ADVANCED
ENGLISH April 12, 1954
STONEY STURMSS

Call me Stoney. I am the son of
John Jacob Sturmss and the grandson
of Cabel Sturmss. Cabel left my
grandmother, Persis, in Boston,
Massachusetts and never returned.
My father, a bitter man, died young.
My mother and stepfather raised me.

From the time I was young, I was
told I was exactly like my father, a
man with a heart of stone. So I was
called Stoney and have kept the
name.

In 1868, I read that the Percival
Robinson Trust Company, run by
Cabel Sturmss and Percival
Robinson, was selling farmland in
California. On the chance that Cabel
Sturmss might be my grandfather, I
decided that someday in my future I
would venture to California.

My mother died in 1870 and I
had no wish to remain with my
stepfather. He had no wish for me to
stay. He told me, "You didn't cry
when your mother died. I won't cry
when you go."

I walked to the pier, boarded a
ship and sailed around the bottom of

South America. By the time I
reached California, Cabel Sturmss
was dead. Having little money, I
signed a piece of paper promising I
would abide by the town of
Westbruk's rules, which included
staying away from liquid spirits and
going to church. In return I was
granted a half acre of land on a mesa
at the Westbruk Wetlands.

The weather was warm the first
day I saw my land. The mesa
overlooked the ocean. I thought I
had never seen such a beautiful
place. I bought a horse and a plow.
The horse and plow sunk in the
ground. How do you plow when
your horse sinks into the ground?
How do you plow when the ground
is always wet?

On the twenty-first day of
botched plowing, I gave up.
Walking through the mud I noticed a
hut made of thatch and Tule on a
pocket of land in the middle of a
small stream. As I splashed through
the warm water, a man came out of
the hut with a bow and a quiver of
arrows and aimed his weapon at me.

The most beautiful woman I'd
ever seen walked out of the hut and

put a restraining hand on the man's shoulder. "No, Papa," I heard her say. "It isn't necessary."

I had no weapon, but I kept wading toward the tiny island. It was as if I could go neither right nor left, only toward the beautiful woman. "My name is Stoney," I said when I reached the sand. "Stoney Sturmss."

"I am Lunathree," the young woman said. "Lunathree Bandino."

The man aimed his bow and arrow toward the sky and shot a duck. Lunathree built a fire out of willow twigs and cooked the bird. The man invited me to share their dinner. I'd never eaten duck before. It tasted something like a fat, sweet chicken or maybe rattlesnake. I'd killed a snake the second day I started to plow the mesa. Actually the duck was better than chicken or snake. Really delicious. So were the red berries we ate with it.

"I never want to leave here," the Papa said. He chomped on the duck's leg, smacking his lips and gums after every bite. He didn't have teeth. "There is enough food here to last our lifetime," he continued.

He wanted to stay forever and I was ready to leave. He thought the place had food. I couldn't plow. It hadn't occurred to me that I could have food without plowing. Besides I didn't want food only for my own use. I planned to sell my crops. I'd heard my grandfather had been one of the richest men in California at one time. Like him, I was ambitious.

"The law will come." Lunathree was a dainty eater. Only tiny bites went into her mouth. I liked the way that mouth curved. I wanted to touch it. I wanted to see her breasts. I wanted to lie atop her. I'd been alone too long.

Papa's bow and quiver of arrows were too close for me to ask why the law was after them. But I did want to know. Because the fog that often covered the marsh blurred one's vision, the wetlands were a good place for outlaws to hide. During the day people could conceal themselves and nap under drought resistant shrubs. Of course it would be hard to sleep because of the noise. There were so many birds and ducks screeching and screaming in the sky, I could hardly see the sun.

I slept on the island sand because I was too tired to walk anywhere after eating. It was cold after the fire went out.

In the morning, I felt the Papa shake me. It was still dark but I could see he held a knife in his hand. "What are you doing?" He looked too weak to kill me. But you never can tell about those things.

"Sit up!" he ordered. "I need to talk to you."

I sat. I would have liked to stretch. It was cold and damp that morning.

"Do you like Lunathree?" he asked.

I shrugged. She was beautiful and I wanted to bed her, but I didn't know if I liked her.

"Would you like to sleep with her?" the Papa asked.

What kind of man offers up his daughter? "I don't have any money," I said.

"She's a virgin," he said.

"I still don't have any money."

"I have other requirements." He looked so weak.

"What?" I felt very uncomfortable.

"First you must let me cut you." He brought his knife close to my hand.

"I'm not going to let you cut me, old man."

He showed me a tattoo on his right hand. "Do you know what this is?" he asked.

"A sun tattoo." It looked like a crude drawing of a sun with small spokes sticking out from its perimeter.

"It's a tattoo," he said. "But not of the sun."

"What is it?" I asked.

"It's a cog stone." The man showed me a cog stone, a rock with teeth like projections coming out of its round rim. I had seen similar rocks on my property on the mesa and had cursed them as one more obstacle to plowing.

"I want to tattoo you."

"Nope," I said. "I don't want your daughter that much."

"Lunathree, come out," he yelled.

She came out of the hut naked to her waist. I was lost.

LUNATHREE

My name is Lunathree Bandino. My mother was half Spanish, half Maritime Shoshone. She was the Bandino. My Papa took her name. He's from far away, calls himself American, but likes living in the old Maritime Shoshone manner. He hasn't been the same since my mother died. He says he is old and sick and will find me a man before he turns east, gets into the fetal position and dies. He says he will die soon. I will put the cog stones on his shoulders when he leaves to go to the Catholic Heaven.

I don't want Papa to go to Hell. So we only steal when we need to. Only in the cities. If the real estate men would stop selling or giving away the property under our huts, we could live on the wetlands and never have to steal.

I am seventeen years old and have never been with a man, but Mama told me what to do before she died. We didn't have to turn her east or fold her into the fetal position. We only do that with men. We did bury her with the metate and mano that she used to grind acorns. I miss the acorn mush. But, we don't walk

to the oak trees anymore. Papa
doesn't feel like walking without
Mama and I don't either.

Papa has watched this man,
Stoney Sturmss, for twenty-one
days. He tells me that he thinks he is
the right man for me. If he is the
right man, Papa will die happy.

"Don't you think I can be by
myself?" I asked Papa.

"Maybe. But I don't want you to
be lonely."

Mama told me how she got Papa
to like her. But, that isn't the
important thing, Mama said. The
important thing is to make a man
keep liking you. To make a man like
you forever. Then she told me the
secrets.

This morning Papa told me if he
called, I was to come out of the hut
baring my breasts.

Papa told Stoney he could touch
my breasts. He did. It was a very
nice feeling. I wanted him to touch
more. I wanted to move closer to
Stoney. I liked the way he looked,
but Papa pulled his hand away.

Stoney nodded. Papa cut a cog
stone tattoo on his hand and rubbed

the deep blue and violet flowers that we call sky lupine into the cuts.

"You will wait till night," my Papa told us.

Then he told Stoney how to farm. He showed him how to cut slabs of wood to attach to his horse's feet so they wouldn't sink into the ground. He told him the right way to dig ditches to drain the water from the swamp.

At night fall Papa slept outside and Stoney came into our hut. He put his big stick into my private parts. It hurt. My mama said the big stick was the best thing that happened to her. It wasn't the best thing that happened to me. Stoney fell asleep and snored. I pushed him off me and remembered Mama said it was the best thing that ever happened on the third time. After that she couldn't get enough of it. *How will I get through the second time?*

"It hurt," I told my Papa in the morning.

"It takes a while,"" Papa said.

"That's what Mama said," I told him.

"I miss her so much," Papa said. "She was so beautiful."

"I miss her too, Papa." I felt so sad. I loved my parents very much.

"When it's good," he said. "Call out. I'll be listening."

"What should I say?"

"You'll know what to say." He kissed my forehead and smiled.

My second time was not as bad as the first. It was in the afternoon. Stoney tried to be gentle. He put his lips on my lips. He put his tongue on my tongue. He fondled my breasts before we got serious.

That night we did it again and then I knew what Mama was talking about. I started feeling good when we touched tongues. When he tongued my breast, I couldn't wait for his stick to be inside of me. When his stick was inside of me I couldn't get enough of it. He moved up and down. I moved up and down. More. More. I wanted more. I was screaming. It felt so good and then it was perfect and I yelled, "Perfect!"

In the morning, I walked outside. The sky was pink in the east. Papa was sleeping on the ground. I bent over to kiss him. He was so cold and still. I shook him just a bit. "Wake up!" I said.

Stoney came out of the hut. "What's wrong?"

"I can't get Papa to wake up."

Stoney took Papa's wrist. Then he put his hand on his neck to feel for the pulse. "He's dead, Lunathree."

My chest hurt, my eyes burned and I was too sad to cry.

Stoney and I dug Papa's grave, folded him into the fetal position, which wasn't easy because he was stiff, and turned him toward the east. I put a cog stone on each of his shoulders. That afternoon we burned the hut and made our way to Stoney's land.

For the next two years we coupled all the time, even when I bled, and sometimes twice or three times a day. Mama was right about how good it was.

Stoney followed my Papa's farming advice. By the end of the first farming year, we had harvested potatoes, lima beans and celery and sold them for good money. I missed my parents, thought about them at the first pink of sun rise, and at the last red of sun set. I heard their voices when the fog rolled in and my vision blurred. I remembered their love for each other and me when I looked to the sky and saw the birds, when I looked toward the ocean and saw Catalina, San Pedro and Long Beach on the horizon, even so, until 1889, my time with Stoney was wonderful.

It was the summer of 1889, when I first saw Count Dietmar Von Baumschlager and could tell he was trouble. Not by the way he looked. He was well dressed. A flat Panama hat covered his dark hair. A brown hatband with the smallest of brown bows decorated the hat. He wore a fancy brown jacket over his fancy brown vest. The white cuffs that peeked out at the end of his jacket sleeves were ironed crisp. I could see the heavy gold chain of his pocket watch hanging from the edge of his vest. He carried a carved wooden walking stick but didn't use it to walk. He must've had the most exquisite of eating habits for his white collar and lavender cravat were immaculate and there were no crumbs in the beard that covered that aristocratic face.

COUNT DIETMAR VON BAUMSCHLAGER

My name is Count Dietmar Von Baumschlager. I saw that beautiful girl, called Lunathree Sturmss, but had no interest in her. My love isn't beautiful. But I would give up a kingdom for her.

COUNTESS ELLA VON BAUMSCHLAGER

I am Countess Ella Von Baumschlager, the legal wife of Count Dietmar Von Baumschlager, a man who doesn't exist. Well he exists, of course, but we are not Von Baumschlagers. We use the Von Baumschlager name to hide my husband's true identity.

When my husband was asked to find a place for a new gun club, I was delighted. My husband is an anomaly in our country. He doesn't work or own a business. He was trained to do nothing but be charming. On Chester Avenue in Los Angeles, where we live, men work and women take care of the households, seeing to the servants and paying the gardeners. We give a lot of parties and I arrange them. My poor husband has nothing to do. He spends the day drawing pictures, waiting for the children on our street to come home from school so he can entertain them. All the children on Chester Avenue love Dieter. Today I watched him hand out chocolate drops wrapped in silver paper that he ordered especially for them. This morning Dieter drew a picture of a flea family to share with the children. The fleas were dressed in ballroom attire, and were amassed in a miniature dining room that looks exactly like the dining room in the Schoenbrun Palace in Vienna. Momma and Poppa Fleas sat at both ends of the long table. Lit candles ensconced in two large chandeliers provided the light in the room and were reflected in the gold-framed mirrors hanging on the walls. Each flea sat on a tiny red velvet chair. Gold urns and tall bowls of peaches, plums, grapes and apricots graced a long dining table. "The fleas eat very fast," my husband told the children. "Because when Momma

Flea and Poppa Flea finish eating, everybody else has to stop eating too."

My husband had told me that Emperor Franz Joseph and his wife, "Sissy", that's what my husband called her, were small eaters. They would take a few bites and leave the table. When they left nobody else was allowed to eat. So the whole hungry crowd went to a restaurant. My husband was part of the crowd. It was after one of those very short dinners that I first talked to him.

I was in Austria on one of those grand tours of a lifetime. My Uncle and Aunt, John and Mary Dreer, had said, "Come along." And of course I did. I thought of it as my last opportunity to do something interesting. I didn't expect romance. I wasn't rich enough to lure a fortune hunter and not pretty enough to attract anybody else.

When we arrived at the Hotel Imperial in Vienna the desk clerk handed my uncle an envelope with an invitation enclosed. It was from Joeseph Weibel. Herr Weibel used to conduct business in Philadelphia where he had met my Uncle. Uncle

John was the President of the Pennsylvania Locomotive Company before he retired.

Herr Weibel and my Uncle liked each other because they both loved music and secretly wanted to be musicians. Uncle John played the piano and harpsichord. Joeseph Weibel played those two instruments and a violin as well. Instead of talking business they played music. They played composers that they both knew and their own compositions. This made them so happy they both decided to retire while they were in their early fifties and devote the rest of their lives to music. Unfortunately, except for Herr Weibel, nobody liked my Uncle's music. To me it sounded like a screaming cat in the throes of a painful kitten birth.

The invitation from Herr Weibel stated that he had arranged for us to go to the court theater in the Schoenbrun Palace to listen to a singer sing Weibel's music.

"What an honor," my Uncle said, "to have your music sung at Emperor Franz Joseph's summer palace." Nothing would have pleased my

Uncle more than to have his own music accorded such laudation.

Two nights later, we were in the theater, sitting on gold gilded seats with new red velvet coverings, listening to the worst music I've ever heard. If I thought my Uncle's music sounded like a cat, Herr Weibel's melodies sounded like nothing I have heard in this world. I think that if I end up in hell and am told that I have a choice between listening to Weibel's music and suffering eternal fire I'll tell the Devil, "I choose to endure the flames."

I excused myself, walked into the vestibule and leaned against a tall marble column. Though the chandeliers were lit and the candles were only half burnt, the corridor was dark, restful and empty. Luckily, I couldn't hear Herr Weibel's music.

Suddenly, a gold gilded door opened. Emperor Franz Joseph walked into the hall. I was sure it was him and gasped. His portrait hung in the Hotel Imperial where we were staying and I'd studied it each time I descended the staircase. The man had hardly any hair on the top of his head and all sorts of brown hair on his face including a large handlebar moustache and mutton chop side burns. This emperor was distinguished. I held my breath and thought I would die but he didn't notice me.

When he scurried away, an attractive, older woman came out from another one of those gilded doors. It was the Empress. "Oh my!" I said and curtsied.

The Empress smiled and then slowly walked down the hall in the same direction her husband took.

Eight other people entered the hallway after she left. I hid behind my column, feeling very uncomfortable. "Dieter," a man called out, "we'll be dining at the Imperial."

Dieter didn't answer. I couldn't understand the rest of the conversation. There was too much laughter. In school everybody had remarked about my talent with languages. In Vienna, I learned I could only understand German if somebody spoke directly to me and there was no distracting noise, such as laughter. The voices and the people disappeared and I walked out from behind the column and bumped into the most distinguished looking man, I'd ever seen.

"Oh my!" I said. *What do I do now?*

He smiled.

"I'm lost," I said.

"Are you English?" He looked something like the Emperor, except he was handsome as well as distinguished.

"American," I said. Was he royalty? I guess he had to be royalty. He wouldn't be there if he wasn't. Was I supposed to bow? That's what I did.

He also bowed.

"Do you like Vienna?" He asked in English.

I nodded.

"Dieter," someone yelled.

Dieter smiled at me, bowed again, then turned and walked away.

I went back into the theater and was so involved with thoughts of the man called Dieter, I didn't mind the awful music.

When the program was over, Uncle John asked Herr Weibel to

join us for dinner. "Choose a place," Uncle John told his friend.

"Why don't we eat in our hotel?" I proposed and felt my face heat up. It was the first time I'd offered a suggestion on our trip. I was so thankful for the opportunity to travel; I would have gladly eaten on the street.

"We always eat at the Imperial," Aunt Mary said.

"It has the best food," Herr Weibel said.

The reason I wanted to go to the Imperial had nothing to do with the food.

COUNT DIETER VON BAUMSCHLAGER

People call me Count Von Baumschlager now. But I'm really a Hapsburg and a minor archduke. So minor that a whole lot of people would have to die before the question of my succession would be brought up.

At the time I met Ella I was enjoying my life. I read. I drew. I'm somewhat of an artist. And I was quite popular with the women. The pretty things flocked to me, and

I liked them. I especially liked going to bed with them.

That night everybody who was anybody dined at the Imperial Hotel. All of us sat at a large round table. The schnitzel was outstanding. The tortes slid down my throat. And the café mit schlagg was just the way it should be, dark, hot and creamy. I sat between two countesses and joked about the music of Herr Weibel. I don't know who had the idea but we'd decided to sponsor a man with no talent and say he was good. And that's what we did. Herr Weibel was everybody's darling because nobody would argue with a member of the Hapsburg family. I felt somebody's eyes at my back and turned to see the woman who had curtsied in the vestibule at Schoenbrun Palace. For some reason, I felt like I was looking at my conscience and it suddenly seemed crass and unworthy to make fun of Herr Weibel.

I excused myself from the table and left the hotel. But, I couldn't get the woman's eyes out of my head. It was a silly situation. At the time, I could have bedded any pretty woman in Vienna and I was spending my time thinking about a homely woman with odd-looking eyes. How do I describe Ella's eyes? They are hazel, brown and have flecks of yellow. They are not shaped in a pleasing manner. Her right brow is a little bit higher than her left giving her eyes and the rest of her face a lopsided look. Yet to this day I watch other men look at my wife, turn away, and look again. They, too, cannot get enough of those arresting eyes, those eyes that inspire you to be a good man. For two days those eyes followed me day and night. Then I had a nice tumble with Frau Schoenfeld and forgot Ella's eyes. And I wouldn't have remembered her, except I promised to bring Frau Schoenfeld a torte from the Imperial and upon entering the hotel lobby I saw the American woman trying to talk to the Hotel Clerk.

I stood for a minute before walking up to her. "May I assist?" I spoke in English and told the woman that I could translate for her.

"I speak German," she said in German. Her accent was atrocious.

I laughed. "Of course you do," I said. "I just meant to help."

She smiled and I was in love for the first time in my life.

"I left some packages with the other clerk," she said. "Nobody seems to be able to find them."

"Everybody has their own place to put a package," the clerk said. "If she could come back when Herr Faerber returns, I'm sure we'll find the packages."

"Why don't you come with me?" I said. "We'll have a coffee with cream. Maybe a chocolate torte. What do you say?"

She smiled again, then, nodded.

The violinists played Strauss. But after a minute I couldn't hear them. The coffee at the Imperial was the best in Vienna but I didn't drink it. Both of our tortes went uneaten. I just wanted to look into her eyes.

ELLA VON BAUMSCHLAGER
Dieter walked me to my hotel room and kissed me gently on my lips. That kiss sealed our fate.

COUNT DIETER VON
BAUMSCHLAGER

I took Ella to meet my mother.

After the meeting, my mother arranged an appointment for me with Emperor Franz Joseph.

The Emperor and I sat on red velvet chairs in a large room in Schoenbrun Palace. I could see my reflection in the many large mirrors hanging on the cream and gold walls.

"You know," he said, "You could be Emperor one day."

I didn't answer because I knew I couldn't be Emperor. There were too many people that stood between that awful responsibility, I didn't want, and me. "I want to marry my Ella and get on with my life," I told the Emperor.

"How will you support this commoner?"

What a question? There were trust funds. Why did he ask?

"I repeat," he said. "You can become emperor. If you never have that office forced on you like I did when I was only eighteen and not ready for such a responsibility, your child could have a throne foisted on him."

It was true. A child of mine could become an emperor. Things like that happened in my family, my strange royal Hapsburg family. There were a lot of countries in the world. Any one of them might like a member of the Hapsburg family to rule them.

"Your American is not of royal blood." The man sat so still. Everything about him was regal.

"No American is of royal blood." I did not like the turn of the conversation. What did the Emperor want of me?

"If you marry her, I need you to do some things. If you are willing, I will see that you are supported in the manner you are accustomed to. If you don't do what I say, I will bankrupt you."

I had my own money, a lot of it. Could he take it away? Of course. He was the Emperor. "What do you want me to do?" I asked.

"I want you to renounce your title and give up your Hapsburg name."

I liked my Hapsburg name. It afforded me the best seats at the opera, the best service in the restaurants. Before meeting Ella my name opened women's legs.

"Is there anything else?" I asked.

"You will move to a place where nobody's heard of the Hapsburg family."

I laughed. "There's no such place."

"America," he said.

I winced. I loved Vienna. There is no better place to live if you like gaiety, great music and good food. Even so I knew I would be glad to renounce my title, change my name and go to America for Ella.

What the Emperor asked for next was too big to give.

"You can't have children." He stood and walked to a large chest of drawers and pulled out two red apples. He handed me one. "Do you need a knife?"

I nodded. I didn't know what else to do. I couldn't say anything. How do you expect me not to have children? I wanted to ask. Ella and I hadn't coupled yet. We wanted to wait for our marriage.

The Emperor handed me a knife. I cut my apple into thin slivers but didn't take a bite.

He cut his into large chunks that he gnawed on as he talked. "I can't have one of your children." He paused to chew before he continued. "I can't have one of your partially non-royal children come back to Vienna and claim the throne."

"What if I sign papers promising that my children will never usurp the throne?" I asked.

"Nobody can foresee the future." He bit into an apple chunk. "Nobody can make promises for their children."

The slivers of apple felt sticky in my hand.

"I wish you well," the Emperor said. "But I must protect the throne."

ELLA VON BAUMSCHLAGER

"Ella! Ella!" I heard Dieter knocking on my door. I let him in. We'd never been alone in my hotel room before. We'd never been alone in any room before.

There were tears in his eyes. I didn't know what was wrong, but I opened my arms and he rushed in. Then he moved away. We both looked at the unmade bed. When the maid had come by to make it, I told her not to bother. I had wanted to stay in my bed and luxuriate. Uncle John and Aunt Mary had been invited to a house in the country and I'd decided to stay in my room and think about the fact that this homely spinster had snagged a prince.

I walked to the bed, got under the covers and beckoned him to come to me. This was the man I planned to give comfort to for the rest of my life.

At first, he shook his head. "We can't, Ella," he said. "I promised the Emperor."

What had he promised the Emperor? "Come here," I said.

I took off my clothes. It wasn't easy. I'm fairly modest and wear a lot of clothes. But I was under the bedclothes and Dieter couldn't see what I was doing. He stood there with his eyes closed, looking like he was praying. "Please, Dieter" I said.

"Dear God!" he said. Then he got under the bedclothes with me. He tentatively reached his hand and touched my stomach. "You're naked," he said.

He pulled the feather bed off me and looked. At first I closed my eyes and then I opened them.

"You are the most beautiful woman I've ever seen," he said.

COUNT DIETER VON BAUMSCHLAGER

After we coupled, I told Ella what the Emperor had said.

"You must marry a royal personage," she told me. "I will stay in Vienna and be your mistress for as long as you wish. And when you don't wish, I'll leave."

It was a good idea. We could have illegitimate children. Then we could couple when we wanted and I could stay in my beloved Vienna. We talked and talked. In between words we coupled over and over again. I was so happy.

In the morning, I left and had a coffee and a sweet roll in the Imperial Dining Room. Looking around, I saw many people I knew and felt lonely. I didn't want a mistress. I wanted to marry Ella.

She let me in her room again at midnight. We took off our clothes. Her skin had a pink glow in the candlelight. She smelled of fresh roses. I put my hands on her breast, then, I sucked the places that my hands touched. I put my fingers between her legs and touched her core. "You must touch me, Ella," I said.

She put her fingers on me. It was such a delicate, hesitant touch.

"Please, Ella," I said. "You must move your fingers, move your hand. Please Dearest."

"Show me," she said.

I did.

ELLA VON BAUMSCHLAGER

Every night Dieter came into my room. We kissed and touched, but we didn't couple. We wanted to marry and if we did, we knew we could never couple again. It was so difficult. We couldn't get enough of each other.

Two and a half months later Aunt Mary called me into her room. "Your Uncle bought steamer tickets," she said. We're leaving Vienna early."

I could feel my heart beat. If I left Vienna, I'd die. "Why?" I asked.

"Because the Emperor asked us to. You're a foolish girl, Ella." My Aunt sat on the huge pink settee in the parlor of her suite. "I hope you're not a pregnant foolish girl."

I started to cry. I was pregnant. I had coupled five times on one night and never again and now my blood was already more than two months late.

"Does he know?" My Aunt looked so sad.

I shook my head.

"We need to go home," my Aunt said.

Did she really think it would be all right for me to go home?

That night I waited and waited and waited for Dieter. He didn't come. In the morning I took the hatpin that held a pink flower to my favorite blue straw hat and looked at it a long time before I inserted it.

COUNT DIETER VON BAUMSCHLAGER

Ella's Uncle John came to my rooms. "I have to talk to you," he said.

"Of course, sir. Please come in." I showed him to my parlor and bade him sit on the most comfortable chair in the room, a high back green silk with a matching ottoman.

I rang the bell and my man Johann entered. "Please sir," I said. "Name your refreshment, Johann will be delighted to get you anything you want."

"I want privacy," Herr Dreer said. "I need to tell you some things." The man looked angry.

I dismissed Johann and sat across from John Dreer. "What can I do for you?" I asked.

"You can't do anything." He pulled his hand across his eyes as if he were about to cry.

I waited for him to say more. I didn't know what else to do. My foot was going to sleep but I didn't shake it.

Finally he looked at the portrait of Emperor Franz Josef on the wall over my gold gilded cadenza and said, "How do you talk to a cad?"

I will need this man's help to meet the right people when I go with Ella to America. "I love your niece, sir," I said.

"Love. Is that what he calls it?" He was still talking to the portrait of Franz Josef.

"I want to marry her," I said.

"When?" After she has her baby?"

Ella was pregnant and she hadn't told me. *Oh God!*

As soon as Herr Dreer left I got in my coach and went to see my mother.

"You'll have to get married." My mother has a regal carriage and looked as cool and stiff as the ice blue dressing gown she wore.

"I can't marry Ella," I said. "I promised the Emperor that there would be no issue."

My mother told me to sit down. "I can't stand your pacing."

I didn't want to sit. I wanted to wage a war, ride the fastest horse and yell in the language of the guttersnipes. But, I sat on a yellow satin chair in my mother's grand parlor and willed myself to stay still. Only my wiggling right ear revealed my restlessness.

"Of course, you can't get married to Ella. You can never see her again." My Mother's knees shook under her gown. She was probably having as difficult a time staying still as I was.

The bride would be suitable and approved by the Emperor. Though it would look as if a substantial dowry had been proffered, in reality, we would pay the bride's family.

"It doesn't matter," my Mother said. "We can afford it."

I agreed. It didn't matter. It didn't matter if my heart ceased to function and my soul descended to hell.

Mother went into Saint Stephen's Cathedral while I stayed in the coach. Duke Rudolph IV, one of my Hapsburg ancestors, had built this gothic church. Sitting there, I realized for the first time how strange the Cathedral with its geometrically shaped tiled roof looked. The north bell tower was tall and imposing. The south tower was never finished. It went half way up, then was capped off by a make shift renaissance spire and looked temporary as if it were going to be finished any day instead of existing for hundreds of years.

I spent more than an hour waiting for my mother, pondering my fate. I would bed my legal wife until she became pregnant, but I wouldn't give up Ella, no matter what my Mother said. No matter what the Emperor said.

Mother came out of the Cathedral accompanied by Father Eckhel, the middle aged man who my Mother always said had the kindest eyes and the best smile. I thought him to have the saddest eyes and no smile.

"Father Eckhel will go over the arrangements with you, Dieter," my mother said. "I'm too tired to think anymore."

After we took my Mother home, I told the driver to take Father Eckhel and me to the Imperial Hotel. "Come," I said. "We'll drink coffee while we discuss the details."

"Good," he agreed.

As soon as he was seated in the Imperial Restaurant, I excused myself and ran up the wide staircase to Ella's room. She didn't answer my knock. I rapped harder. "Let me in, Ella." I pushed the door. It didn't give. It was thick and hand carved. The shiny brass lock worked too well. I looked around the empty hallway, walked a few paces, then turned and ran as fast as I could, slamming into the door. The door gave and my shoulder hurt.

I lit the candles in the wall sconces to produce enough light to see. Ella was in bed. Her face looked pale on her pillow. She made soft moaning sounds. Her breathing was shallow. "Wake up, Ella."

She didn't stir. I felt her feverish brow, pulled the bedclothes back to cool her and saw blood on the sheets. I took her blood-covered hand from between her legs and saw that she was holding a large hatpin. Taking the pin from her, my hand started to tremble and the pin dropped to the floor. "My God!" I said. "My God! My God!" My Ella had committed a mortal sin.

I put the sheet between her legs to staunch the blood and couldn't stop shaking. Not knowing what else to do I ran down the stairs. "I don't know how to save her," I told Father Eckhel.

"I'll get help," he said.

I went back to Ella's room, sat on the bed and held her hand. "Don't die. Don't die," I repeated over and over again. The sheet was soaked. I exchanged it for a pillow sham.

Father Eckhel brought Sister Elena Maria, a drab efficient sort who wore her brown religious habit well. The nun cleaned Ella's legs, put a pillow under her bottom and said, "There. There. I know. I know."

In the morning, Ella opened her eyes. "I'm so tired, Dieter."

"You'll be all right," Sister Elena Maria told Ella. "Lots of people lose babies."

"She's committed a mortal sin," Father Eckhel said.

"Some people don't know when to keep their mouths shut," the sister said. She wiped away perspiration from Ella's face with a dry wash cloth. "Some people should go and eat breakfast before saying another word."

"I want to marry Ella," I told Father Eckhel when we were seated in the hotel dining room drinking our coffees.

"I understand." He looked into his coffee cup. How could he look at a man who wanted to marry a mortal sinner?

"We won't have intercourse again," I told the Father after telling

him the Emperor said if I married
Ella I couldn't have children.

"You can pleasure yourselves
without intercourse," the Priest said.

How did he know? He looked at
me and I knew why my Mother had
said he had the kindest eyes. I didn't
know what he was thinking. But I
felt his empathy.

Father Eckhel married us two
months later. I changed my name
from Hapsburg to Von
Baumschlager. We immigrated to
America but didn't go to live near
the Dreers in Pennsylvania. We
weren't welcome. Ella's Uncle John
made that clear.

ELLA VON BAUMSCHLAGER
We've had a good life in
California. And it turned better for
Dieter when he was asked to
establish the Westbruk Gun Club.
He finally had an occupation and a
place to go and things to do to fill his
days. That he wasn't paid for his
work didn't matter to either of us.

COUNT DIETER VON
BAUMSCHLAGER

I spent the day tramping through swamps. Clear and cool there were so many birds and ducks overhead; the sky was a squawking, screeching aviary. The ground was covered with fragrant low-lying plants and bushes that bloomed purple, lilac, and yellow blossoms. The place had the fresh smell of ocean. In the early afternoon, I chose the perfect spot for the gun club. It was on a mesa. To the west was the Pacific. To the south were streams, ponds, a low lying swamp and another mesa.

It took four hours to ride the more than fifty miles to our home in Los Angeles. Ella had the Butler draw my bath.

By eight we were dining in Henry Millington's house. Our chops were served on gold etched, bone china. The linens were hand crocheted and the flatware was polished silver. I could have been among the Hapsburgs, I thought. Rarely does anything seem so civilized in Southern California.

The woman sitting next to me talked and talked and talked. "We are so lucky to have this lovely weather in January," she said. "In

New York, where I hail from, my aunt is suffering the arthritic pains of a blizzard."

I didn't hear what she said next because my wife's nimble fingers were touching me. We had gotten in the habit of pleasuring each other in public because there was no chance that we'd be carried away and couple. If we had a baby, we'd be lost. We would never be able to find another Father Eckhel to forgive us for losing it. If my wife didn't end her pregnancy, we'd lose the money provided to me. If we lost this money, we'd starve. I have no skills that could provide employment.

The woman to the right of me droned on. I looked at her as my wife's fingers moved up and down and I continued to eat. I wanted to scream. I wanted to kiss my wife. I thought I was in heaven and prayed that I wouldn't yell.

Mrs. Millington came to our table and told us the dancing had started in the ballroom. "You must excuse us," I said to the woman next to me. "I want to dance with my wife."

On the wood parquet dance floor,
other men held their partners
decorously away from their bodies.
Ella and I moved as close as we
could to each other, moving to the
rhythm of the Strauss Waltz.

Later, in Henry Millington's
small library, I showed the men my
drawings of the Mesa. "It's the
perfect place for a gun club." I
explained how we would dig lakes
and ponds and bring new flowers and
shrubs to plant around the lagoons.

The following week the men that
had listened to me in Henry's library
bought 2000 acres that included the
beach, as well as the wetlands. They
paid $50.00 an acre for the land atop
the mesa and only $5.00 per acre for
the marsh. This may have seemed
cheap. But we weren't cheating
anybody. What can you use
marshland for? You can't farm it.
I've seen the puny efforts of the men
who try to plow the wetlands.

ELLA VON BAUMSCHLAGER
Dieter was elected the first
president of the new Westbruk Gun
Club. He didn't get paid to oversee

the building and see that everything was done right. But he was good at what he did and couldn't have been happier. Every morning we had our butler fill our tub with hot water before we bathed together. I soaped him. He soaped me. There was no crevice in our bodies that wasn't clean. Because of our abstinence life wasn't perfect but at times it seemed pretty good.

STONEY STURMSS

One day in the summer of 1899, my wife, Lunathree, and Judy and Bob, our children, and I walked over to see the progress of the gun club. As usual, Count Von Baumschlager, the fancy gentleman with the funny accent, was watching everything.

My wife said the club was being built on property that was once occupied by her ancestors and nobody had offered to repay her for the land. I asked the Count, "How come?"

"We bought the land from the Westbruk family. They were the owners of record," he said. "It was a fair transaction."

I didn't know what to say so I didn't say anything.

Count Von Baumschlager, a polite man, offered to take us through the almost completed red wood planked and cedar shake roofed building.

We accepted his offer and entered the meeting room, which was enormous. It had a burnt brick fireplace that looked as if it had been there for years even though it had yet to be used.

The gun room was smaller than the meeting room and had a similar, but smaller fireplace. The card room was identical in size and shape to the gun room.

"Do you like to play cards?" the Count asked my daughter, Judy.

She nodded. He tousled her hair and smiled.

Each wing housed six to ten bedrooms. Double wardrobes and hand bowls were already installed. When we walked through the third bedroom Judy said, "This room is bigger than our whole house."

I felt my cheeks redden.

LUNATHREE

After the Count climbed on his buckboard and rode off, Judy said. "It's beautiful here."

"I love it!" Bob was running about, dancing.

I ran after my five year old and watched him jump higher than I'd ever seen anyone else jump. He could hop further, hold a handstand longer, and somersault faster. He could swim like a fish and climb like a goat. He couldn't stay still. How would we harness his energy?

We followed him as he explored the land around the club, the recently excavated lagoons and ponds. When it was just about dark, we happened upon a mound of bones. Judy counted 34 skeletons and 274 cog stones. I started to cry. "How can they dig up dead bodies to build a club?" I asked. "This is sacred ground."

Judy saw me cry and she cried too. Bob jumped and landed on the skeletons. I grabbed his arm and slapped his face.

ELLA VON BAUMSCHLAGER
Dieter saw to everything. It was his idea to mount stuffed birds over

the Gun Club's dining room
fireplace. After installing tables for
dominos as well as cards in the card
room, he had a plaque attesting to the
purity of the water from the artesian
well on the property hung at the card
room entrance. A scientist had said
the water found on the Club's
grounds was probably the purest in
the world.

The first night I ate in the club
dining room the waiters brought the
first course, consommé, in tiny silver
bowls. My husband walked from
table to table, telling jokes and
asking about the members' health.
He didn't sit until the duck was
served.

One of the white jacketed, white-
gloved waiters held a silver tray
topped with eight, perfectly browned
ducks swathed in orange sauce while
the other waiter, also wearing a
white jacket and white gloves,
served. I took a bite of the duck and
was delighted with the delicious
taste. It had to have been the best
fowl I'd ever eaten. I scraped the
bone before I noticed that nobody
else at our table was touching the

ducks. "You should try," I said.
"It's delicious."

Nobody made a move. I put my
fingers on my husband's thigh. He
took a nibble of the bird and
remarked, "Ella, you're right. This
is delicious."

Phillip Luten, a man with
premature silver gray hair that belied
his good fortune as well as his age,
took a bite of the duck. He was
chewing on the bone and licking his
fingers before he turned to his wife
and ordered her to taste it. After that
everybody at our table "oohed" and
"aahed" as they ate. I would have
sucked the marrow out of the bone if
I had been alone.

"This has to be fresh water
duck," Mrs. Luten said. "Nothing
else could taste so good." She also
had silver gray hair. It didn't look as
good on her as it did on her husband.

"You're right, dear," Phillip
Luten agreed. He bit a bone and
sucked the marrow.

Doctor Milbank, a chubby, jovial
man who sat across from me said,
"Dieter, you should give our
compliments to the chef." He licked
his fingers, sucked the marrow and

used his crisp white napkin to remove the slivers of duck from his curly brown beard.

"Maybe something should be done so that only fresh water ducks are served at the club," Mrs. Luten said.

"You're right, dear." Phillip patted his wife's hand. "Count Dieter, here, is our man. If anybody can see to the ducks, he can."

My husband smiled his most charming smile and patted Mrs. Luten's hand. "Of course," he said. "If you want fresh water ducks you will have fresh water ducks."

COUNT DIETER VON BAUMSCHLAGER

Guaranteeing fresh water ducks seemed an easy enough task. I walked into the kitchen and told the chef, "From now on you will only serve fresh water ducks."

"I would like to. Ducks bred in fresh water taste much better than those bred in salt water." The chef was stirring an enormous pot of oxtails. "But how do you expect me to get fresh water ducks?"

"Get them from fresh water," I said.

The man stopped stirring and laughed.

"You will provide fresh water ducks." I believed in being firm with the help.

"If you can stop the ocean from flowing into the fresh water pools, I'll provide the ducks you want." He laughed again. "That's a mighty strong ocean."

ELLA VON BAUMSCHLAGER

In the morning Dieter and I walked around the grounds while the other men took to the duck blinds to shoot. It was a short walk to the place where the ocean met the fresh water. My husband kissed me and laughed. "How easy to fix!" he said.

"How easy to fix what?"

He laughed and kissed me again. "Ah, Ella." He was beaming. "We're going to build a dike. This Club will always serve fresh water ducks."

STONEY STURMSS

The stench of dead animals made it difficult for me and my family to breathe. Clap-tat-tat. Clap-tat-tat. The sound of gun-shot started early in the morning. So many birds and ducks fell from the sky. How could the members of the gun club possibly eat all they killed?

Feeling like something should be done to abate the constant noise and horrible smell I walked the short distance from my farm to the inlet that runs next to the club. The harbor for small craft was closed. "What are you doing?" I asked a workman.

"We're building a dike." The man pounded a large piece of wood into place.

"Why?" I asked.

"To stop the salt water tides from going into the fresh water."

"Why?"

"Because the members of the gun club are paying us good money to do it," another workman said. He moved a large boulder next to the piece of wood placed by the first workman.

When I came back to see the dike two weeks later, the workmen were gone. There were dead fish on the mudflat. Shutting off salt water from the fresh water had destroyed the beds of clams, oysters and other shellfish. I thought I would throw up from the stink. God, how would we be able to continue living here?

On January 30, of this year, 1901, I went to the meeting of the Westbruk Farmers Society. We discussed our grievances and made plans to sue the Gun Club. Our secretary wrote the following letter to the Honorable United States District Attorneys.

Dear sirs,

The Westbruk Gun Club that is located adjacent to our farm lands has placed obstructions to a natural inlet which entirely closes it as a harbor for light sail and fishing boats. The blockage of this inlet, a navigable water way of the United States, is in violation of the national navigation laws. By erecting these obstructions this said Westbruk Gun Club has appropriated to their own private use the said Inlet to the entire exclusion of the people from the same, not only as a harbor but also

*as a hunting and fishing ground. By
shutting out the salt water valuable
beds of oysters, clams and other
varieties of salt water shellfish have
been destroyed, and salt water fish
have died in large numbers. The
stench arising has caused malaria
and typhoid to an extent never before
known in this vicinity. More over the
said Westbruk Gun Club has recently
used the said obstructions to the
positive damage of farming lands
adjoining, by backing up the water
flowing into the said inlet from a
drainage ditch to such an extent the
water is now standing in the furrows
of plowed land.*

*We earnestly request you to take
steps to have these obstructions
speedily removed as the law directs.*

*Earnestly hoping that you will
take prompt action in this matter for
the relief of our people, we are
Very Respectfully
Westbruk Farmers Society
O.B. Cyram sec.
Route #2 Westbruk, Cal.*

LUNATHREE STURMSS

I am so tired. Our farm reeks
from the smells of decay. My

husband is always gone. He spends his time with the members of the Farmers Society. They want to sue the Westbruk Gun Club. There are so many sick people. So many people dying because a few rich people want to eat fresh water duck.

Judy is only eight years old, but she is the one who provides our meals. My son, Bob, and I have a hard time eating. I used to ask to myself, why Bob couldn't sit still? Now he stays in bed and moans. He is so pale, I can hardly tell the difference between him and his dirty white sheet. Judy is the one that puts the wet cloth to his brow. I am too weak to walk across our small room from my bed to his. Whenever my husband finds me sleeping in my own throw up, he heaves too. Only Judy is strong.

My throat hurts. It is so dry. The water in our artesian well used to be clear. Now it is brackish. Judy lugs the water in buckets that look as big as she is.

STONEY STURMSS
I watched my wife and son die and didn't cry. But when my

daughter Judy died, I gave up. I tried to die too but didn't know how. I wanted to kill somebody.

ELLA VON BAUMSCHLAGER
In April, Henry Millington invited to us his new house in San Marino. His Italianate palace, though much smaller, seemed to me as grand as the Schoenbrun in Vienna.

Dieter told me that Henry's Uncle Collin had left him eleven million dollars.

Though we are wealthy, I can't imagine that much money. Henry waited for us at on the top of the stairs in front of the columned entryway. He stood with his Uncle Collin's widow, Arabella, who was helping him to pick out his new furniture. I though it odd that Henry's wife wasn't the woman picking out the furniture but didn't say anything.

Arabella showed me some remarkable Adams chairs in the sitting rooms and bedrooms and acted as if they were hers.

Henry showed us around the enormous grounds. There were so

many plants and each was planted in the perfect place to make it look like a splendid piece of art. Quite a botanist, Henry. His seedlings were imported from all parts of the world. Arabella seemed to know as much as Henry did about the flora that covered the grounds.

When Henry took Arabella's elbow to help her over a rough spot on the walkway, I saw his fingers caress the soft part of her under arm.

Later, when Henry and Dieter went into the smoking room to discuss the plans for the Fourth of July celebration at the Gun Club, Arabella and I sat across from each other in the front parlor and drank coffee from tiny demitasse cups. I didn't know what to say to this lady who I knew was not acting as an aunt to my friend, Mr. Millington.

"I won't cause a scandal," she told me. "My late husband, Collin, was married when I met him. We waited till his wife died before we got together."

"Why do you tell me this?" I took a sip of my coffee.

"Because I know enough about you to ensure that you won't talk about me," she said. She smiled but her eyes weren't friendly. "I know your husband is a Hapsburg."

I didn't say anything. I was tired and wanted to go home.

On the Fourth of July in 1904 Dieter and I boarded a red electric car with other members of the gun club. It was the initial ride for the route that went from Los Angeles to a stop just outside the gun club.

What a ride! I was told we were going fifty miles an hour. I'd never gone anywhere so fast. Dieter sat next to me and covered our legs with a blanket. It wasn't necessary. Everybody was busy looking out the windows. We could have been naked and nobody would have noticed. My husband's hand was working his way to my privates. I gasped out loud and put my hand in his belt. Every time the train made a slight turn everybody yelled. The pleasure was so intense. "I love going fast," I told my husband.

Henry Millington turned around to look at us. I prayed he couldn't tell what was happening under the blanket. He said, "I wish Aunt

Arabella was here," then turned away.

When we reached our stop, we got out. Some people cheered. Others weren't so happy to see us. One man grabbed Dieter's shoulder.

My husband took off his hat and removed his gloves. "My dear Mr. Sturmss, how good to see you. I want to introduce your precious children to my wife."

Mr. Sturmss spit. His spittle landed on my husband's shoes.

"What was Sturmss' problem?" I heard my husband ask when he and the other men gathered in the card room to play dominoes.

"They still hold it against us," Phillip Luten said. He shuffled the tiles face down.

"Hold what against us?" my husband asked, drawing the first tile.

"Some of their families got sick from typhoid and malaria." Luten's tile had the most pips. So he took the first seat. "A lot of people around here lost their children," he said. "Pretty sad to lose your children."

My husband looked as if a boulder fell on his head. He wiped his hand across his face. "We couldn't have caused the children's deaths," he said. "Could we?" His pip count was the second highest. He sat on his wooden chair.

"Some people say we did." Phillip Luten tapped his tile with his pointing finger. "The farmers started to get sick after we built the dike."

"That's a bunch of hoolycock," said the man who sat down next. He was sitting out of turn.

"Get up, sir," another man said.

The out of turn man laughed, "Of course."

The conversation had already turned to pleasanter topics when Henry Millington walked into the card room and said, "I hear they're renaming this town Millington after me."

"Because you arranged the Red Car stop?" I asked.

He nodded.*

(*Westbruk is still Westbruk. It was never called Millington.)

That night, when we were in our rooms, my husband took me in his arms and made love to me. It was the first time in our marriage and felt so good.

"I like Mr. Sturmss' children," Dieter told me. "I want us to have some of our own."

"How will we manage?" I asked.

"I don't know." He entered me again.

"We'll manage, Ella," he said afterwards. "I can't spend my life as a non-paid manager for a rich man's club. And you can't spend your life giving parties."

He was wrong. I could spend my life giving parties.

BARON DIETER VON BAUMSCHLAGER

Ella didn't get pregnant and we didn't try anymore.

On a Tuesday in the early part of 1907 I met Stoney Sturmss again. He stood at the Gun Club entrance. "Why are you here?" I wanted to know why the man had spat at me. His spittle had changed my life. His saliva had made me realize what an empty life I lead.

"I need a job," he said.

We walked through the ivy-covered arbor. There were only three ducks hanging on the hooks that we kept in rows, individually labeled for that purpose. At that time, I was proud that shooting was only allowed on Wednesdays and Saturdays; that we stopped at 4 PM and only shot from blinds and boats; and that we conformed to United States laws and California game regulations.

"What are your qualifications?" I asked.

The man looked dirty. I led him to the back of the building, where the small apartments of the live-in employees were located.

"How are your children?" I asked before he could recite his talents.

He put his hands in his pockets and looked straight in my eyes. "My wife and children are dead."

I didn't know what to say.

"I can't work here," he said. "They died because of this damn club." He took off running.

Early the next morning, I took my gun out of the gunroom and tramped down to the lagoon with three other gentlemen. The sky was alive with birds and ducks screeching and squawking. But there weren't as many of the flying creatures as there had been the year before. We'd been lamenting the loss of the bird population since 1901. I wondered why. Were we shooting too many? Had building the dike changed the topography too much?

Before I could think more about the lack of birds and ducks Phillip Luten said, "Would you look at that snowy egret?" Phillip's hair seemed whiter and thinner each time I saw him. "Wouldn't my wife be glad to have a new white plumed hat!" he continued.

Ella had a straw hat adorned by egret feathers. She hardly wore it. I thought about Stoney Sturmss' children and it didn't seem very important to provide feathered hats for our women.

The other men started to shoot. I held my gun on my lap. The sound of the gunfire snapped, snapped, snapped in my head. The birds fell. My companions were good shots.

The shooting stopped when the butlers brought our food from the club. Silver lids atop the China kept our eggs, bacon, toast and potatoes hot. Silver urns kept our coffee scalding. Our juices, fresh fruit and cream were icy cold.

"We have to thank you," Phillip Luten told me after he finished chewing and swallowing his toast and jam. "You're the one who initiated eating in style while we hunt, Dieter."

How wonderful, I thought. I initiated dining in style and the sickness and death of women and children. A real success! I turned to my companions and said, "I'm going back to the club."

Phillip aimed and shot the snowy egret. "I guess somebody's going to have a new hat." Then he turned to me. "Dieter," he said. "Enjoy yourself for a few hours. The club can carry on without you."

I agreed with Phillip and resigned from the Gun Club before the day was out.

Dear Mrs. Hopkins,

It's late, this paper is due tomorrow and I'm not sure how to end it. So I'm jumping to the epilog or what I call the epilog to let you know what happened to these people. I hope this is all right with you.

Sincerely, Jean Sturmss

EPILOG
STONEY STURMSS

In 1912 when Adelita Bandino
Sturmss died I was one of the many
people who petitioned the court for a
piece of her inheritance. I was able
to prove my relationship with Cabel
Sturmss, my grandfather. I also told
the judge that my wife Lunathree
was a Bandino and he believed me. I
was awarded $500,000.27. Why the
twenty-seven cents? I don't know
and don't plan to ask. As soon as I
received the money I decided to look
into the Jewish religion of my
ancestors. So I went to a Synagogue
and tripped over a box at the door.
When I looked up I saw the most
beautiful red head and fell in love.
The love was reciprocated. I married
her and we have two sons.

ELLA VON BAUMSCHLAGER

The day my husband resigned
from the Gun Club, he came home a
broken man. We didn't host parties
any more. He didn't make up
stories for the neighborhood
children. When World War I started

we went back to Austria to stand with the Hapsburgs. They didn't welcome us and my husband died from the pain.

I was in Paris when Henry Millington married his Aunt Arabella. They were in their sixties and both seemed very happy to see me. I wished them well and never saw them or anybody I met in California again.

Dear Mrs. Hopkins,

It's 4:30 in the morning and I have a few more things to say. Stoney Sturmss is my grandfather on my father's side. Arabella and Henry Millington are the ones that started the Millington Library. My great grandfather on my mother's side was Phillip Luten. I've been to the Westbruk Gun Club. It's a great place to go if you don't have a good nose. The club is surrounded by stinking oil wells and over looks a smelly beach called Cardboard. The last time I went I didn't see a duck or a bird in the sky. People still shoot, but only for target practice.

Even so it's still fun to go there. There's a room with a player piano, radiola, and all sorts of books and games. People have told me that a lot of this stuff was supplied by the Von Baumschlagers.

Well, I'm done and I'm hoping my paper works.
J.S.

16.

Dear Dessa Dreams,
I'm lonely and sad. My grandparents divorced. My parents divorced. Will I get divorced too? It's beginning to look that way. Always Arguing in Anaheim.

Dear Always Arguing,
If your parents and grandparents divorced statistics show that you have a good chance of divorcing too. I dreamt about a woman whose parents and grandparents divorced. She decided not to get married. So she never got divorced. Hopefully, there are other ways to break the cycle. Stop arguing.
Sincerely, Dessa Dreams.

In July of 1959 my parent's divorce was final. *What kind of statistic am I going to be?*

I called Jean. "That was quite a paper," I said.

"Did you like it?" She was imitating me again. *Why?*

I decided to ignore her. "How did you get away with all that sex stuff? How did you know about all that sex stuff?"

"I read a lot," she said.

"Didn't Mrs. Hopkins give you any trouble? I mean—"

"You put sex in your Juan Sebastian Cabrillo paper," she said. "I read it."

"I said that people coupled."

"Well, I like to be explicit."

"And I noticed you named your character Lunathree after I named my characters Lunaone and Lunatwo."

"How many times do I have to tell you imitation is the sincerest form of flattery?"

It didn't feel like flattery. "Jean did you get in trouble with the sex part?"

"Here's what happened," she said. "Mrs. Hopkins said, 'I'm going to call your parents and discuss your paper with them.'

"I said, 'I'll tell my mother to expect your call.' I smiled. Hopkins frowned.

So I didn't leave the house until she called. Every time the phone rang, I ran to answer it and said, 'Caroline Luten Sturmss here, how may I help you?'

"And if you think I can imitate your voice well, you should hear what I can do with my mother's. "Jean sounded exactly like her crisp, clear speaking mother. "Hopkins said that she was calling about my final paper.

"I said, 'Wasn't it a wonderful paper?'

"Hopkins said, 'Wonderful? Maybe you didn't read the same paper I did.'

"'Oh,' I said.

"'The paper with an abortion and explicit sex,' Hopkins said.

"'I said, 'That's the one I read. Quite a writer, my daughter! We're all so proud of her.'

"Mrs. Hopkins gave me an "A"."

"Oh Jean," I laughed.

"Oh Jean," she parroted.

"Goodbye," I said and hung up. I didn't like her aping me. But I did like having such an audacious friend. Actually I loved having Jean for a friend.

Then I called her right back. "Jean," I said. "There's no way Mrs. Hopkins would have let you get away with that paper."

"Yeah! Yeah!" she said.

"Well?" I said.

"Okay. I turned in a shorter version without the sex."

"Without the hatpin abortion?" I said.

"Without the hatpin abortion."

"I knew it," I said.

"I wrote the newer version a couple of months ago. I was daring in high school," she said. "But not stupid."

"Yeah! Yeah!" I said.

"Yeah! Yeah!" She was imitating me again.

I laughed. For the first time I thought her mimicry was funny.

She laughed too. "I told you imitation is a compliment."

"Bye Jean."

I hung up and dialed Micah. I had never called him before. But I felt like talking some more. "Hello," I said.

"Hi!" he said. "How is my little Scherezade today?"

"What?" He'd never called me Scherezade before. The name didn't fit. I wasn't a storyteller.

"I have my coffee ready waiting to hear your newest," he said.

"My newest?" I wished I had some coffee.

"I love your stories," he said. "I plan to wake up every morning for the rest of my life and listen to them."

"Are you telling me that I call you every morning and tell you a story?" I asked.

"Of course," he laughed.

"You're making fun of me." I felt my eyes tearing.

"What's wrong with you, Dessa?" I could hear him gulp the

coffee. "Are you coming down with a cold?"

"Yes." I pretended to cough. "I have to get off the phone."

I drove to the mansion that Jean Sturmss' family called home. Her parents had fenced in one block in our tract for the gardens that surrounded their estate. The place was enormous, the gardens were immaculate, and the flowers looked like they were raised by a graduate horticulturist. I rang the bell at the outer gate and was admitted immediately.

Jean was in her bedroom, sitting on her dark green silk bedspread. Jean's mother had picked out the furniture and color scheme for this bedroom and Jean loved it. She once told me that there was nothing as impeccable as her mother's Luten taste which included the thick rose carpet that I was standing on.

"I've figured out why you keep imitating me," I said.

"Don't worry," Jean said. "I can supply you enough stories for a life time."

"I don't want to use your stories to keep Micah." Just then, I had an epiphany and realized I didn't want to keep Micah. The question was, did I want to keep Jean for a friend? I only had one best friend.

17.

Dear Dessa Dreams,
My best friend used to be poor just like me. Now she's a rich bitch and a snob to boot. What's the best way to show her up and make her feel awful?
Wanting revenge in Reseda.

Dear Wanting,
I dreamt about people who suddenly got rich. Be nice maybe she'll share. If not, forget her and find some other friends. There are a lot of people in this world.
Sincerely, Dessa Dreams.

I told myself I didn't want to become my mother. I didn't want to

go to bed and fall asleep whenever
there was a problem. But I was so
unhappy; I went to bed and took my
cog stone with me.

* * *

GOD says, "It's 1920."

Leo sits on a piano stool, playing
the piano in the Westbruk Gun Club
game room. I stand beside him. He
knows all the words to "*You're The
Cream In My Coffee,*" "*Swanee,*" "*A
Good Man Is Hard To Find*" and
"*Lovin' Sam*". After he sings them
once, I can sing them too. I am very
smart in my dreams.

Leo agrees that I'm extremely
intelligent. "What are you going to
do with your genius?" he asks, then
stands up, and leans over to give me
the perfect kiss. He puts his hand in
my blouse. I don't stop him the way
I would if this were real life. It feels
too good.

Boom! What a loud sound!
Something exploded. A bomb? Leo
and I rush outside, run down the
driveway that extends through an
arbor lined with ivy and look toward
the wetlands. Black liquid shoots up
hundreds of feet into the sky.

"My gosh!" I say.

"It's oil!" Leo yells.

We run toward the dirty goosh and when we get closer to the geyser, I see Grandpa and Luna. They're jumping and dancing. Because I don't like or trust Grandpa and can't tell if Luna is alive or a ghost, I turn and try to run.

But Leo grabs my hand and propels me closer to the oil. "No!" I say. "I don't like Grandpa. I don't want to socialize with Luna and him.

"I'll fix it," Leo says. He claps his hands and Grandpa and Luna jump up and disappear into a smoky sky.

The oil is ruining my clothes.

"Take your clothes off, Dessa," Leo orders.

We take our clothes off and slosh around naked in the oil. Then we hug and kiss until we're ready to do more than hugging and kissing.

* * *

I woke up. I had forgotten to close the window shade the night before and too much sunlight flooded the bedroom. I got out of bed, pulled the shade down, returned to bed, reached for my cog stone and went back to sleep.

* * *

GOD says, "It is 1921."

There are steam-operated, oilrigs surrounding the gun club. I count twenty-seven men at each rig. I'm the only female. I wonder if other girls will come. This is a great place to find a husband if I were looking for a husband which I'm definitely not.

"GOD," I say. "Where do all these men go when they get tired?"

GOD says, "Look, Dessa."

I jump into the sky, fly over a steam cloud and look down. Men sleep everywhere. They're in cardboard houses and tents: big tents, army tents, all kinds of tents.

I see Grandpa. Dropping to the ground to see what he's doing, I land in an open-air bus.

"Welcome to the 'sucker bus'," GOD says.

The women on this bus are 1920's flappers. They wear cloche hats. The hems of their dresses fall to their calves. Their belts clasp their hips instead of their waists. They all seem to be tall, straight up and down, looking like skinny pencils.

The men wear denim overalls and flat caps.

The bus stops in front of a big tent where Grandpa is waiting for us. "Come on in," he says. "Fried chicken and all the fixin's are inside."

I walk in the tent, grab a plate of fried chicken, corn, mashed potatoes and brown gravy and sit down at a long table.

"Try it, Dessa," Luna says. She's sitting next to me. "It's delicious."

"I don't eat gravy," I tell her. "Are you alive?"

"Wait till you hear what Grandpa has to say," she says, ignoring my question. Luna has very nice manners and doesn't drop any food on her flapper dress.

"I think you better watch out, Luna," I say. "You can never tell when Grandpa is going to shoot you with his bow and arrows."

She smiles, keeps eating and doesn't seem one bit scared when Grandpa comes to our table.

"I guess Luna told you about the great deal I have for you, Dessa,"

Grandpa says. He's very dirty and
his teeth are missing again.

I don't know what he's talking
about but I'm not frightened.

Grandpa shows me some papers.
"Sign here," he says.

"No," I say. "I won't sign
anything without reading it."

"Come outside," Grandpa says.

I follow him outside.

"Looky right there," he says
pointing to a percolating pool of oil.
"Tomorrow that pool is gonna be a
geyser. You can buy it today."

"Don't listen to him," Leo says.
He grabs the papers from Grandpa.
"He's trying to fool you. He wants
your money."

Where did Leo come from? I
hadn't noticed him. In fact, until
then, I hadn't noticed the awful
stench and the empty sky either.
"Where are the birds and ducks?" I
ask.

GOD says, "When the farmers
dug the irrigation ditches to drain the
wetlands so they could plow the
ground, a few birds and ducks left.
When the members of the Gun Club
erected the dike, lots of birds and
ducks flew away. When the oil

riggers built roads so they could get to the oil wells more of the birds left."

"It used to be beautiful here," I say.

"All right. All right," Grandpa says. "Let's talk about important things. Birds and beauty aren't important. Money is."

Leo and I follow Grandpa back into the tent. The tables and benches are gone. So are the people. The tent interior is now the inside of a house.

"It's so cold. Where are we?" I need to find a winter coat.

"You're in a house in Lunenburg, Massachusetts," GOD says.

"I know this house," I say. "I saw it on a TV show. This is where Cabel Sturmss lived when he was a boy."

There is a Menorah in the window. It must be Chanukah, I think as I step as close as I dare to the fireplace and warm my hands.

"Sit down, sit down," Grandpa says.

I'm warmer now, so I sit on one of the wooden chairs as Grandpa drops a box of Encyclopedia Britannica's on the polished dining table. "If you buy this set of

274

Encyclopedias, I'll give you a Westbruk Wetlands lot. It's a very good deal," he tells me.

"No," I say.

"Grandpa may be right this time, Dessa," GOD says. "Some of the people who hold the deeds to the Encyclopedia Lots will get rich."

"I don't care," I say. "I don't want to buy anything from Grandpa."

"You're making a big mistake," Grandpa says. He puts his hand on my shoulder and starts to shake me.

"Stop it!" I say.

* * *

"You have to get up," my mother said.

I opened my eyes. "I need to go back to sleep."

"You gotta get up! They're in the living room."

"Who?" I stretched. My cog stone cut into my fingers.

Micah sat on the rose silk couch in our living room, hugging the armrest and turning the pages of an art book featuring Vincent Van Gogh. Jean sat at the other end of the couch. Neither of them noticed

me. Micah was giving his full
attention to the book. Jean was
staring at Micah.

"Okay. Okay," I faced them,
sleepy eyed and morning breathed.

"What do we have here?"

Micah jumped up from the
couch. "I love you, Dessa," he said.

Too late, I thought. Who cares?

Jean said, "It's my fault."

"I want to marry you, Dessa"
Micah said. "Nobody but you."

I looked at the man who I had
thought was the best thing that ever
happened to me and knew I wouldn't
marry him. I looked at the female
who had been my best friend since
we were twelve and cried, "Why?"

"Because I was stupid," she said.
"It was just so much fun imitating
your voice and telling him my
stories."

"It doesn't matter, Dessa." Micah
kept his right hand in the art book.

"What doesn't matter?" I sat on
the green chair in the corner of our
living room. The walls of our living
room were the softest of greens. Our
thick, plush carpet matched the
walls. The ceiling was the rose of
our couch.

"I don't care if you never tell me a story," Micah said. "It's not important. I can read stories."

I took Micah's hand and pulled him outside to the front porch. I wasn't going to break off an engagement that didn't feel like an engagement in front of Jean. On the porch, I said, "Micah, I'm sorry. I can't do it."

He looked down at me, shook his head and handed me the Vincent Van Gogh book. "Can you take Jean home?" he asked.

I nodded but he didn't see. He got into his shiny black Jaguar and drove away.

"I don't know what got into me, Dessa." Jean said.

"Go after Micah," I told her.

"I don't want him," she said.

"What do you want?" I asked.

"This book." She touched the art book I was holding.

"You want the Van Gogh book? Why?"

"Because it's valuable and belongs to you," she said.

"Take it!"

Jean Sturmss has been writing best sellers since 1965. Her pen name is Jean Halom. When asked why she uses that name she always says, "A long time ago, I knew somebody named Halom. Halom means dream. I'm still waiting for my dreams to come true."

I don't know what her dreams are. I do know that she married Gilbert Stoneman. Last year Doctor Gilbert Stoneman and his partner, Doctor Marion Rickbin, were awarded the Nobel Prize for applied science. I think it would be interesting to know Jean and her husband. They'd probably be great company at a dinner party.

I haven't heard about Micah since the Ollie drug store chain went belly up in 1964. My dad told me that Micah's s parents sold their Hillwood Country Club membership and Micah went to work for another law firm. Maybe he's still the best catch. I don't know. I've never run into him again.

In the late 1950's the steps in front of the UCLA library was the place where Jewish students met other Jewish students. I was sitting on those steps telling myself not to cry about Jean and Micah when I noticed familiar, scuffed brown loafers with familiar, white socks inside.

"Vat's new, Dessa?" Leonard Lechmann sat next to me.

I looked into his brown eyes and said. "The stone is only good for dreaming. My wishes don't come true."

Leonard stared at me then laughed. I remembered the laugh of the boy who thought it was funny that I didn't eat fish. "You still laugh the same," I said and showed him the cog stone. After I broke up with Micah and severed my friendship with Jean, I carried it everywhere I went.

He touched the stone. "Is this supposed to be for wishing?"

"No," I said. "You warned me. You said it was only a one wish stone."

He smiled.

"You should give me my money back." I didn't really want my money back. I didn't want to give up my cog stone induced dreams.

"How much money do I owe you?" he asked.

"I think you should have to pay interest," I said.

He laughed again.

"What happened to your grandpa?" I asked.

"Which one?"

"Do you have more than one grandfather?"

"Most people have two grandfathers," he said.

"Oh!" *How could I make such a dumb remark?*

"The grandfather that owned the cigarette factory died smoking."

What is this garbage? Leonard was obviously poor. His cheap clothes and red, rusted jalopy with a missing top did not speak the wealth of somebody whose grandfather owned a cigarette factory.

"You smoke," I said.

"Not anymore," he said. "I miss it though."

"What happened to your other grandfather?" I said. "The one who shot the arrows?"

"My other grandfather died in Auschwitz with the rest of my mother's family."

I got up and walked away. I couldn't stand liars then and I still can't.

18.

Dear Dessa Dreams,
 Pops is crazy. Moms ran away. What should I do?
Don't know how to take care of my self in Tarzana.

Dear Don't Know,
 I dreamt about some crazy people. They swam in the ocean and drowned.
 You need to talk to somebody quick. I suggest a psychiatrist, a psychologist, or a clergyperson. If you're still in school, talk to your favorite teacher or counselor. I'm also including a list of telephone hotlines for you to call.
Sincerely, Dessa Dreams.
   * * *

 GOD says, "It's 1928."

I'm in the ocean, treading in cool water. I like the feel of going up and down in the waves. I look east toward shore. From here the Gun Club looks like an oasis on a hill surrounded by ugly, spewing oilrigs. "Westbruk isn't beautiful anymore," I say.

"You're right, Dessa." GOD agrees with me.

The current changes. The undertow is strong, forcing me out to sea. There's a lot of tar and I'm getting tangled in seaweed. I know this is a dream but I don't like what's happening. Maybe I'm going to drown, I think. "Help! Help!" I call.

Leo swims toward me. He's swimming a leisurely sidestroke. Why isn't he swimming the crawl? How will he get to me with a sidestroke? Grandpa rows his dory toward me. What will Grandpa do when he gets here? The dory is moving slower than Leo. How strange! What kind of stupidity is this? Lifeguards using the sidestrokes and slow dories to save drowning people. I'm going further out to sea. I'm so tired. I'm going under. There's an alarm clock at the bottom of the ocean.

* * *

The alarm didn't waken me. My mother did. "Dessa," she said. "I've packed my suitcase. The cab is here. I'm leaving."

"What?" I was still asleep, deep in the ocean with a ringing alarm clock.

I reached for the clock and turned off the alarm. "Where are you going?"

"Don't worry," she said.

By the next morning, when I still hadn't heard from my mother, I got scared and my throat hurt. Dad was in Chicago. I had lost the slip of paper with the name and phone number of his hotel. *Who should I call? The police?*

The following afternoon a Mrs. Chillingwort called to inform me that after running back and forth through traffic on Slauson Avenue, my mother told the arresting policeman that the FBI was after her and had stolen her toothbrush. Mrs. Chillingwort said my mother was now incarcerated in the Metropolitan State Hospital for the Mentally Ill.

In July of 1959 the grass was brown and the plants looked tired in front of the pink stucco building that housed Metropolitan State Hospital. A man in a white jacket let me in then locked the door behind me. *Is he going to let me out again? Can the people in charge tell that I don't belong? Or do I belong? What would these people think if they knew I had cog stone induced dreams?* I shuddered as I wrote my name on the Visitor Sign-In-List.

A man in a white jacket led me into a poorly painted, large room with a gray linoleum floor. People sat on metal folding chairs in a large circle. A fortyish woman was facilitating a group discussion. She sported a pressed white blouse with a peter pan collar, and a name tag announcing that she was Norma Popper.

Another woman dressed in Salvation Army faded discards said, "If I have to live the same way, I'll go crazy again."

"She can't work," a man, dressed in overalls, said. "She's not capable."

"I can't go home with him," the woman said. "I can't."

"Who will take care of her?" the man said.

"I want to take care of myself," the woman said.

I sat on the chair next to my sleeping mother and touched her wrist. She woke up, looked at me and screamed, "You always sided with your father!" Then she went back to sleep.

"I want to take care of myself," the woman in the faded discards repeated.

My mother woke up again, stood, then ran across the room screaming, "Wicked man! Evil incarnate!"

I gasped when I saw that "Evil Incarnate" was Leo's Grandpa. He rose from his chair, looked at my mother, ran out the door, and jogged down the hall. My mother darted after him yelling, "Hitler reincarnated! Hitler reincarnated!"

I ran after them. My stomach hurt. The man in the white jacket grabbed Grandpa's arm. Grandpa slugged White Jacket's nose and grabbed his keys. White Jacket slumped to the ground. Another

White Jacket came to help but by
then, Grandpa had unlocked the door
and was off to somewhere.

Two weeks later, Norma Popper,
the social worker/facilitator, told me
why my mother was so angry with
Grandpa.

19.

My mother, Leonora Purlmun
Halom, and her first love, David
Melberg, took the red car from Los
Angeles to Westbruk on July 4,
1928. My mother was eighteen and
had already completed two years at
UCLA. David Melberg was my
mother's true love, not my dad,
according to Norma Popper, my
mother's social worker and
facilitator. (This information gave
me a stomach ache and made me
want to throw up.)

My mother and David only dated
in the summer. The rest of the year
David attended Stanford University
in Palo Alto, where he'd met "Duke"

Khanamoku, the champion swimmer from Hawaii who, in the 1920's, introduced the world to surf boards.

David had heard that the Duke was going to be at Westbruk Beach on the Fourth of July. Wouldn't it be great to swim with the famous guy!

Mother wore a bathing suit that covered her from shoulders to mid thighs under her skirt and middy. In her big red cloth bag, she carried her towel, some sandwiches, fruit and two novels, "*So Big*" by Edna Ferber and "*The Murder of Roger Acroyd*" by Agatha Christie.

David dragged a beach umbrella and a large blanket on the red car, the one car train that zoomed back and forth between Los Angeles and Westbruk.

During the hour ride the passengers on the red car sang "*Only a Bird in a Gilded Cage*", "*Ida, Sweet as Apple Cider*", "*Give my regards to Broadway*," "*Down by the old Mill Stream*," "*Let Me Call You Sweetheart*," and other songs. My mother and David knew all the words. David didn't make my mother feel badly because she couldn't carry a tune the way my dad had. He was too much in love.

The red car stopped near the Westbruk Gun Club. It was an ugly place to stop, my mother had told Miss Popper, the social worker/facilitator. The Gun Club was nice enough but the smoke from the steam-operated oilrigs on both mesas that flanked the wetlands weren't a pretty sight and didn't smell good. Added to the stench was the fact that the red car stop was a long way from the Westbruk Beach Pier where they expected to find the "Duke".

But neither the stink nor the distance deterred David and my mother. They kept singing and telling each other how much they loved each other as they walked. When they reached their destination my mother suggested they swim in the saltwater plunge just north of the pier. After stowing their gear on covered benches, David dove into the deep end and my mother walked into the shallow. My mother had to crawl over the restraining bar to get into the deeper water. They asked other swimmers if anybody had seen the "Duke". Nobody had. Nobody knew a Duke.

"The 'Duke' wouldn't swim in a plunge," David told my mother. "It's too tame."

They went to the beach where they laid the blanket and put their stuff on top of it. David stuck the umbrella pole into the sand. Then they walked about asking everybody they met if he or she had seen the "Duke".

Everybody said no until two men said yes. The "Duke" had taught them to surf, they said. Their names were Bud and Gene and they asked if David and my mother would like to watch them surf.

David nodded.

Mother said, "What a pleasure!"

Bud and Gene pushed enormous redwood boards out to sea. Mother thought the boards must have been at least thirteen or fourteen feet long.

When the men waded to a place too deep to stand, they climbed atop the boards and stayed in a prone position until a big wave came. Then they stood and rode the boards back to shore.

"It was flabbergasting," my mother told Mrs. Popper. "I'd never seen anything like it."

Bud asked if David and my mother would like to try.

"Yes!"

"Double yes!"

My mother was a wonderful dancer and had remarkable balance. Though she was a mediocre swimmer, she pushed the board out to sea, climbed on, stood up on her first try and rode a wave to shore. She was so happy.

David, a great swimmer, couldn't stand on the board. He kept trying and failing till the sun went down.

"It was a spectacular sunset," my mother told the social worker/facilitator. "Pinks and yellows, going down in a few seconds."

It had been a great day, Mother said. "Not hot. Not cold. Just perfect."

People built bonfires at dusk. Gene and Bud stowed their surfboards and invited my mother and David to their bonfire. Mother and David shared their sandwiches. Gene and Bud and their dates shared their marshmallows. Gene's girlfriend had ugly bunions on her feet. Mother had to concentrate so she wouldn't stare at them.

The tide was high that night. One wave almost touched the edge of the bonfire. When that wave receded, hundreds of grunion wriggled on the sand. Everybody on the beach, including my mother and David ran after those slender, mostly silver fish with bluish green backs. "They made soft squeaking noises when they laid their eggs," my mother said. My mother didn't have a gunnysack to put them in and wondered what to do with the ones she caught.

"Fry them!" the woman with big bunions on her feet said.

"In the bonfire?" My mother was more interested in the bunions than the grunion.

When the grunion disappeared the fireworks started. Strings and dots of bright colors lit up the sky. It was so pretty, my mother told Mrs. Popper. She leaned against David. He kissed her neck and her cheeks. And he touched her breasts.

(I wished Norma Popper hadn't told me this part. But I didn't say anything. I wanted to hear the rest of the story.)

Before the fireworks ended my mother saw her new friend, Bud, climb to the top of the pier. She watched as he wrapped himself in flannel and doused himself with alcohol. "What is he doing?" she asked Bud's friend Gene.

Gene laughed and told my mother to watch.

Bud climbed to the top of a tall diving platform at the end of the pier. There he lit a match and set himself on fire.

Mother screamed. Her chest hurt. She couldn't breathe.

Bud dove into the ocean. He looked like a ball of fire during his descent. "It was amazing," my mother told Norma. "I thought the man was trying to kill himself. But it was just a trick. People all over the beach were cheering."

David and my mother didn't leave the beach when the other people did. Instead they stayed on their blanket and kissed and kissed. And they did more than that.

Mother didn't tell Norma Popper what more they did or if she did, Norma didn't tell me. Thank the Gods!

My mother did tell David that she didn't want to get pregnant.

He told her, "I'll do what I always do when I get too hot."

David ran to the ocean, waded to a place where he couldn't stand and swam toward the horizon.

Mother put her feet in the water. It was cold but felt good. She told Norma she never felt more alive. It wasn't a dark night. She could see David. He was the strongest and most graceful swimmer she'd ever seen. Then he stopped swimming. His head bobbed up and down. He wasn't going anywhere. Just bobbing. My mother screamed, "David!"

He continued to bob up and down. Disappearing. Reappearing.

My mother panicked. She ran the beach, screaming, "Help! Help!"

A scruffy looking man, with dirty brown hair, caught her by her shoulders and said, "What are you screaming about, girlie?"

"My boy friend. I think he's drowning."

"Good thing ya run into me," he said. "I'm a lifeguard."

"He's right over there!" My mother pointed toward David, who was still bobbing in the water.

"I gotta get the dory." The man didn't look strong enough to be a lifeguard.

"Just swim out there!" my mother yelled.

"I gotta get the dory."

My mother followed the man. He looked in a shed attached to the plunge. "Dory's not here," he said.

"Why do you need a dory?" my mother screamed.

"Don't worry!" the man said.

My mother was more than worried. David was still bobbing.

They found the dory on the other side of the pier. My mother helped push the small boat into the ocean.

She looked toward where David had been. He wasn't there.

My mother told Norma that she'd never felt so bereft. Certainly not when my dad left, she said.

When the scruffy looking man returned with the dory there was no David.

She shook the man. "Where's David?" she screamed.

"I couldn't find him," he said. "Sorry."

Sorry. Did he say he was sorry? My mother said she couldn't believe what she was hearing. "Why didn't you swim after him?" she yelled.

"I don't know how to swim," the man said.

"How can you be a lifeguard?" my mother screamed.

"I know somebody."

"What?" my mother screamed.

Another man flashed his flashlight at them. My mother saw the cog stone tattoo on the lifeguard's hand. "I've never forgotten, Mrs. Popper."

(I've never forgotten Grandpa either.)

"Couldn't be helped," Grandpa said.

"When are you guys gonna learn to swim?" the man with the flashlight said. "Somebody's drowned at this beach every day this summer."

My mother took the red car back to Los Angeles the next day. She told Norma she was never the same again. "I don't know why David stopped swimming. I don't know what happened to him," she said.

I wished I would have known my mother when she was younger. I wished I could have seen her ride the waves on a surfboard.

20.

Dear Dessa,
    My boyfriend wants me to go all the way. What do you think?
Want to from Waukegan.

Dear Want To,
    Don't!
Sincerely, Dessa Dreams.

This is the kind of advice a woman born in 1937 gives.

I sat in the Beverly Hills Branch of Reed's Shoe Store examining the four shoes I'd picked off the display stand while waiting for somebody to wait on me. It was January of 1960 and I would be graduating in February with a major in theater arts, specializing in television. My dad was in New Orleans chasing down steel. My mother was still in the Metropolitan State Mental Hospital. I hadn't made a new friend since I lost Jean. I hadn't met a new man since I broke my engagement to Micah. And, one day, while working on a stage set, I'd spilled paint on my one pair of good shoes.

The store was filled with people. I had finals to study for, decisions to make and dreams to dream but I sat quietly waiting for somebody to help me. That's when I spotted Leonard Lechmann. "Where are you going to wear the shoes?" he asked his customer. He was a shoe salesman.

"Winter prom," his customer said.

"What color is your formal?" Leonard asked.

"Green. Light green. Green apple green."

"All right," he said. "We can dye a satin shoe to match. But I suggest you take this off white. Then you can wear it with more than your prom dress. Don't you think?"

The prom girl bought the off whites.

So did the "out to dinner" woman.

So did the woman who wanted the shoes for "just around the house."

In ten minutes, Leonard sold eight pairs of shoes. I wasn't surprised. He had sold me a cog stone when I was ten.

The other salesperson, a pretty high school girl, offered to help me.

"No thanks," I said. "I'll wait for him."

She grimaced. "Yeah," she said. "He knows more about shoes than I do. He's our best salesman."

She walked across the beige-carpeted floor and said something to

Leonard who turned to look at me and, then, went back to his customer. Ten minutes and four shoe sales later Leonard got to me.

"What kind of shoes do you want?" he asked. The best shoe salesperson still wore white socks inside of scuffed brown loafers. He looked at the four single pumps at my feet. Black, beige, white and brown leather. "Do you want all of them?" he asked.

"If they're comfortable. In the right size," I said.

"Let's measure your feet."

He unlaced my tennis shoes while I prayed that my socks didn't have holes and my feet didn't smell.

"Lets look at your feet under the fluoroscope."

I put my feet in the large x-raying contraption that every shoe salesman used to determine foot size in 1960.

"Size eight, wide" he said. "I hadn't noticed how big your feet are."

How did he get to be Reed's best salesman? "Do you have any size eight wides?" I asked.

"I get my break in a few minutes. Do you want get some coffee?"

"Why?"

"To talk." He put my shoes back on and tied my laces.

We sat in the brown Naugahyde booth in the well lit, smoked filled coffee shop next to Reed's Shoe Store. I sipped my usual, half coffee, half cream, six spoons of sugar.

His coffee was black. He had been glib with the customers in the shoe store. *Why isn't he talking to me?*

"Do you like movies?" I asked, needing to break the silence.

"Would you like to see NORTH BY NORTH WEST?" he asked.

"With you?" *Is he asking me for a date?*

Mr. Silence nodded.

"I don't think so," I said.

"Why not?" he asked. "Most Hitchcock's are good."

Why would I go out with him? He was a liar who had just insulted my big, wide feet. "I don't date liars."

Leonard grimaced. "I don't lie," he said.

"When are you going to graduate?" I asked, wondering if we were going to graduate on the same day.

"I've graduated," he said.

"I didn't know you had to graduate to sell shoes." *Why am I being so mean?* I didn't like myself. So I went back to Reed's Shoe Store, bought four pairs of shoes from Leonard and went to see NORTH BY NORTH WEST with him.

He bought me popcorn and a coke. We didn't talk once the movie started. This was a plus for Leonard. I couldn't stand people who talked during a movie. Still can't. When Cary Grant ran from the crop duster I grabbed Leonard's thigh for security. And then I let go of it like you would a hot pot of soup that you accidentally touched. But during the finale filmed atop the presidential faces of Mount Rushmore, I grabbed Leonard's thigh again. He patted my hand.

After the movie, we drove back to my house and I learned that Leonard knew how to kiss.

Our next date was at The Silver Bull, a steak house in Santa Monica with red and white gingham cloths on the tables and sawdust on the floor. That was the night I discovered we both loved steaks. I also found out that Leonard had atrocious eating habits. What could you expect from a boy who had been homeless on the beach when he was young?

This is what he did: He held his fork in his left hand, knife in the right, cut the meat, pushed it on to the fork with his knife, and with his left hand put his fork into his mouth. *Didn't he know that he was supposed to change hands and put his fork into his right hand after cutting?* I decided to be nice and not say anything. But, Leonard did. "Americans have odd eating habits!" he said. "Not practical."

My eating habits were odd? Not practical! What was he talking about? What was wrong with him?

"You should do it like this." He proceeded to show me how he did it.

People were looking at us. A man with a string tie at the next table said, "He's right, girlie. Europeans do eat more refined."

"They're more practical," said his heavily jeweled dinner partner.

I was not happy about the situation and didn't like Leonard Lechmann.

When he left me off at the door, he kissed me. It was the best kiss.

Our dates were predictable. We spent the first hours arguing. We argued about the weather. About what building looked the best. About the advice I gave in the Dear Dessa Dreams column. About politics. About what was good entertainment. Leonard said watching and reading about sports was the best way to use one's leisure time. I hated sports. Leonard said that burnt to the crisp steak was the only way to eat it. I ate it rare. Leonard wouldn't eat fish. I started ordering it. I liked making him mad. Leonard said the best meal was radishes and pumpernickel bread slathered with sweet butter. Imagine!

After we argued, we necked. Then we petted. And then we almost, but didn't. There were so many almosts; we decided to talk to a rabbi.

Rabbi Louis Allen sat behind his Danish Modern desk across from us, pushing his fingers together to form a pyramid. He licked his thick lips before he said, "So you want to get married."

"Yes," Leonard said.

"I'm not sure," I said.

Leonard and the Rabbi said, "What?" in unison.

"I think I want to go to bed with Leonard." I looked down at my lap. *How could I say such a thing?*

"I've known Dessa for a long time," Rabbi Allen smiled. "I've always liked her."

I looked at the Rabbi in his nice gray suit with his clean-shaven face and realized I didn't know him at all.

"Since Dessa's parents aren't here, I'll stand in for them and ask the questions." The Rabbi put his fingers together to form another pyramid. "How do you plan to support her?"

"He sells shoes," I said. "He's good at it." I put my fingers together and made my own pyramid.

Rabbi Allen smiled with his teeth. His eyes were somber. "Dessa's used to the best," he said. "I'm curious, Leonard. Do you own the shoe store?"

"He's poor but we'll make do." I had no idea if we could and hoped we weren't going to end up at Cardboard Beach living in a box.

"Are you expecting her father to help you?" Rabbi Allen asked.

"The day I decided to marry Dessa, I knew I would have to earn more money." Leonard took out his wallet, counted out ten one hundred dollar bills and put the money on the Rabbi's desk.

I was stunned. The Rabbi looked more than stunned. "How did you get the money?" he asked Leonard.

"I earned it," Leonard said.

"How?" I asked.

"I've gone into commercial real estate," Leonard said. "That's my first and second commission." He pointed to the money on the desk.

"Working on commissions, negotiating. Real estate isn't easy," Rabbi Allen said.

"I was born in Subotica, Yugoslavia in 1936, stayed in

Bucharest during World War II and escaped to Vienna after the war," Leonard said. "I lived in a displaced person's camp before coming to United States. Nothing in my life has been easy."

"I thought I detected an accent."

Detected an accent? Was the Rabbi hard of hearing? Leonard couldn't pronounce 'r's or 'th's.

"I've heard commercial real estate is a good business." Rabbi Allen smiled.

Leonard smiled.

I didn't say anything. I was too angry.

"Why didn't you tell me you were going into commercial real estate?" I asked Leonard when we were outside standing on the cracked sidewalk in front of the red brick temple. "Don't you think I should know how you make a living?"

"Why?" Leonard asked.

"We're getting married. Don't you think you should confide in me?"

"I'll tell you everything and all things," Leonard said. "When I want to tell you."

"That's not good enough."

"It's the best I can do," he said.

"Do you love me?" I asked.

"Do you love me?"

I wasn't sure.

"If you don't love me, why do you want to marry me?" *Could Leonard read my mind?*

"I want to go to bed with you." Nice single girls didn't get pregnant in 1960. I was a nice girl, wasn't I?

"We'll be stuck together for a life time," he said.

"People get divorced," I said. "My parents did."

It was over. A kaput relationship. Better now, I told myself. Besides, I didn't care. *Did I?*

I miss you Dessa," Leonard said when he called six months later. His boss had died. "Emphysema." He owned the commercial real estate business now. Life seemed sort of empty, he said. He was doing well. Not real well. But he was making a living and wanted to see me.

I wanted to see him, too. I didn't know if I loved him. I had thought about him when I went to see

"Psycho". I was so scared during the shower scene I wanted to grab my date's thigh, but hadn't. I'd spent great chunks of time fantasizing the arguments I would have with Leonard over the Kennedy-Nixon debates. Listening to the first debate on the radio, it sounded to me as if Nixon won. Everybody said Kennedy would give all our state secrets to the Pope. The Pope would say, "You have to confess, Jack. Tell me everything you know." And Jack would say "yes, of course" in his Boston accent.

We sat on the green front seat of Leonard's ugly yellow Dodge Coronet sedan.

"Who did you vote for?" I asked.

"Who did you vote for?"

"Well I was going to vote for Nixon," I said.

"But you didn't, did you?"

"Who did you vote for?"

"Kennedy," he said.

"If I knew you were going to vote for Kennedy, I would have voted for Nixon," I told him. "No matter the Jewish thing." Every

Jewish person I knew believed
Nixon was a covert anti-Semite.

Leonard laughed. "How Jewish
are you, Dessa?"

"Jewish enough. Why?" I didn't
know how Jewish I was.

"It's important to me," he said.

We spent the next hour arguing
about how Jewish we were and came
to the conclusion that if we were
ever so dumb as to get married it
would be a disaster for both of us.

Two weeks later on Sunday,
December 18, 1960 we were married
in Rabbi Allen's study.

21.

Dear Dessa Dreams,
I've been married a month and
am ready to get divorced. What's
the best way to get his money?
Had it in Herrin, Illinois

Dear Had It,

I dreamt about some people who had a horrible divorce. She wanted all the money. He wanted all the money. Their lawyers got all the money. So if you want all the money, become a lawyer.
Sincerely, Dessa Dreams

"You have to do some cleaning, Dessa," Leonard told me.

"When?" I asked.

Our upstairs one bedroom apartment in Long Beach, California was little and should have been easy to clean.

Leonard said he needed to work seven days a week to get ahead in real estate. "I have no time to clean," he told me.

"I don't have any time either." I was the new Recreation Director for the Robertson Playground in Los Angeles, directing plays and teaching dance, exercise and arts and crafts classes. I made up verses for preschoolers to march across the stage of the Robertson recreation room. "We march to Stage Left. We March to Stage Right. Then we turn our selves around and we clap with all our might." "We run to Stage Left." "We skip to stage right." I also created rhymes about elephants, ducks and caterpillars. In my spare time I visited my mother at Metropolitan State Hospital, talked to my dad on the phone and answered Dear Dessa Dreams letters.

"Men don't clean," Leonard said.

"What do you mean?" I yelled.

"You exhaust me, Dessa."

We stripped and got into bed. He threw his clothes to the floor on his side of the bed. I threw mine on my side.

"Men don't clean," Leonard repeated.

"My dad did," I said. "He used to sweep dirt under the rug."

Leonard laughed. And then we did what we always did before I took my cog stone from under my pillow and went to sleep.

* * *

GOD doesn't say anything. I'm on the lower wetlands with the members of the Gun Club. The men pick up their guns, aim and shoot. Pop! Pop! Boom! Boom! All the egrets fall out of the sky. The grounds of the wetlands are covered with white feathers.

"Where are you GOD? I need to know."

GOD doesn't answer. The hunters are gone. It's just me, sitting by myself with dead birds and thousands of white feathers.

"Everything's ruined, GOD. Please do something."

"Close your eyes, Dessa," GOD says.

"Okay." I say. The silence of the dark behind my closed eyes is better than the silence of dead birds and a sea of white feathers.

When I open my eyes I'm sitting on the mesa in a field of green gray plants and blooming flowers. I inhale the pleasant odor of coastal sagebrush while looking at the dazzling yellow blooms of Bladder pods and Coast Sunflowers. Clusters of whitish-pink flowers sprout on the top of the branches of California buckwheat. "This is much better," I say.

Two Great Egrets stand like statues at the edge of a clear pond in front of me. *Didn't all the Egrets die?*

The female moves her neck back and forth. "Kroow." She has a deep gravelly croak. The male cranes his neck back and forth and jumps up and down, wiggling his legs in the air. "Karrrr." His voice is lower and coarser than the female's. Both voices sound unpleasant to me. But watching the birds is miraculous. This must be some kind of mating dance. "Will there be a baby?" I ask GOD.

"Yes."

* * *

I was pregnant. I suffered morning sickness for a short time and had one horrible stomachache. Tubular pregnancy was mentioned over and over for three hours. Then the miracle happened. I felt great. My husband was happy. He said I was beautiful. We didn't argue about house cleaning because I kept our apartment spotless. We could have eaten off the floors and the ceilings. I took a mop and scrubbed those ceilings. I had endless energy and couldn't stand dirt.

I would have gone on scrubbing and scouring if I hadn't visited my mother at the Metropolitan State

Hospital on a day when Norma Popper was facilitating one of the circle discussions.

Sitting next to my sleeping mother, I listened to a woman dressed in a faded purple bathrobe say, "I notice everything and feel nothing."

"What do you mean?" Norma Popper asked.

"I was raped and didn't feel it. I looked up at the ceiling and watched the dirt."

"Hmmn." Norma fingered her peter pan collar.

The purple robed woman fingered her collar, too. "The doctor gave me a shot. I counted the pieces of lint on his jacket," she said.

Like the purple robed woman I noticed everything, too. Was I feeling anything? I wondered about craziness and heredity. Besides my mother, had there been other crazies in our family? Would my baby be okay?

22.

Dear Dessa Dreams,

I'm pregnant and don't know nothing about babies. Neither does my husband. I don't feel good and puke constantly, not only in the morning. When I'm not puking, I'm crying. What do you think I should do?
Miserable in Mendocino.

Dear Miserable,

I dreamt about a pregnant person. Her morning sickness passed. She stopped crying and had a beautiful baby. Read Doctor Spock and stay away from Simone de Beauvoir. If you read a book by Simone, you may want to run away to Paris and eat croissants and drink hot chocolate at an outdoor café. Then who will take care of your baby?
Sincerely, Dessa Dreams.

I read Spock and Beauvoir. And there were times that I did want to run away to Paris. There still are.

My mother smiled and seemed happy when I told her she was going to be a grandmother. But then she kept smiling as she told me that having a baby could kill me. Didn't I remember all the miscarriages she had? I did. Didn't I remember that every time she had one of those miscarriages she almost died? I did. Didn't I know that when she had me she also almost died? I hadn't known so I took my cog stone to bed with me to ponder the situation.

* * *

GOD says, "The future is here, Dessa."

I look around. Everything seems so fertile. Baby Legless and Western Fence Lizards creep between the Yellow Beach Evening Primrose and Lilac Verbena that bloom on the wetlands sand dunes trail. Baby snakes slither out from hiding places under large rocks. Monarch butterflies dart through sage and buckwheat. Baby Belding's Savannah Sparrows eat baby insects on the pickle weed. I look up. The sky is filled with baby birds. A baby red-tailed hawk darts above me. "It doesn't have a red tail," I tell GOD.

"Baby red tailed hawks don't," GOD says. "Come on up. You can see better."

I jump up to the sky and look down. From this angle I watch baby White-tailed Kites, Brown Pelicans, Great Egrets, Snowy Egrets, and Blue Herons hatch from eggs.

A baby coyote chases a baby Black-tailed jackrabbit. A baby skunk sprays me. What a dreadful odor! The stench hurts my stomach. I try to pull my knees to my chest and my big, pregnant belly gets in the way. Then I fall from the sky and land on my stomach. The pain is so bad. Couldn't be worse. I'll concentrate on something else.

Through the clear water of a pool a few feet away I watch tiny, newly spawned Fiddler Crabs, Sea Hares, Round Stingrays, California Halibut, Arrow Goby, Staghorn Sculpin and Top smelt.

"Everybody has a baby but me," I tell GOD.

Then an invisible iron fist punches my abdomen and I scream.

"What's wrong?" Leo asks and takes my hand.

"You always come when I need you Leo," I say. Then the pain is too much and I scream again.

* * *

"Dessa," Leonard said. "Are you all right?"

He pulled me toward him. It took me a minute to get used to the surroundings and realize that I wasn't at the wetlands with Leo but in bed with Leonard in our apartment in Long Beach. It was dark. "What time is it?" I asked.

Leonard switched on the lamp next to his side of the bed. "It's two-fifteen," he said. "How do you feel?"

How do I feel? I answered with a scream. My back hurt. My stomach hurt. I couldn't breathe. Did he expect me to answer him with words?

"I'll time the contractions," Leonard told me. "Maybe, I should get dressed." He got out of bed and walked to the closet.

Who cared if he got dressed? I wanted to go back to the Westbruk Wetlands. I wanted to fly with the birds. "Oh my gosh! Going to hell. I'm going to hell."

"Five minutes," Leonard said.

Five minutes? He was completely dressed. It was the middle of the night. Where did he get the energy to put clothes on? "We don't have to worry till it's ten minutes," I said.

On my last routine visit Leonard had gone with me to see Doctor Cranstern. "When she has contractions every ten minutes, call me. Not one minute before," the doctor had told him.

"I think we better dress you," Leonard said.

I didn't want to get dressed. I wanted to take my dream inducing cog stone, go back to the wetlands and discuss my rotten situation with GOD and Leo. "Damn it to hell!" I needed stronger words to describe the large pole of steel slashing through my back to my stomach. But screaming the foulest language I could think of didn't help me and it scared Leonard. I could see the fear in his eyes. On his down turned lips. I didn't care. *Let him suffer*.

"I'll call the doctor," he said.

"It's not ten minutes between contractions yet," I said.

Leonard laughed.

"This isn't funny." I was perspiring and scared. My mother almost died having me. Maybe I would die. I screamed.

"Four minutes," my husband announced. He picked up the phone and dialed.

"I don't want you to bother the doctor until it's ten minutes," I said.

"Doctor Cranstern, this is Leonard Lechmann. . .Four minutes." He bit his cuticle. "She didn't want me to bother you till there were ten minutes between contractions." Leonard started to laugh again. "She is very funny. Always has been."

I'm not funny! I screamed again.

Outside I sat on the curb.

"We need to get to the hospital," Leonard said.

"I can't go," I said.

"You have to get in the car," he said.

"I'm not budging," I said.

In the hospital, I had my legs in stirrups when Leonard walked into the room. "How do you feel?" he asked.

"Where's the doctor?" I wanted to know.

"Don't push yet," the ugly woman dressed in white said. "We can't locate the doctor."

The doctor was hiding and I wasn't supposed to push. What did push mean? I may have gotten through college but I was really ignorant about this stuff.

"My back is killing me," Leonard said.

Who are these people? This "don't push" female and my husband with a sore back. I was the one having the baby. I needed to sit on the toilet and have a bowel movement. I needed to push. Aha! Now I knew what "Ugly in White" meant by pushing. I pushed and pushed and screamed.

"My back hurts so bad, Dessa."

I hated him. He had no right to a backache. I pushed again.

"I told you to hold off pushing," the woman in white yelled.

Doctor Cranstern arrived eight hours and some minutes later. "Ready for some help?" he asked me. "She's ready for the saddle block. Set her up," he told the nurse.

Where the hell had he been? I wanted to ask. Instead I screamed and pushed.

"The head. Too late!" Ugly nurse yelled.

"Okay," the doctor said.

I closed my eyes. I was getting ready to push again and opened my eyes. The doctor had a scissors in his hand. *What is he doing?*

"The baby's coming," he told me.

I screamed, pushed and yelled, "What are you going to do with the scissors?"

"You're ready for your episiotomies." Doctor Cranstern wore a white mask over his face but I could tell he was smiling. I hated him.

Snip. Snip. Snip. The cuts didn't hurt. But I could feel the pressure and hear them.

I pushed the baby out. Eight pounds two ounces of perfection. Arthur Michael Lechmann was born on August 28, 1962.

On June 26, 1965 I went to a deli, ate sweet and sour cabbage and had a contraction. Two hours later Eli Stephen Lechmann was born.

By 1967, we lived in a tract house in Westbruk, California. It was, then, when I was living in a house that looked like everybody else's house, had two babies, a husband to fight with and not much sleep that I discovered Simone De Beauvoir. When Jean Paul Sartre, her lover, got a teaching job on the other side of France he asked Simone to marry him.

"No. No," she said. "I don't believe in marriage. Too bourgeois." Instead she stayed in Paris, went to cafes, drank hot chocolate, ate buttery croissants and wrote her thoughts on big tablets.

What am I doing here? I asked myself. What happened to the arty theater arts major? She would have never lived in a tract house. I had thoughts. I could learn to speak French and go to France. I don't belong in Westbruk, California, I told myself.

23.

Dear Dessa Dreams,
*   I can't stand my husband or my*
kids. I want to run away. Where is
the best place to go?
Can't stand anything in Chicago,
Illinois.

Dear Can't Stand Anything,
*   I dreamt about a woman who*
couldn't stand her life. She ran away
to the circus. If there's no circus
near you join a Community Theater.
Community Theater takes up lots of
time so you won't have to see much
of your family.
Sincerely, Dessa Dreams.

In 1967 Johnny Johnson, my
boss at WEEK SAVERS, bought
four California newspapers with
small circulations. My "Dear Dessa
Dreams" column was syndicated in
the Westbruk Bulletin Gazette,
Caruthers Bulletin Gazette, Rawley
Bulletin Gazette and the Ridley
Bulletin Gazette. For the same
amount of work, I earned more

money. And Leonard's commercial real estate business was thriving.

Barry, a second cousin and a junior at Cal Berkley who wanted to be a psychiatrist and was studying psychology, phoned me periodically to check on my mother's progress after she'd been declared mentally ill by the state of California, called April 13th in the morning. "Hi! Dessa," he said.

"What's new?" I asked.

"I'm going to march tomorrow," he said.

"March where?"

"Thousands of people are going to demonstrate against the Viet Nam war. In San Francisco."

"Will it be dangerous?"

"Don't be silly?" he said. "Would I do anything dangerous? Don't worry Dessa."

"I'm going to try out for a play," I told him.

Instead of running away to Paris or joining the circus, I auditioned for a part at the Westbruk Community Theater.

"Speak louder," the tall, motherly, redheaded director said.

She was sitting in the back row of the small thrust theater.

I spoke louder and got the part of the ingénue Girl Friend in the play *LOOK HOMEWARD ANGEL* by Ketti Fring, based on the book by Thomas Wolfe.

I told the director, "Mrs. Macefield, if my second cousin goes to jail, I might not be able to be in the play." I was pretty sure that I was the only one in our family that knew about his marching and, if necessary, it would be me that would have to bail him out.

"Of course, you should help your cousin." The director hugged me, "Call me Mace," she said.

Barry called to report the "awful" experience on Saturday. He'd walked twelve blocks before his group got lost and turned around. There was going to be another march in a week, but he couldn't go. He had a makeup test he couldn't miss.

Thank you GOD for makeup tests. I really wanted to be in the play.

The cast and crew of *LOOK HOMEWARD ANGEL* talked of

things I wanted to talk about. They didn't discuss the best way to clean a cloth diaper, what baby formula they used and what nursery school they thought most ideal for their children.

If I hadn't had to kiss Eugene Gant, the boy coming of age in the play, everything would have been perfect. The thought of the kiss made me so queasy I couldn't remember my lines. I knew Leonard would come to the play, see the kiss and want a divorce.

Sam Goodman, the eighteen year old who had the role of Eugene, was a gangly younger Jimmy Stewart type with a large bulge in his pants.

I was ready to quit but didn't because of Sharon Morgan. Sharon played Eliza, Eugene's mother. On stage Sharon/Eliza was electric. Her speaking voice was clear, unique and projected to the back row. Off stage she was a pocked marked woman who talked from the left side of her mouth and said nasty things to me. "You can't remember your lines, can you?" she said. "You're not much of an actress, are you?" "You look really tired." "Take care of yourself.

The Girl Friend is supposed to be good looking."

I wasn't going to quit.

One night in the second week of rehearsal Eugene/Sam threw his arm around me. His fingers were too near to the top of my breast. "We should rehearse the kiss," he whispered in my ear. "We don't want to make fools of ourselves."

"Huh?"

"There's nobody in the greenroom," he continued. "We could have some privacy."

Mace told Sam and me to get on stage.

"We want to rehearse alone first." Sam/Eugene pulled me closer to him.

"That's an idea." Mace laughed.

"I don't know my lines," I said.

"Of course she doesn't." Sharon/Eliza's pocked-marked face was beaming. "I can't wait to watch the amateurs kiss."

Mace looked at her watch. "Maybe we should call it a night," she said. "My mother hasn't been feeling well."

"Let's go into the green room," Sam/Eugene said. "We need to work this out."

"No," I said.

Sam/Eugene grabbed me. "We can fix the problem in a jiffy."

I looked directly at his bulging pants and said, "No."

"Okay," he said. "But you really should grow up. Great actors do it. If you have the sex off stage, the electricity shows. We gotta do it, Dessa. You know it and I know it."

Why didn't I laugh?

Mace's mother died that night.

After a three-night break in our rehearsal schedule, Mark Schamberg hired on as our new director.

"Oh no!" Sam/Eugene said. "I loved Mace."

Maybe there was more to the guy than bulging pants, I thought.

"Oh hell," Sharon/Eliza said. "Schamberg's the meanest guy alive. Be forewarned, Dessa."

If Sharon was forewarning me, I thought I might like Mark Schamberg. When I first saw him, I loved the way he looked. Long, thick brown hair, silver bracelets on both arms, he resembled James Dean or maybe Marlon Brando.

"Give me a few minutes, guys." Mark sat in the front row. He dumped Jack Kerouac's "*On the Road*" and Alan Ginsburg's "*Howl*" on the seat to the right of him, then looked at the script.

Sam/Eugene said we should go into the green room and shake out our kinks.

"No," I said and sat by myself in the back row of the well-lit theater, picked up my script and thought about using the time to memorize my lines but couldn't concentrate.

Mace's mother was dead. Mothers died. I hadn't visited my mother since I started rehearsing.

I had taken the boys to see my mother on the Wednesday after my last call-back (audition). She'd been living in a board and care facility in the Fairfax area of Los Angeles for the last year and a half.

A tiny bit of sanding, stripping and a new paint job to replace the missing beige paint would have improved the looks of the dilapidated building that housed the board and care.

Inside, the Orthodox Rabbi who ran the facility always smiled when I saw him. Women sat on old green and brown couches that hugged the walls of the large reception room. Some slept. Others stared. A few carried on a conversation about my sons and me as if we weren't there.

"So she's finally come to see her mom."

"Doesn't come very much."

I had been there three days before.

"Just like anybody else's child. She's lazy."

"No, I'm not," I said.

The women carried on as if I hadn't defended myself. "She wears pretty clothes."

"Her mother wears schmates. Rags."

My mother once used her new blue sweater to wipe herself after a bowel movement. She spilled food at every meal.

"Her kids are cute."

"If you like boys."

Where is my mother? I needed to get away from the harpies.

Arthur spotted her first and ran across the room to where she sat in the corner watching me. Her hands were folded in her lap. There was no smile on her face.

"I want to go in the elevator, Bubby," Arthur told her.

"Me too," Eli said.

My mother didn't look at my sons.

"Please," Arthur said. "I really want to use the elevator. I really like elevators, Bubby."

The elevator was small. Only two could fit. Arthur went with me. We got off the elevator and walked through the hall to my mother's room. The flowered bedspread and matching window curtains gave the stark white-walled room some life. Arthur and I sat on the two flower patterned, quilted chairs. I told him, "You'll have to get up when Bubby comes."

He grimaced.

When my mother came into the room, Arthur asked where Eli was.

"Eli?" My mother acted as if Eli was a name she'd never heard.

I grabbed Arthur's hand and ran down the hall as fast as I could.

How would I get in the elevator? Be calm, I told myself. I pushed the button. Nothing happened. I couldn't hear the elevator. Where was it? I pushed the button again. The door opened. Eli sat in the corner. My toilet trained (for a week) child sat in his mess, crying, nose running and sucking his thumb. He was too heavy to lift but I lifted him, pulled Arthur into the elevator with my free hand. "Push the Down Button," I told Arthur, thankful that he was smart and could read.

After that I called the Rabbi to ask about my mother at least three times a week; but didn't visit. What kind of daughter was I? Why was I rehearsing? I needed to go and see my mother at night when Leonard could watch the boys. I felt guilty. Too heavy a feeling for an ingénue; I needed a heavier part or a lighter feeling.

Mark, the beatnik looking director, sat in the back row of the theater, jangled his silver bracelets and watched the kiss scene between Sam/Eugene and me.

Sam/Eugene pushed his big bulge into my privates. I pulled my rear end back to avoid him. He whispered through tight lips that I was supposed to be seducing him.

"Sam, back off!"

"Think Eugene," he whispered. "Get into this play! Seduce me!"

"Okay," Mark said. "Take a break."

Forty-five minutes later, Mark's girl friend, Cheril, a pretty blonde, had my part and I had the part of Helen Gant, Eugene's sister. Charlotte Weidameyer, who had *owned* the Helen Gant part but was more than an hour late or absent to every rehearsal, was out.

Because there was so much of Helen to learn, I didn't have time to rehearse her non-speaking scenes. Saturday, June 3, opening night, was the first time that I was on the stage while Sharon/Eliza and Tom Goodvil, the man who played Oliver her drunk husband, had their big fight scene in the boarding house. They screamed their lines with ferocious energy. They threw stage props. I stood upstage center and watched these two people act like my parents did when I was little. My dad had never been drunk. My mother never had Sharon/Eliza's vigor. But what happened was the same. I was terrified as a child and horrified under the spotlight. I was caught up in the action, reacting.

Mark grabbed me and gave me a hug as soon as I walked off stage. "You stole the show," he whispered. "You were so good!"

Sharon heard him. "I've never worked so hard in my life and you are praising Dessa? What's wrong with you?" She threw one of the prop dishes at him.

On Monday, June 5th a rave review about me appeared in the Westbruk Bulletin Gazette. My boss, Johnny Johnson, wrote the article.

That evening a meeting was called at the theater. We actors sat in the front row. Mark stood on the stage. "Does anybody have anything to say?" he asked.

"I loved reading the rave about Dessa," Sam/Eugene said. There had to be something about the boy that I overlooked.

"I have something to say,"
Sharon said. "Dessa should not be
upstage-center during the blowout
scene in the boarding house. She's
too distracting."

"Where should I be?" I asked.

"Behind the potted palm pouring
water."

"Okay," I said. "But, I'm still
going to react."

"No need, lambie." Sharon
smiled her crooked smile at me.

I'm not your "lambie".

Leonard was waiting for me on
our front porch.

Oh no, I thought. He's going to
argue with me in front of the
neighbors. He doesn't care that I got
a rave review. He probably wants
me to quit the play. Please, let him
be quiet until the play is over. It's
only three more weeks. If he wants a
divorce then, I'll give it to him. I'll
admit that I'm the worst wife, that I
spend money foolishly on take out
food, that I'm never home and if and
when I am home, I'm tired and
cranky.

"Israel's gone to war," he said.

"Who is Israel?" I couldn't think of anybody named Israel.

"Israel is a county," he said. "Do you care?"

I didn't know what to say.

"Your mother died," Leonard said next.

Had I heard right? The mother that I hadn't visited for seven weeks was dead?

"The Rabbi thinks she starved herself," he said.

I walked into our front room and sat on the couch.

"We have to arrange a funeral." Leonard sat on our big burnt-rust chair across from the couch.

I didn't want to look at Leonard. I wanted to take my cog stone and go to bed. At the age of thirty I still wanted things to be all right. I wanted my mother to be well. I wanted my parents to have a happy marriage. I wanted to have a good life.

I called my cousin, Barry.

"Your mother used to be so lovely, Dessa. My father always said so." Was he crying?

I didn't feel like crying. *What's wrong with me?*

"Should I come down?" Barry asked after telling me that his finals would start the next day.

"No," I said. "Take your finals." Why should he come? He hardly knew my mother.

I called my dad.

"What can I do, Dessa?" He sounded so sad. Was he crying?

Dad paid for the funeral that only my husband and I attended.

The Rabbi who ran the board and care facility told me my mother put her food in paper bags and hid them in back of her closet and under the quilted chairs in her room. He hadn't noticed her weight loss, he said. There were so many women living in the board and care. When one of the ladies had somebody who came to visit on a regular basis, he didn't worry about the woman. "You always came, Dessa," he said.

But I hadn't come. I hadn't been there for weeks.

The first few days after the funeral, I sat on the couch in my nightgown and told Leonard that I was watching Israel's "Six Day War". But when the war was over I still sat in front of the television.

I was watching the *MERV GRIFFIN SHOW* when Leonard dragged the long extension cord across the room and tried to hand me the phone.

"I can't talk," I said.

He told the black receiver, "Of course she wants to talk to you, Sharon."

Sharon/Eliza told me how great *LOOK HOMEWARD ANGEL* was doing without me. Charlotte Weidameyer, who had *owned* the part of Helen before I took over, poured water in the potted palm during the boarding house scene and did not upstage other actors.

"Good," and "Bye" were my only contributions to the conversation.

I started my day with Hugh Downs on the THE TODAY SHOW. On Monday June 26, Hugh told me that President Johnson met with Soviet Premier Kosygin in Glassboro, New Jersey on the 23rd and yesterday four hundred million viewers had watched The Beatles sing *All You Need Is Love* on the first satellite television production.

My son Arthur asked me, "What should we do about Eli's birthday, mommy?"

"I have to watch Hugh Downs," I said.

Leonard looked at me. "You can't sit there the rest of your life," he said.

"Why not?"

Leonard took two cookies out of a pack of cookies, put them on two plates and stuck a large red candle in one of the cookies, struck a match and lit it. "Come here, Eli," he said.

Arthur and Leonard sang happy birthday. Eli and Arthur blew out the candle. I watched the rest of the broadcast.

When Leonard took our sons to Day Camp, I watched *GUIDING LIGHT* and *SEARCH FOR TOMORROW*. I couldn't seem to hear the dialogue. I used the bits and pieces I was able to catch of Virginia Graham and her panelists on *GIRL TALK* to answer the letters in my Dear Dessa Dreams column. I never took a writing break.

When the boys were home, they sat next to me and we watched Mr. Rogers and Captain Kangaroo. I

wanted to meet Mr. Rogers. He
wouldn't tell me that I was a bad
person for not going to see my
mother. He would say that
everything was going to be all right
in our neighborhood.

I read somewhere that laughter
was the best medicine, so I watched
*THE LUCY SHOW, JACKIE
GLEASON, RED SKELETON*, and
GOMER PYLE. Were they funny? I
didn't laugh.

I was watching Ralph
Cramden/Jackie Gleason argue with
Alice when Barry called. "I didn't
take my finals," he said. "Nothing
seems relevant so I've quit school."

"Oh." I felt like crying but didn't.

I didn't cry three weeks later
when I received a letter from him
postmarked Kabul, Afghanistan.

Dear Dessa,

*This is the life. I've gotten high
on hashish, tripped out on LSD,
painted the most vivid water colors
and have written mind-altering*

poems about your mom. I may send
you some.
Fondly,
Barry.

Barry's second letter came from
Katmandu, Nepal.

Dear Dessa,
I'm in Nepal. Big bats fly around
my head. It is the festival of some
important Goddess. I feel at home
and am off drugs.
Fondly,
Barry.

Big bats. Off drugs. I didn't
laugh but I smiled.

Barry called at the end of
August. "I'm back," he said.

"I'm glad," I said.

"I'm 4F," he said. "I didn't take
a physical but I've been declared 4F.
What do you know about it, Dessa?"

"I know I'm glad," I said.

"Did your father pay someone
off?" he asked. "I think my dad
asked him to. Your father has the
pull."

From time to time I asked my
dad if he got Barry out of the army.
He never answered.

Barry eventually went back to school, studied psychology and never became a psychiatrist. Instead he teaches creative writing at a community college in Eureka, California and when I see him he brags about his "gorgeous", "genius" granddaughter.

At the end of that summer, Johnny Johnson called me and asked me to come down to the Westbruk Bulletin Gazette. "I'm mired," he said.

"I'm not in a good mood," I said.

"Please, Dessa," he said. "Just for an hour."

I can't," I said.

"A half hour," he said.

"No," I said.

"I'm thinking of tossing the Dear Dessa column," he said.

I dressed myself, threw the smelly nightgown I used for watching television in the trashcan and went.

The Westbruk Bulletin Gazette was located in the last building in a down town Westbruk strip mall, next to a laundry. The parking lot needed repair and there were no white lines to demark the parking spaces.

There was a small roll top desk, a wall full of metal file cabinets and two chairs in the Westbruk Bulletin Gazette office. Johnny sat at the desk chewing his cigar tip and spitting. Reams of papers were piled high all over the gray cement floor.

"You shouldn't threaten me," I said.

"I'm already done with the 'A's' to the 'V's'," he said. "Let's attack the 'W's'".

He pointed to a low stack of pages.

The Westbruk Wetlands pile was my domain. I was to sift through anything that pertained to the Wetlands and put them in the "W" drawer of the file cabinet.

I tossed most of the pages. I kept, sorted and filed the following items:

1.   There is going to be a Nuclear Power Station on the Wetlands. President Johnson signed the papers. Funds are approved. The Viet Nam War ate the funds. There will be no

Nuclear Power Station on the Westbruk Wetlands.

2.	There will be an airport on the Wetlands. The airport won't be built.

3.	There will be a Marina Residential Complex on the Wetlands and a major highway going around and through the Wetlands. Citizens living in the area don't want a highway. The highway won't be built.

Citizens didn't want a highway and they were able to stop the process. Active citizens could do something about things they didn't want to happen. How wonderful!

I could do things. My mother was dead and I couldn't bring her back. Maybe I could do something else. What?

24.

Dear Dessa Dreams,

*I can't get out of the house.
What is the best way to kill the
children?
Stir crazy in Syracuse.*

*Dear Stir Crazy,
    Don't kill the children. Make
them hot chocolate and cinnamon
toast instead.
Sincerely, Dessa Dreams.*

I didn't know sugar can make
children hyper when I doled out this
advice.

On rainy days I gave my sons hot
chocolate and cinnamon toast. They
were hyper.

I was thirty-two, Arthur was
almost seven and Eli was four. 1969
was the year that Leonard and Arthur
decided to be "*clean in body, pure in
heart, 'pals forever', to love the
sacred circle of their family, to be
attentive while others spoke, to love
their neighbor, to seek and preserve
the beauty of the Great Spirit's work
in forest, field and stream.*" They
joined the Indian Guides.

Leonard was busy scouting new
locations for REALLY REST

MATTRESS Stores. So it was me who sat with my squirming sons on cold metal folding chairs in the meeting hall of Merkel Family Funeral Home with the other Indian Guides and their fathers.

Bill Kettler, a cheery, dark haired man, dressed in an expensive looking gray suit, stood in front of the long, narrow room. He wore a black string tie that was laced in silver and turquoise. His jacket was open so I could see his silver belt buckle inlaid with turquoise. He sported silver and turquoise bracelets on his right arm that were visible because his gray jacket sleeves were pushed up. "On March second, 1932 it poured in Westbruk," he said. "And I saw two white balls on the north mesa and those white balls were skulls and the skulls were attached to skeletons and I took the bones home and hid the skeletons in my closet."

"Could you find some skeletons for our closet?" Arthur asked me.

"My skeletons are over nine thousand years old," Mr. Kettler continued. "People who lived at the Westbruk Wetlands nine thousand years ago were kind to each other and to the land and ate delicious food."

"What kind of food?" Arthur wanted to know.

Mr. Kettler smiled before he said, "Snails, grubs and worm soup."

One child said, "Ycch!"

Arthur said he'd like to taste some snails, grubs and worm soup and would I cook some for him.

I told my son I wasn't a very good cook. That evening, I told Leonard that the next time there was an Indian Guide meeting; he would have the privilege of going. And if there was any insect soup to be cooked, Leonard would have the cooking privilege, too.

Years later, I ran into Bill Kettler again.

"What happened to the skeletons in your closet?" I asked.

"An Apache Chief arranged for them to be buried in an unmarked grave at the Westbruk Cemetery," he said. "If I could find them, I'd dig them up."

"What?" I was gob smacked.

"People want to build houses on the north mesa of the Westbruk Wetlands," he said. "If the mesa is developed the birds on the lower bench of the wetlands won't have a place to go on rainy days when their nesting places are flooded. If I could find those skeletons and have them carbon dated maybe I could save the wetlands. People don't usually build over burial grounds."

If he found the skeletons, and if he could have them carbon dated, and if the carbon dating proved that the skeletons were over 9000 years old, how would he be able to prove he unearthed the skeletons on that particular piece of earth?

"People would believe Bill," SOMEBODY whispered in my ear. *God?*

The white haired man who still sported beautiful turquoise and silver jewelry smiled at me and, then, reached into his jeans pocket and took out a cog stone.

"Do you use the stone for dreaming?" I blurted.

"Are cog stones good for dreaming?" he asked.

I nodded, feeling like a fool.

"I'll try it," he said.

I've run into Bill Kettler a lot in recent years. I've never asked him again if he used his cog stone for dreaming. I have asked about the missing skeletons. So far he hasn't found them.

25.

Dear Dessa Dreams,

My husband is being transferred from Nyack, New York to Gallup, New Mexico. I'm too shy to talk to new people. What should I do?
Don't want to be new from Nyack.

Dear Don't,

I dreamt about somebody that moved from east to west. In the east she was shy. In the west she was friendly. So when you move to Gallup, get friendly. Join the community theater. Lots of friendly people hang out at community theaters.
Sincerely, Dessa Dreams.

In 1974, we moved from our tract house in Westbruk to a more expensive tract house in Westbruk. The new house was located on a landfill which used to be part of the Westbruk Wetlands. (I've heard that landfills liquefy in earthquakes and houses built on them disappear. So far, this hasn't happened in Westbruk. Thank you, God!)

If I leaned over the railing at my tenth stair on my new curved staircase and looked through the window over my front door, I could see swamplands covered with brown weeds and oil wells and a bit of the Pacific Ocean beyond. This view resembled and, yet, didn't resemble the wetlands in my cog stone induced dreams.

To buy the new house we had to sign a paper stating the realtor had not informed us that the nasty looking quagmire within walking distance from our new house might be turned into a magnificent marina. It was true that the realtor hadn't mentioned it. But other people had. I found it exciting to think that somebody was going to take the ugly marsh and make it a place to watch colorful sailboats. Maybe there would be restaurants and little shops. The possibilities seemed endless.

After we moved and my boys were enrolled in new schools, I spent my time answering Dear Dessa Dreams letters, reading best sellers, going to the beauty parlor, and shopping for things to make our house look good. I didn't like to shop then and I still don't.

So after a few months I quit shopping and in early 1975, I hopped down to the Westbruk Community Theater and signed up again. Though the name was the same the venue had changed. The theater was now located in a barn on Main Street in down town Westbruk. I volunteered for everything but acting, because I'd promised myself I would be a better wife and mother in the new house and I realized rehearsing ever night would probably not allow me to realize this ambition.

I handled costumes, built and painted sets, saw to program printing, did errands, arranged cast parties and was an all-around gopher.

In a pinch, I acted as stage manager. Mostly I begged props and other materials from local merchants. I was good at scrounging. Johnny Johnson, my boss and publisher, usually told me where to go to find what I needed and who to ask.

"I need office furniture for Act II of *The Aimless Plan*," I told Johnny.

"Go to the Westbruk Corporation," he said. At that time the Westbruk Corporation owned most of the oil rigs on the Westbruk Wetlands.

"Who should I talk to?" I asked.

"Benny Sherman. We're doing a story about what happens to the people who are named the Westbruk Man or Woman of the Year". Benny Sherman, the president of the Westbruk Company, was once a "man of the year"."

"Thanks," I said. "I'll talk to him.

"If you interview him, you could make some extra cash." Johnny tamped his cigar.

"I don't need extra cash."

Leonard was earning big time money in his commercial real estate business.

By 1973 Johnny had taken over sixty-three failing newspapers in small to medium towns all over the United States and had turned them into thriving Bulletin Gazettes. I was syndicated in all of them and he raised my salary every time he acquired a new paper.

"I've done you a lotta favors," my boss said.

He had. "What do you want?"

Johnny Johnson dialed the phone on his oak, roll-top desk. He owned the same desk in 1953 when I'd first started to work for him. Every cubbyhole and drawer was packed with stuff. Even so Johnny never had any trouble finding stuff.

"I'm organized," he'd once told me. "And when organization fails I have a hell of a good memory."

I don't know about his organizational skills, but I never saw him look up a phone number.

"Mr. Sherman, please," Johnny said. "Benny. This is Johnny Johnson. Yeah, my wife is fine. What about your family? . . . Good to hear it. Always good to hear positive news. Listen I have a reporter who wants to talk to you.. . .

Dessa Lechmann. We're doing a story on what happens to people who were named "Men of the Year". . . Benny, you're too modest."

"Office furniture," I hissed. "Say something about how I want to borrow office furniture."

Johnny smiled, bit on his cigar and chewed. I backed up and moved out of his way, not wanting to be in his spitting distance.

"She's a volunteer for the Westbruk Theater and wants to beg some--. Of course, you can say no. But, I guarantee when you see her, you'll say yes."

Wow! I was thirty-eight. Did Johnny Johnson think I was pretty?

"Am I pretty?" I asked Leonard that evening. I was at home, making a good dinner for my family; kosher hot dogs, a can of Franco American macaroni and tomato sauce with added Italian seasonings, sliced tomatoes and Jell-O with bananas. Arthur and Eli couldn't stop praising this gourmet meal.

Come on boys," Leonard said. "Let's take your ugly mother for a drive. It's the least we can do."

"She's not ugly," Eli said. *What a great son!*

"Numbskull. Dad's just teasing," my thirteen year old Arthur told his ten year old brother before he cuffed him on the shoulder.

"Oww!"

At the top of Edwards Hill we could see city lights to the north and the wetlands below.

"Imagine how nice this place would look if it were developed," Leonard said.

"It would be awful," I wasn't sure why I said it. But developing the wetlands felt like the worst thing that could happen. "Um," I said. "Um. Um."

"What?" Leonard asked.

"Nothing," I said.

"You have to have a vision," Leonard told me. "This weed-covered land just sits there and looks ugly."

"I like it," I said. "It's empty."

"Exactly," Leonard said. "Who wants ice cream?"

At the coffee shop, I said, "We need some building free spaces on this earth." The coffee ice cream tasted so good on my spoon.

"Chocolate tastes better than strawberry," Eli said.

"Are you nuts?" Arthur said.

"Don't you see?" Leonard inhaled his vanilla milk shake. "It would be beautiful. Just imagine a planned community where the wetlands are. Little parks. Maybe some good restaurants." He slurped the dregs in the glass.

"We could live there," Eli said.

"Use your napkin," I told him.

"We could have ten bedrooms." Eli licked the ice cream off his lips. "I'll have two just for me."

"I'll have three," Arthur said. "Nobody named Eli will be allowed in any of them."

"You're so lucky to live in America," Leonard told our sons. It was his usual litany. "In America when you have an idea, you're free to do something about it."

You're right, Dad," Arthur said. "Nobody can come in my room again. This is America. I'm going to enforce the rules."

"I'm going to do something about it." Leonard licked the rim of his glass.

"What are you going to do?" I asked.

"I'm going to see to it that the land is developed. If you have an idea, you have to go forward. This is America." Leonard slammed his empty glass down.

"America!" Eli slammed his glass.

I stopped eating. My stomach hurt. The ice cream had attacked my throat. "Um," I said.

Leonard and the boys looked at me.

The minute I got home, I found my cog stone and went to sleep.

* * *

GOD says, "It's the future, Dessa."

"I remember the future," I say. "There aren't any oil wells. The plants bloom and the wetlands are populated with a slew of babies. Baby birds and ducks. Baby rabbits and coyotes. Baby snakes, squirrels and skunks."

Babies fly and scamper around the clear waters of the wetlands. A

stream swirls down to meet the sea.
Fish swim among the sea lettuce.
Then a mosquito bites my cheek, a
thousand bees swarm around my
head and a shiny black and white
skunk sprays me.

"GOD," I say. "Do you think we
could get rid of the mosquitoes? My
cheek is so itchy."

The ocean swishes around. The
tide goes in and out. And the
mosquitoes disappear.

"Where did they go, GOD?"

"Mosquitoes don't breed in
moving waters, Dessa."

"Maybe we should get rid of the
bees, too," I say. "They sting, you
know."

"Look, Dessa!" GOD orders.

I look. The wetlands are covered
with plants. Lavender-blue sea
lavender grows on the tops of long
stems that rise from gray-green
leaves. Pickle weed with red tips on
their stems sit near the water as
Belding's Savannah Sparrows eat the
insects that surround the plant.
Yellow Beach Evening Primrose and
Lilac Verbena hug the sand trail.
Coast Goldenbush with their bright
yellow, circular puffs stand up on the

mesa. The whole Westbruk Wetlands are alive with yellow and lilac blooming plants. The bees hum, swarm and do not sting.

"How did you get them to stop stinging?" I ask GOD.

"Native plants. Gentler bees," HE answers.

Then a skunk walks right up to me. "Hi," I say to the skunk. "You're very good looking."

The skunk sprays me. Ycch! "Do you notice how skunks smell up the place? You could throw up, GOD."

"Never satisfied, are you Dessa?" GOD says, "How about a different future?"

The birds and ducks fly away. The insects disappear. The animals run off. The fish swim out to sea.

Houses build themselves. Big mansions and medium size tract houses. Town houses next to strip malls appear. Gardens with exotic blooms and grass that seem to need constant watering materialize.

"It doesn't look bad," I say. "Why does my throat hurt?"

"It's awful and you know it,"
Leo says. He's standing next to me.
Where did he come from?

"You're right," I agree.

"We have to do something," he
says.

"What can we do?" I kiss Leo on
his cheek.

"This is America," he says. "We
can do something." He kisses me on
my lips.

"What?" I ask, kissing him back.

He inserts his tongue into my
mouth. He has a wonderful tongue.

"We'll talk to the man in
charge," he says.

"GOD?" I ask.

"GOD is not a man," Leo says.

"Is SHE a woman?" I ask.

"I have an appointment with the
head man of the Westbruk
Company."

"Close your eyes, Dessa," GOD
orders.

I do.

When I open them again I'm
sitting next to Leo in a small office.
Our chairs are small, cozy-
comfortable brown leather. We face
a mahogany desk.

A tiny man in a gray suit has his back to us. He's writing numbers on a paper pinned to the wall. "Gotta get the facts down," he says. "I do it every day. High and low tide. Prevailing winds. Temperatures. No number can be left out."

I wish he would turn around. I'm holding on to my cog stone but as usual it doesn't work for wishing. "I wish you sold me a wish cog stone instead of a dream one," I whisper to Leo.

"Mister," Leo says to the man's back. "We have to bring back the natural life to the wetlands. It will be good for the people, you know."

"I have to design jewelry." The man holds up his hands displaying gold rings on every finger.

"The wetlands used to be wonderful. Now too much water is needed to maintain it. The sewers are clogged. The fish are dying. What will the fish eaters eat? The non-native plants grown in the gardens have brought non-native bees that sting the people. And there are so many people and so many houses. Soon it will be too polluted to breathe," Leo says.

The man still has his back to us as he opens his window and starts to fiddle with a window box of cactus. "Do you know," he says, "I have one of the largest collections of cacti in the world?"

"No, I didn't know," Leo says. "But, the wetlands are important."

"I do important things, young man. Open my top drawer and look."

Leo doesn't move. So I open the drawer and look inside. It's full of stamps.

"Look at the Christmas Seals," the man says.

I look.

The sound of people coughing cascades through the office; but there are no people. Only coughs. Invisible people are coughing harder and harder. I can hear their hampered breathing.

Over their din, the man says, "We're going to eradicate their coughs, young people. The Christmas Seals Organization is going to do it."

"I'm here about the wetlands." Leo sits so still.

"Did you know in 1945 T.B. cases declined? Do you know what happened next?" the man asks.

I shake my head. I don't know what happened. But if the tuberculosis cases declined, why do the invisible people keep coughing?

"They cough because the cases of lung cancer have increased. That's why!"

How does the man read my mind?

"Because, I'm a psychic," he answers.

"Oh," I say.

"We're here about the wetlands," Leo says again.

"I have to do something about the coughing," the man says.

The coughing is getting louder and louder. The breathing in between coughs is harsh short rasps. I'm in a room full of invisible people with some kind of pulmonary disease.

Cough. Cough. Cough.

* * *

When I awoke, Leonard was coughing.

"Coming down with something?" I asked.

"No," he said. "I have a great idea, Dessa."

"What?" I asked. As long as he wasn't sick, I worried about my morning breath and sleep filled eyes. As long as he wasn't a coughing invisible person dying from who knew what, I wasn't really interested in his great idea at 6:30 in the morning.

"It's a secret," he said.

I was wide-awake. "Tell me."

He laughed. "As long as it's a secret, you're interested."

He was right.

"I'm here to beg," I told the skinny man in the gray suit who sat across from me. Both he and his office looked vaguely familiar.

"You don't have to beg," he said.

Great, I thought. The President of the Westbruk Company is going to donate a whole office full of furniture to the Westbruk Playhouse.

"Here's the latest temperature ledger." Benny Sherman put a blue loose-leaf notebook on his desk. "I record the highs and lows every day."

"I thought you wrote the numbers on the wall," I said breaking my new year's resolution for the umpteenth time. I had promised myself that I wouldn't blurt anymore, that I would think before I said anything and that I would not discuss my dreams as if they were true. (But, I had dreamt about a man who recorded the high and low temperatures. Hadn't I?)

"What?" the skinny man said.

"Nothing." I looked at my broken fingernails with their peeling polish.

"You wanna see my other notebooks? He put two other notebooks on top of the first one. "Tides and prevailing winds. Mostly Santa Ana or northeast," he said.

"Do you collect stamps?" I asked, knowing from my cog stone induced dream that he did.

"How did you know? Are you psychic?" The man smiled at me.

"I'm not. But you are, aren't you?" I knew he was. I'd dreamt it.

"Why do you ask?"

"I guessed. Because of your books," I said. Five books titled *"Ghosts I Have Met"*, *"Yankee Ghosts"*, *"Ghosts in American*

Houses", "*Haunted Houses,*" and
"*Psychic Phenomena*" rested on top
of his desk between two elephant-
shaped, bookends.

"Because I'm interested in a
variety of topics doesn't make me
psychic, young lady."

I didn't like the way he said
"young lady". *Is he angry?*
Remember, I told myself, I'm here to
scrounge office furniture for the
Westbruk Playhouse. "You're right,"
I said. "Maybe I jumped to a false
conclusion. It's all those "Fates". I
pointed to the pile of "Fate"
magazines piled neatly on his desk. I
knew the periodicals were a
compendium of paranormal
phenomena because I had perused
them often in the Westbruk Library
to see if I could find any information
about cog stone induced dreams. So
far, I hadn't.

"Okay," he said. "I've had one or
two psychic experiences. Nothing I
care to discuss. And for all I know
they could have been more
coincidence than psychic."

It was then I spotted a cog stone
on his desk. "What do you dream
about?" I asked.

"I just met you, young lady. Do you think that I'm going to discuss my dreams with a stranger?"

"I own a cog stone, too."

"What are you talking about?" he asked.

I pointed to the cog stone.

"I picked it up yesterday on the wetlands," he said. "I like the way it looks."

I nodded.

"Tell your husband I can't help him, Mrs. Lechmann."

"My husband?"

"That's the real reason you're here, isn't it?"

What is he talking about?

"You coming here doesn't have anything to do with what an old man does with his life after he's been named "Man of the Year", does it?" He placed the temperature, tide and wind notebooks in a catch all box.

"No," I said. "I'm here to ask you—"

He reached in the top drawer of his desk, took a letter out of an envelope and handed it to me. I recognized Leonard's handwriting and read:

"I am prepared to execute the large task of developing the land because of my many years of experience in property management, developing strip malls and leasing of such. I will be able to recommend other qualified people to take over the housing section of this big and necessary Westbruk Wetlands project."

I felt betrayed to the core. I stood there hoping the tears that I felt forming in my eyes would not wash down my face.

My husband wanted to take over the commercial development of the wetlands. That's what he did. Commercial development. He made a good living at it. Why did I feel so badly?

"I'm here to ask for office furniture for the Westbruk Community Theater," I said.

Benny Sherman smiled. "Too bad. I don't have any to give."

I had some choices.

I could go home and take my cog stone to bed with me.

I could drive to Leonard's office and yell at him.

I could find some office furniture for the playhouse.

I spent the rest of the day going to almost every merchant in Westbruk. By nightfall a desk and a chair sat on the Playhouse stage.

I stuck with the theater when it was cold and I had to wear a heavy coat and cover myself with a blanket to watch a performance or rehearsal. The audience never complained about this hardship so neither did I. I didn't complain when the ghostly white barn owl that lived in the rafters shrieked one of its hissing screeches that sounded like cssssssshhH whenever an important line was spouted. I tried not to complain about the flock of pigeons (or what I thought of as pigeons then but now know to be Mourning Doves) flying through the theater. Their wings produced an airy whistling sound when they took off which wasn't too bad. But their mournful "ooAAH cooo coo coo" was awful and made the audiences laugh harder during serious dramas than people who watched old Marx Brother movies.

I didn't grumble about having to go down the hill in the dark to use the portable chemical bathroom. Sitting in the poorly lit smelly enclosure, I could hear the laughter, the owl and the morning-doves. I was sure the tear jerker play "Pulliver's Train" was going to be a disaster and didn't care. What I wanted to know was why I was taking a dirt trail to use porto-potty in the night?

How important was theater in my life? Pretty important, I guess, because when the jaws of the bulldozer razed the barn in 1976, I cried.

In 1978 the Playhouse was relocated to the Main Street Shopping Center in a renovated storefront building. Seven years later, I directed "*Michael Malone*" by Ricardo Mentis in that renovated building. I was forty-eight.

In Act One, Michael Malone, a cab driver picks up a mysterious old lady from a hotel. She, hidden by a black hat and veil, asks Michael to take her to a factory on the bad side of town. When they arrive at their destination, he asks for the fare. She

tells him to wait; she'll pay him
when he takes her back to the hotel.
Michael says he doesn't want to
wait. There are no streetlights. He
doesn't feel good about this place.
"Sorry lady. No can do."

"If you want to be paid, you'll
wait," the lady says before
disappearing into the factory.

Michael says he's dependent on
strangers. They make the decisions
as to where he should drive. Though
he is supposed to work eight hours,
he often works ten to sixteen. "What
kind of life is this?" he asks.

Then there is a bloodcurdling
female scream. Lights go out. Act
One ends.

Act Two is set inside the factory.
Michael shines the flashlight over
the floor and bare walls. "Where is
she?" he asks.

Strange sounds emanate from the
walls. A cat meows. The floor
creaks. The wind howls. Then out
of the shadows a child walks toward
Michael.

"Where's the lady?" he asks.

"I am her." The child shows
Michael the hat and veil.

"You couldn't be her," Michael says. "She was old. She had wrinkles. I got a glimpse."

"I am her," the child sings. "I live again. I live again. I can't tell you why or when but I live again."

Michael sings, "You can't live again. You can't live again. I can't tell you why or when but you can't live again."

Then people come into the warehouse and sing and act out the mysterious lady's life. When she's a young woman, Michael falls in love with her. She turns old before his eyes.

At the end of Act Three, Michael takes the old lady back to the hotel. He doesn't feel sorry for himself anymore and likes being a cab driver. "I've had my chance for love," he sings. "And though it was short, it was enough. I have loved and that's enough."

The first night of tryouts the perfect Michael Malone auditioned. He must've been about thirty and had the ideal tenor voice. He was a younger version of Leonard and looked exactly like the Leo of my dreams. He sported a cog stone tattoo on his wrist just like Grandpa did.

told the producer, "Cast him. He's perfect."

Monney Jackson, my new friend and producer, said, "It's not right, Dessa. You have to let everybody try out."

"I'm doing them a favor," I said. "It's not right to waste everybody's time."

Monney stared at me. *Is she my conscience?*

"Okay," I said. I watched and listened to thirteen other men. And it was a good thing I did. Because when Monney tried to get in touch with Ishmael Arons, the perfect Michael Malone, she couldn't. His phone had been disconnected.

I thought him so perfect, I picked up Monney and we went to the address that Ishmael Arons left on his audition file. I couldn't get him out of my mind. Was he related to the boy, Leo, I had met on the beach? He was thirty. Could Leo have been his father?

"This is silly," Monney said. "Ishmael wasn't any better than Daniel Crayburn or Ned Chalmers."

"He was a lot better." I didn't want to tell her the real reason I wanted to find Ishmael. She would think me crazy.

Ishmael's address proved to be an eight-unit apartment house.

"He had to take off," the manager said. "He's in construction and his dad got him some work in Wyoming."

I was so disappointed.

"It doesn't make any difference," Monney said. "Two or three of the other actors were better than him."

The apartment manager, a man who stood behind his screen door clad in a bathing suit and a sleeveless white undershirt, seemed to sense my disappointment. "Ishmael told me to tell anybody who came around he would call soon."

Two days later Ishmael called Monney and apologized. He thought he could do the play and then go to Wyoming to help his dad, he said. He hadn't known that his father would need him so soon.

"Did he tell you his father's name?" I asked Monney. "Did he tell you exactly where he is? Did he give you an address? Did he say his father's name was Leo?"

"Why would he tell me his father's name?" Monney asked. "Sometimes you say the oddest things."

"Yeah! I guess I do," I said.

Monney put her finger on her square chin. "Ishmael looks like Leonard," she said.

Ned Chalmers was a great Michael.

"*Michael Malone*" was a big success until closing night. That night all the toilets, which were shared with the other shopping center tenants and were more than one hundred yards from the theater, clogged up.

I called the property manager on the pay phone.

Mr. Perkus answered on the first ring.

I explained the situation.

"How in the hell do you think I'm gonna get a plumber on a Saturday night?"

"Well, maybe you can fix them," I said.

"I don't fix toilets," he said.

"What should I do?"

"Fix the toilets yourself," he said. "Haven't you heard that necessity is the mother of fixed toilets?"

"No. I haven't heard that."

Mr. Perkus hung up without saying goodbye.

I went in the Women's bathroom. It stank. The audience would show soon. Members of the cast were relieving themselves between the dumpster and the wall of the building that was behind the stage.

"Not to worry," Ned/Michael Malone told me as he stood at the door of the women's room. "We're doing it in pairs. One reliever. One watch out. Heaven help us if somebody needs to make the big dump."

"Heaven help us," I agreed. Why hadn't my cog stone been a wish stone? I could have wished for a magical plumber. I sent up a quick prayer toward the dirty ceiling of the women's rest room. "Send a plumber, please," I whispered. "Please. Please. Please."

Monney walked in with three plungers. Ned, Monney and I went to work. The toilets were fixed. What else could go wrong?

In Act II when Michael was shining his flashlight on the dark parts of the factory and the creepy sound effects had started, the theater shook. Was it a sonic boom or an earthquake? I still don't know. I was standing back stage, acting as stage manager because the stage manager said she would have a very unpleasant emergency if she didn't go to the toilet. "Thank goodness the toilet works," I whispered.

The theater shook again. The pipes over the stage broke. And an enormous amount of water fell on my head. And kept falling and falling. Not only was I suffering from the deluge, the stage was flooded. My actors carried on as if this was an occurrence that happened every night and they were used to acting soaking wet. The audience gave them a standing ovation.

When we finished cleaning the mess it was two o'clock in the morning.

The actors and most of the crew went to the cast party.

I was too tired and went home. Twenty three-year old Arthur was in his Los Angeles apartment. Eli was in his dorm at UCLA. Leonard was in bed asleep. I took my cog stone from under my pillow and joined him.

* * *

GOD says, "It is March 10, 1938.

"My goodness," I say. "It's raining hard."

"This is worse than the 1933 earthquake," Luna tells me.

"Where are we?" I ask her. *Is she alive or dead?*

"We're staying at the Evangeline Hotel," she says. "We needed a vacation."

I look around the room. Two beds with thin quilts and a small wooden dresser make up the furnishings.

The sound of the rain is scary. It rains harder and harder.

"Where's the closet?" I say. "Maybe we should change for dinner."

"There's no closet," Luna says.

"All hotel rooms have closets," I say.

"Not in 1938," she says.

We're both dressed very nicely.
Our sleeves end at the elbow. Our
hems fall just below our knees.
Luna looks wonderful. Her neckline
flatters her beautiful face. Her silk
sash, which ties in the front,
emphasizes her perfect figure. My
dress is just as posh as hers but I
know I look dumpy. I've put on
twenty pounds in the last three years.
Why does Luna still look like she's
twenty? I'm forty-eight. She has to
be in her fifties. Maybe she's had
plastic surgery. Do they have plastic
surgery in the 1930's?

The rain pounds against the
outside walls harder and harder.
Louder and louder. I don't like the
sound of it.

"This is scarier than the 1933
earthquake." Luna says but she
doesn't look scared.

I remember something about the
1933 earthquake. "I think I dreamt
about it," I say.

"You did," GOD says.

Luna laughs. "I hate
earthquakes," she says.

"Me too," I say. "What
happened in the dream about the

earthquake, GOD? I can't
remember."

"Close your eyes," GOD says.

"Okay," I say and close them.

When I open my eyes again
GOD says, "It is March 10, 1933 at
5:53 PM."

"My goodness," I say. "GOD,
you've never mentioned the exact
minute before."

I'm sitting at a small square table
playing Snakes and Ladders. I've
never played the game before, but I
know its name and how to play it. It
is a racing board game. Luna and
Leo are my opponents. I plan to beat
them. All I have to do is push my
token around the track to the finish.
I'm concentrating.

"Somebody has to get dinner
ready," Luna says. "It's getting
late."

"I don't cook in dreams," I say.
"You'll have to do it."

Luna moves her token too many
places.

"Not fair," I say.

"I'm getting hungry," Leo says.

"How old am I?" I ask.

"What a silly question!" Luna says. It's her turn and she's cheating again.

"You're twenty-three, Dessa," Leo says.

"Where are we?" I can't afford to look around. If I don't keep my eyes on Luna's token, she'll cheat and beat me.

GOD says, "We're in Westbruk."

Then the table shakes. I shake. And the room shakes.

"What is that smell?" A disgusting odor wafts through the shaking room. The tokens flip off the table, so does the game board. The table falls over. I know what the smell is.

"It's Grandpa's beer," Luna shouts.

Grandpa runs in the room. "I gotta get outta here," he screams.

I hear glass break but can't see the source of the sound.

"Let's get outta here," Luna yells. She and Grandpa push against a plain brown door. It doesn't budge.

"Help us, Leo," Luna shouts.

The shaking has stopped. I sit on the floor and cut my hands on small shards of glass from a broken aquarium. There is a dead gold fish in front of me.

"You let the goldfish die, Dessa," Grandpa aims his bow and arrow at me.

"I don't like this dream, GOD," I say.

"We gotta get out of here," Luna says. She and Leo are still pushing the door.

"Maybe we should climb out the window." I try to focus on a window framed with white lace curtains instead of Grandpa's arrow that is aimed straight at me."

"You're really stupid," Luna tells me. "We're on the second floor."

Water rushes at me. Where is it coming from? I close my eyes.

When I open them, GOD says, "It's March 10, 1938 again."

A shaft of water rushes through our window. I'm so wet. "My shoes will be ruined," I say. My black heels are just the kind I like, not too high, not too low.

"They are ruined," Luna says. "What about our hats?"

We're both wearing cloche hats with wide brims. "Why are we wearing hats?" I ask.

"Ladies wear hats," she says.

"Are we ladies?" I ask.

"We're not gentlemen." She laughs. It's a nice laugh. Luna changes her moods often in my dreams. She can go from mean to nice to mean in single instants.

"My feet are cold," I say.

Too much sound! The rain is too loud. I've never heard anything like it. It is as if the raindrops have been amplified by a microphone.

"I want to wake up," I say. "I don't like it here."

"We don't have to stay here," Luna says. "I think it would be nice to go on vacation."

"I thought we were on vacation," I say.

"Hmmmn," she says.

"We're so dressed up. Are we rich?" I ask.

"Of course we are," Luna says.

"But in the 1930's everybody was poor," I say. "I've read about the depression."

"Leo is doing well," she says.

"Leonard is doing well, too." I wish GOD would do something about the rain. Doors bang. Wind blows. It's too noisy. I need to concentrate. What if the rain knocks the building down?

"Who is Leonard?" Luna asks.

"I can't remember," I lie.

"We should survey the situation," Luna says. She pushes up the window sash and we fly out of the window. Luna hands me a black umbrella. I suspect we look like two Mary Poppins flying with umbrellas in the sky. To help the image I turn my wet black shoes outward like a ballet dancer. Sheets of rain slap us. The umbrellas don't help. I'm so wet. I better not catch anything. I'm too busy to be sick.

The cardboard houses on Cardboard Beach fall like domino tiles. I land on the beach and hand my umbrella to a woman holding on to two children. I stick my cloche hat atop her daughter's head.

Luna grabs my arm and we fly east. Buildings are falling down all over Westbruk. The streets are rivers of water. All of the Westbruk

Wetlands are awash. The oil wells
sway.

"There's the earthquake fault."
Luna points to the part of the
wetlands north mesa that cuts
sharply into the lowlands.

"I've never noticed the fault
before," I say. "It's so big."
Lightening! The earth isn't shaking
anymore. Where are the birds? "We
need an ark to protect the animals."
Who's saying this? Sounds like me.
Couldn't be me. I'm scared of
animals. I don't have any pets. I
don't want to be locked in an ark
with a smelly skunk.

We land in front of the Westbruk
Gun Club and walk right in. It's
better than an ark. The fireplace
houses a cozy fire. A waiter brings
me a cup and saucer. He pours
steaming coffee from a silver urn.
For a minute, I can picture the wet
woman on Cardboard Beach with her
wet children. Her cardboard box
house, flat on the ground, offers no
protection.

"She and the children are already
dead, Dessa," GOD says.

I don't want to listen to HIM. I
won't think about it, I tell myself.

I'm rich and belong to a Gun Club. I'm warm and cozy. "I want a wishing cog stone," I tell Luna.

We sit at a table covered with a white tablecloth. Other people, dressed as well as we are, sit at other white clothed tables. The lights have gone out but the lit candles on the tables offer more than enough illumination. Everybody sips coffee and nibbles tasty little pastries. What are the people at Cardboard Beach eating?

"What would you do with a wishing cog stone?" Luna asks me.

"I'm not sure," I say. Would I restore her to life? Would I use the stone to help the poor people on Cardboard Beach? Or would I wish to forget so I could enjoy myself?

Luna walks to the piano and starts to play. Pretty soon everybody in the dining room is singing, "It ain't gonna rain no more."

"It ain't gonna rain no more. No more. It ain't gonna rain no more." We sing almost loud enough to muffle the sound of the wind, the flashing water, the thunder, and the screams of human beings. "It ain't gonna rain no more. No more."

* * *

"It ain't gonna rain no more. No more."

"That's Roger Barkley and Al Lohman singing," the Sunday KFI local news announcer announced. "That dynamic radio duo that we've been listening to so long, will soon be off the air. How are we ever going to get along without them?"

Leonard turned off the radio. "You look very tired, Dessa," he said.

I was very tired.

26.

Dear Dessa Dreams,
My husband is hung up on fat girls. What is the best way to put on weight?
Skinny in Schenectady.

Dear Skinny,
I dreamt about a person who was skinny. Then she went on a

chocolate diet and got fat. If you
want to get fat, eat chocolate.
Sincerely, Dessa Dreams.

June 12, 1987. It was my fiftieth
birthday and I was twenty pounds
overweight. When I got out of bed I
rushed to the full-length mirror in the
master bath and looked at my naked
body. There were furrowed lines on
my forehead but even without make
up, my face didn't look too bad. My
stomach stuck out a bit and my rear
end stuck out a lot. Leonard walked
into the bathroom. I grabbed a towel
and wrapped it around my torso. I'd
never been shy about my body
before.

Leonard handed me six hundred
dollars. "This is for you," he said.
"But with strings attached."

"What strings?" I clutched my
towel as if it were armor.

"You and I are going to buy you
an outfit," he said.

"Not for ten weeks," I said. Did
Leonard think I looked dowdy?
Why did he think I needed a six
hundred dollar outfit? Why didn't he
say happy birthday?

As soon as Leonard left, I drove to Monney's house. She lived on an enormous pie shaped lot on a cul-de-sac that faced the east section of the wetlands. That she had no grass and planted the front and back yards with trees made her home look as if it were perched at the edge of a forest. Her porch was red wood not cement. And while every other person in the neighborhood discouraged wild animals, Monney put out an animal feeder. Muskrats, squirrels and raccoons frequented her back yard. She owned five cats. Her proclivity for animals and my discomfort in their company made us most unlikely friends. But, then I had married the most unlikely husband.

I wanted to discuss the six hundred dollar present. "Do I look dowdy?" I asked Monney. We sat at her Danish Modern walnut dining room table drinking tea and eating croissants topped with butter and raspberry jam. Monney had read Simone de Beauvoir, too.

"Are there times you want to run away to Paris?" I asked her.

"There are times I want to run away," she said. "But not to Paris."

"Where?" I asked.

"I'd run to a simpler place. More back woods. Less people. Slower pace."

"Harder work. Less conveniences. If the toilet got stuck you'd have to fix it yourself," I retorted.

"I can fix a toilet," she said. "But then you're assuming I would have a toilet."

"Yeah," I said. "I am."

She laughed. "Someday, I'm going to live in a beautiful place. I'll grow my own vegetables, bake my own croissants--."

"You'd have to clean your own house. I bet you can't get a cleaning woman in the country."

"I clean my own house now," she said.

We looked at all the dusty stuff piled high on top of Danish Modern tables in her living room/dining room combination and laughed.

"When I feel like it," she said. "I clean when I feel like it."

"I have to do something about my weight," I said.

"Me too," she said.

We were both attacking our second croissant and sipping our tea. To me my short chubby friend looked great. So alive. There was some gray in her dark hair, but it framed a youthful, round face without a wrinkle. Her big brown eyes radiated kindness.

"Why do you have to lose weight?" I asked.

She laughed. "Dessa, I'm shorter and weigh more than you do."

"How much do you weigh?" I asked.

"I'm not telling."

How did she know that she weighed more if she didn't tell me her weight?

"How much do you weigh?" she asked.

I wasn't telling either.

"So what should we do?" I asked. "We better tackle the situation now. I only have ten weeks." I told her about the six hundred dollar outfit.

"Okay," she said. "We're going to stop eating and start exercising."

"Right," I said.

"No driving your car over here," she said. "Walk or don't come."

"Right," I said.

"No more second breakfasts," she said.

"This is my first breakfast." I reached for my third croissant.

"I think we need to walk," she said.

"Walk?"

"Come," she said. "We'll walk on the berm. Down at the end of the street."

She was talking about walking the wetlands. "I've never explored the area the whole time I've lived here," she said.

I looked down at the bedroom slippers I was wearing. "Tomorrow," I said. "I'll wear tennis shoes."

"Old tennis shoes," she said.

We ate the rest of the croissants. Tomorrow we'd be walking. Tomorrow it rained.

One week later we walked on the wetlands for the first time. Though it looked like country with wide dirt trails it wasn't a pretty place. And we weren't used to walking. We were out of shape and after seven minutes we turned around. In two weeks we were up to an hour, a half hour out and a half hour back. I

didn't notice what we saw because
we were too busy talking. But I did
notice that I felt good walking
around the wetlands. Sometimes,
when we stopped talking and I
listened to the whine of the oil wells,
the hum of the insects, the caws and
croaks of bird song, I felt as if I were
at some special place on earth. I
didn't talk about this to Monney
because I chalked the good feelings
to exercise and attendance to good
diet.

In the middle of July, Monney
started to take her camera with her.
She had enrolled in a photo class. I
couldn't figure out why she took
pictures. I loved the wetlands, but
would a tamped-down dirt trail that
meandered through brown weeds and
skirted rusting oil wells make for a
pretty picture?

The unsightliness didn't register
in Monney's photos. The first
picture she showed me was of a plant
with large green leaves that looked
like they were made of leather and
the tips were dipped in red ink. Tiny
white flowers grew on a conical
spike. Large white petals surrounded
the bottom of the spike. The plant

looked like it could have been in one of the premiere gardens in the world not on the wetlands with its rusted oil wells and brown weeds.

That night I took my cog stone to bed.

* * *

I see Monney's photo of the plant with the leathery blooms. Then the edges of the photo disappear and I'm looking at Um people picking the plant.

"What are you doing here?" I say to an Um old lady. "Didn't you die years ago?"

"She can't understand you," Luna says. She's also picking the plant.

Leo walks by.

"Hi, Leo," I say.

Luna shakes her head.

Leo says, "Um. Um. Um."

"I wish I could still understand Um," I say to nobody at all. Luna has disappeared.

The Um old lady takes a leaf of the plant and rubs it against some blotchy red spots on her legs. The leaf erases the spots and the woman sighs. She says, "Um. Tum. Um."

I think she's content but can't tell
for sure. Why can't I understand Um
anymore?

GOD says, "This is a Yerba
Mansa plant. My people use it to
treat asthma, skin cuts, muscular
aches, indigestion and skin disease."

"Am I one of your people?" I
ask GOD.

"Do you speak Um? HE asks.

"No. I used to," I say. "Can I
learn again?"

"Maybe."

* * *

Monney knew about the Yerba
Mansa plant. She had bought a
California Coastal Plants book at the
Westbruk Central Library's Used
Book Sale.

She took pictures of sedge that
looked like small dome shaped
buildings. She photographed sea
lavender with tiny blooms that grew
on top of long spindly stems. She
snapped succulent Pickle weed and
Cattails. She even shot the cord
grass that I once used to build a
kiicha in a cog stone induced dream.

One day we walked along the
side of a private strawberry field and
ran into some block wall structures

that seemed to lead to an underground edifice. "What do you think this is?" I asked Monney.

"Beats me," she said. "It looks like an underground bunker."

"Maybe it's a bomb shelter," I said.

"Hmmn," she said.

"Um," I said.

Leonard and I bought my six hundred dollar outfit; the silk skirt and matching vest at Abercrombie and Fitch, and my blouse, underwear, and shoes at Nordstrom. I had lost ten pounds. My stomach was almost flat again but my rear end still stuck out, though not as much as it had ten weeks ago. Leonard said I was beautiful. That night he made love to me and I fell asleep holding my cog stone.

* * *

GOD says, "It is Sunday December 7, 1941."

I'm boogey woogeying on a flat brown area rug in an unfamiliar living room. Crocheted doilies cover the arms of stuffed chairs and a wide green sofa. *Chattanooga Choo Choo* plays on the Victrola.

Grandpa rushes in. "Turn that awful music off," he yells. "I can't be abiding frivolous stuff."

I hate Grandpa. He has the worst attitude. He pulls my record off the Victrola and tries to break it. I'm able to rescue the record because Grandpa's attention is now focused on the radio.

"We'll be interrupting all day," the voice on the radio says. "I can't believe it. I can't believe it. Oh. Hawaii."

What can't he believe?

I jump out the window, fly across the ocean to Hawaii, and check out the situation. Bombs are dropping everywhere. A ship named "Arizona" is sinking. This is so sickening. I fly home to check on the wetlands.

GOD says, "It's 1942.

Leo wears a soldier uniform.

"Are you in the army?" I ask.

We're standing in front of a small house near the Westbruk coast road.

"I can't talk, Dessa," Leo says. "We gotta move these houses and get the wetlands ready. You can never tell when the Japanese will attack."

I watch. Leo lifts the house all by himself. I didn't know he was so strong. Other soldiers toss other houses up to the sky. Where the houses were, Leo and the other soldiers dig holes in the dirt with shovels that drop from the sky. What are they doing? Why are they doing it?

Careful not to get in the way, I walk through the tunnels while soldiers dig them, then, later, fortify them with ten feet thick walls of block concrete.

In the evening Leo leads me to the back of the Gun Club. I see new buildings that look like army barracks. "Welcome to Fort Westbruk," he says. "Do you want me to show you around?"

I nod.

Leo takes my hand. We walk along the north mesa toward two big guns that are mounted on large circular tracks. "These are our Log Tom Panama Mounts," he says pointing to the guns that look like cannons and are pointed west toward Japan. "They are 155 MM guns," he continues as if he thinks that I would know something about 155 MM guns.

"Oil wells pump, men work on road construction and farmers farm." Leo smiles at me. "Life goes on," he says.

"But we're at war," I say.

"Even in war," he says, kissing me on my lips. Who is a better kisser Leo or Leonard? I'll have to decide this important matter someday. I kiss Leo back for research purposes.

"Come into the bunker," he says.

"Monney said it was a bunker," I say as we enter an empty tunnel.

"We're going to store ammunition," Leo says and kisses me again.

He helps me take off my short blue jacket. Two days ago, on March 8, the War Production Board issued Regulation L-85. Everybody has to use less material for clothing. My jacket is straight and only 25 inches. My skirt is too short.

Leo unbuttons my blouse.

"Leo," I say. "Why don't I speak Um?"

Leo stops unbuttoning. "Um," he says. "Um tum um um."

"I don't understand."

"Um!" He shouts as if shouting will make me understand. "Um! Um! Um! Ummer!"

* * *

"Dummer," my son Arthur shouted into the phone in the hallway. He was home for the weekend. "It's the dumbest thing, I've ever heard. Dummer than that."

Why was my late sleeping son up so early in the morning? I wanted to go on dreaming.

Roger Marek, a columnist at the WESTBRUK BULLETIN GAZETTE, ended one of his columns: *The "Log Tom" Panamas installed on the Westbruk Wetlands north mesa were never shot. After World War II the two guns were removed and the bunkers were used as mushroom farms. Later the bunkers were sealed off with dynamite. The owners of the property probably wanted to get it ready for development and didn't want pieces of history to impede their way. And that's that."*

Roger was a friend of mine and I once asked him why he always ended his columns with "that's that".

He answered by asking, "Dessa, why do you say that you dream your answers?"

I didn't answer. Neither did he.

27.

Dear Dessa Dreams,

I'm just as nice as I used to be but my wife doesn't appreciate me anymore. Should I find somebody else? Where's the best place to look? Looking in Lancaster.

Dear Looking,

I dreamt about a man who looked for the rainbow. He went to Zanzibar and Tinbucktoo but couldn't find it. When he got home it rained in the morning. In the afternoon he saw the rainbow in his own back yard. So stay where you are. And just in case your wife is a little bit right and you're not as nice

as you once were; join an
organization that helps people. And
just in case she's wrong and you are
still nice, organizations that help
people usually attract nice women.
Sincerely, Dessa Dreams.

* * *

GOD says, "Um."

The old lady without teeth says, "Um."

Leo says, "Um."

"I don't understand," I say.

"We don't understand them, either," Luna says. She's smiling at me.

"Should I shoot them, Dessa?" Grandpa asks. He raises his bow and arrow, aims and fires.

The old lady falls.

"No!" I scream.

"You're on our side now, Dessa," Grandpa says

"I'm not on your side," I say.

Luna says, "We're against the Ummers. We don't understand what they say. They don't understand us. Let's kill them."

"Okay," Grandpa says. He aims and shoots again.

Leo falls.

GOD yells, "Um!"
* * *

I turned on my lamp and looked at the clock radio. It was two-fifteen AM, August 13, 1989. I was fifty-two and not sleeping well. Neither was Leonard. He wasn't in bed.

I walked down our circular staircase and found him sitting at the family room table perusing a commercial real estate journal.

"I guess you couldn't sleep either," I said, sitting on the chair next to his.

"Do you have to make so much noise?" he asked.

What kind of noise was I making? The chairs that moved on silent casters over the oak floor didn't make noise. Did they?

"I came down here to be alone," he said.

"Oh." *What's happening here? Who is this nasty man?*

"You snore," he said. "I can't sleep when you snore."

"You snore too!" I said. "You've always snored.

"You go, 'um, um, um, um'." Leonard wiped his eyes, then, looked at me.

He has mean eyes, I thought.

"You've gotta stop umming, Dessa. It makes me crazy."

I took my cog stone and went back to bed.

* * *

"GOD," I say. "I have to stop umming."

* * *

In the morning, Leonard was still sitting at the table.

"Do you want breakfast?" I asked.

"I've already eaten." He left.

"Monney, I'm not happy," I said as we traipsed the wetlands.

"Nobody's happy," she said.

A group of noisy America Crows flew over our head. "Caw. Caw. Caw."

"You're happy," I said.

Monney focused her camera upwards and shot one picture after another of the crows. "I don't have time to think about it, Dessa."

"But—"

"Shh!" Monney ordered.

"Sleep loo lidi lijuvi pluk vidididididididi." A long billed, short tailed, Western Meadowlark with a bright yellow breast, throat and belly sat on the edge of a folding chair that had been dumped on the wetlands. It sang a glorious song. Monney snapped the picture. "If you don't like your life, change it," she said.

"How?" I asked.

"Sometimes you gotta figure things out by yourself."

It wasn't what I wanted to hear.

I was in the Westbruk Central Library checking out *Getting the Love You Want*", "*Crawling Out of the Pit and Flying*" and "*I'm Okay, You're Okay*" when Charlene Silverman waved at me.

Dressed like a fashion plate, well coifed, expensively jeweled she walked over to where I stood and gave me a hug.

I didn't feel like hugging. I was wearing my grungy wetlands walking clothes because I hadn't stopped to take a shower after Monney told me that if I didn't like my life, I should change it. I decided that I was ready and that self-help books were the tools I needed.

Charlene and I walked outside. "Isn't it great? That the library is inside a park?" she said.

"Uh huh." I said. It was great that the library was in a park, but I wanted to get away from her, go home and attack the library books.

"There are 327 acres in the park," she said. "Did you know that Westbruk has more park space per person than most cities the same size?"

That's good, I thought. What other facts is she going to lay on me?

"Isn't this library something?" she said. "But a lot more needs to be done."

"Uh huh," I said. What was she talking about? Could she smell me? I could smell myself. Why hadn't I stopped to take a shower?

"You should join," she said.

"Join what?" I asked.

"The Friends of the Library," she said. "It's only five dollars."

Only five dollars? "Okay." I took five dollars out of my purse and plunked it into Charlene's perfectly manicured hand.

"You need to sign the papers," she said.

"I'm in a hurry," I said and started to run.

"I know where you live," she said.

"Great!" I kept running. Did she really know where I lived? We weren't friends. I hardly knew her.

Charlene not only knew where I lived, she knew my phone number.

"I don't think so," I said when she called to ask me to join The Friends of the Library Board.

"You should join," Monney told me.

"Why?" I asked.

We were walking on the berm at the far end of the Wetlands. A red tailed hawk flew overhead.

"Because we're lucky," Monney said. "Lucky people have to pay back."

"So are you going to join the Friends of the Library board?" I asked.

Monney aimed her camera upward and took a picture of the red tailed hawk. "I already have," she said. "I'm in charge of their mailings."

"What?" I asked.

"I sort the newsletters by zip codes and take them to the post office to be mailed."

"Hmmmn."

Monney took another picture of the red tailed hawk when it swooped over us again.

"Okay," I told Charlene on the phone. "What do you want me to do?"

"What can you do?" she said. "We like to take advantage of people's natural talents."

"What are some of the possibilities?" In a two and half minute conversation with Charlene I became the vice president in charge of finding speakers for the Friends of the Library luncheon meetings.

Monney joined a group called "Los Amigos de Westbruk Wetlands".

"You can be my first speaker," I told her. "You can tell the Friends of the Library about the Amigos."

"I don't make speeches," Monney told me.

"Oh," I said.

"I'll get you somebody," she said. "Don't worry."

We had just finished eating the twelve-dollar awful conglomeration of creamed chicken served over a lumpy white roll, three slices of cucumber and a dab of green Jell-O in the Cabrillo Room of the Westbruk Central Library. Monney's suggested speaker stood before the Friends of the Library members.

I couldn't put my finger on what Monney's speaker had, but when she spoke people listened. She wore a rose colored dress. Her hair was in place. Her clothes fit well. She was the kind of woman you didn't notice until she talked. Then you noticed how attractive she was. Her voice was well modulated, but it wasn't only her voice that attracted the listeners that day, they were interested in what she had to say.

"When I moved to Westbruk from Los Angeles in 1964, I immediately joined the League of Woman Voters. At that time the Wetlands were nothing but working oil wells and they were part of the county not the town of Westbruk," she said. "The question before the League Of Women Voters was: should the wetlands be annexed to Westbruk town proper or stay with the county?"

I looked around. The audience was into the speaker's every word. Everybody was paying attention.

She told them that in 1970 Schlesinger Oil bought the Wetlands from the heirs of the Westbruk Gun Club and came up with a plan for a residential community, a marina, hotels, and restaurants. "Quite an asset to the community, wouldn't you think?"

A male voice shouted an enthusiastic, "Yes!" The only man in the room stood just inside the doorway at the back of the Cabrillo Room. He sported a three-piece gray suit and carried a small American flag.

Some people laughed at the interruption. Others tittered.

The speaker smiled and continued. "With the Schlesinger Plan only150 acres of the wetlands would be left and those acres would be surrounded by the development."

"Don't you think that people who own a piece of property can decide what to do with it?" said the man in gray.

The speaker smiled at the man. "What did you say your name was, sir?"

"I didn't say," he said.

"My name is Mary Ellen Haseuman," the speaker said. "I am the attorney that incorporated the Amigos de Westbruk Wetlands in 1976."

"I know who you are," the man said.

"You know that the Amigos want to protect the environment, right?" Mary Ellen looked directly at the man.

He threw up his arms and then waved his flag again.

Mary Ellen continued, "Schlesinger Oil introduced a bill to take the Westbruk Wetlands out from under the California Coastal Act. That would have made it easier for them to develop the land. Our Westbruk Wetlands lobbyists stopped their bill. We've been effective in stopping other bills that would have adversely affected the Wetlands environment."

"You're a group of unprincipled rabble rousers," the man said.

People in the room were moving their heads back and forth. We looked at Mary Ellen. We looked at the man. We looked at Mary Ellen again. It wasn't high drama but it was interesting.

"Four years ago, in 1985, the California Coastal Commission unanimously approved a plan for 915 acres of wetlands, 1,300-slip marina, I don't know how many restaurants and 5,700 homes," Mary Ellen said. "Everybody said, 'Well, it's done. It's a done deal.' But it wasn't. We had asked for a condition. The condition stated the plan could only be executed as long as there was no environmental damage."

"You kept at them until they caved in, didn't you?" The man waved his flag. "Listen to me people, you're gonna lose your property rights."

"They haven't caved in," Mary Ellen said. "Last year, in November, I spent four hours sitting in Tate's Coffee Shop with the vice-president/project manager of Schlesinger Oil."

Mary Ellen told us that she kept drinking black coffee until her bladder was bloated. Then she excused herself, came back to the table and drank some more.

The V.P./Project Manager told Mary Ellen that he was working very hard.

"I liked him," Mary Ellen told us. "I believed that he was working hard."

He told her that he wanted the project to go forward and that he really needed her help.

She told him that she would give him her help.

"You'll agree to the marina?" he asked. According to Mary Ellen the V.P. was smiling and had a nice smile.

"No," she told him. "You can't have the marina. It would hurt the environment."

The V.P.'s smile morphed to a frown.

"To give him his due," Mary Ellen told us, "I really do believe the man did not realize the environmental damage that could be caused by building a marina."

The man in the gray suit waved his flag. "I wanna tell you folks something. I live in the Harbor section of Westbruk in a lovely house on the water. My house is on a man-made island on a man-dredged canal. I sail my man made boat through the waters brought in by men. It is a good place to live. The Westbruk Wetlands would be a good place to live too. In fact, where I live was once part of the wetlands." The man walked toward the front of the room and stopped next to my seat. He pushed his sleeves up as if he was ready for manual labor and I spotted a cog stone tattoo on his wrist.

He wasn't old enough to be Grandpa. He didn't look like the Leo of my dreams. Who was he?

"You live in the Harbor area just like me!" He pointed his flag at Mary Ellen.

I kept looking at his wrist.

Mary Ellen nodded. "You're right. I do live in the tract known as Westbruk Harbor."

The man turned to smile at the people pasted to their seats in the Cabrillo Room. "I told you so," he said as if he had proved something to us. Then he walked to the back of the room and out the door.

I ran out of the Cabrillo Room in my uncomfortable high heels hoping to spot the man in the gray suit with the cog stone tattoo on his wrist. I wanted to ask him how and where he got his tattoo. Did he know Leo? Did he know Leo's grandpa? But, I couldn't find him.

Mary Ellen was still fielding questions when I came back to the Cabrillo Room.

Charlene Silverman grabbed my arm. "Isn't Mary Ellen a great speaker? Weren't we smart to get her?"

"Yes" I said. What was the "we" about? I thought of the program and Monney had recruited Mary Ellen.

"She puts her money where her mouth is," Charlene said.

I didn't know what Charlene was talking about. But I did know that I loved her ruffle brimmed teal hat. Charlene was the only woman in the Cabrillo Room wearing a hat. And she looked so much better than the rest of us, I decided to go and buy my own hat. Of course, one hat wouldn't do. Charlene had a hat to go with every outfit. Every time I bought a new outfit, I told myself, I would buy a new hat. But I hated to shop. Maybe I could get one of those personal shoppers at Nordstrom.

Charlene said something and I missed it. "What?" I asked her.

"Aren't you listening?" she said. "Holding Hands for Westbruk."

"Holding hands for Westbruk?" What was she talking about? How much had I tuned out? Not a good habit to get into. Tuning people out.

"She's the one who paid," Charlene said.

"I love your hat," I said.

"You always say the same thing."

"You always look perfect," I said. Was I jealous? No. It was somewhat of an epiphany. I wasn't one bit jealous. That's good, I thought. "Holding hands for Westbruk? Somebody paid?"

"You were there, Dessa. Don't you remember?" Charlene said.

"Are you coming down with something?"

Holding hands for Westbruk. Of course!

One day, earlier in the year, when Monney and I had been walking on the Wetlands, we saw a large group, maybe hundreds of people holding hands in a large circle. Most of them were wearing faded, messy, old clothes. Charlene was there looking like a model. Her expensive looking black and yellow hat matched her expensive looking black and yellow sweat suit. "Hi! Dessa," she had said. "Isn't this fun? Why don't you come and join us?"

Monney and I had joined the circle. Monney held Charlene's hand. I held Monney's and the hand of a nice looking man with a gray beard. Gray Beard didn't tell me his name. Charlene didn't introduce us. We stood there only for a few minutes. I can't remember what Monney's hand felt like. But I remember the man's. It was warm and rough and I liked holding it.

One day, after an argument, Leonard and I had discovered that we weren't fitted to hold hands. He was taller, so his hand and my hand were not located in the right place. In order to hold hands, he had to reach down and I had to bend my arm at the elbow. It seemed too difficult, so we stopped holding hands.

"Okay," somebody said. "Thanks everybody." The man with the beard let go of my hand and I felt like crying.

The Westbruk Bulletin Gazette and other nearby newspapers ran aerial photos labeled "Holding Hands for Westbruk". The people holding hands in the pictures outlined the amount of land that would be lost to the Wetlands if a marina were built.

"Mary Ellen and her husband paid for those aerial photos with their own money," Charlene said.

Charlene always looked good and knew a lot of interesting things. I'd seen her holding hands with her husband. But, I wasn't jealous, I told myself.

The March 11, 1990 Op Ed piece in the Westbruk Bulletin Gazette caught my eye.

PROPERTY RIGHTS YES. BUT DON'T MAKE ME PAY FOR THEM.

I live in the Harbor area of Westbruk, California. I'm sending this Op Ed essay to every newspaper in this county. I'm considering sending it to every newspaper in every big city in the country.

When I first saw the Westbruk Wetlands I was appalled. Weeds all over. Trash all over. Smelly oil rigs. When I heard that Schlesinger Oil was going to build a marina and pretty houses like we have in the Westbruk Harbor area, where I live, I was delighted. First of all, it would raise my property value. It would mean more navigable water because the plan was to build a cut between the Harbor and the new development. But when Schlesinger Oil announced that they weren't going to pay for the cut and that every one of us homeowners was going to be assessed for the costs, I got mad. I wave my flag for property rights. There is nothing I believe in more. But when you own property and you want to improve it, it is up to you to pay for the costs of the improvements. It is not up to me. I'll pay for my improvements and you pay for yours. If you decide to pay your own way, Schlesinger Company, I'm still a hundred percent behind you.

Harry Jack Mulganerson.

There was a photo of Harry Jack Mulganerson at the top of the article. He was the man who heckled Mary Ellen Haseuman at the library. I could see his cog stone tattoo. His wrist was visible because he was waving his American flag. I knew the man's name now. What else could I find out about him? His cog stone tattoo weighed heavy on my head.

I didn't meet Harry Jack Mulganerson until Saturday, September 17, 2005. He was grayer and paunchier but I recognized him. How many men sport a cog stone tattoo? His was visible because he rolled up his sleeves.

Charlene Silverman had a fancy catered sit-down dinner party and invited Leonard and me. I'm not sure why we were included. Harry Jack was invited because he was a single man. Charlene had been widowed a few years back and was looking.

It had been one of those great days. The weather was perfect. Leo and I had been at the Rose Bowl. UCLA had beat Oklahoma 41 to 24. The man who sat in front of me in the stadium had kissed my cheek at the end of the game. The two women that sat in back of me had hugged my husband and me before dancing their way out of their aisle.

Leonard was in a great mood.

I plopped myself next to Harry Jack at Charlene's large dining room table set with gold chargers under Spode, Fleur de lys China, Waterford Crystal Colleen pattern goblets and wine glasses and Cristale silver. Leonard sat on the other side of me.

During the gravlax on toast course Harry and I exchanged names.

He said he'd read my Dear Dessa Dreams columns for years.

I let him know that I was familiar with his views on property rights, probably not the best way to start the conversation.

"Did you read the Kelo vs. New London case?" Harry asked Leonard.

I knew about the case. The Supreme Court had decided on June 23 that privately owned real property could be taken with recompense to be used for economic development.

"Yeah, I was appalled," Leonard said.

"People never want to listen to me." Harry handed his unfinished portion of gravlax to the dressed in white server and spooned into the cold cream of tomato bisque that was the next course.

"My gosh!" I said. "Hasn't Hurricane Katrina proved that wetlands must be restored no matter who owns the property? Hasn't it proved that you can't build on wetlands?"

"Nobody's sure about that," Harry Jack said.

"They are sure," I said.

"Don't argue with the man," Leonard whispered. "You won't change his mind."

I looked at Leonard. Had I changed his mind? Where are the open minded people? How do you change minds?

I turned back to Harry. "What an interesting tattoo!" I pointed to his cog stone tattoo. "How did you get it?" I took a spoonful of my cold soup. The cream of tomato bisque was the most delicious bisque, I'd ever tasted.

"Can you believe the Supreme Court?" Harry seemed to like the tomato bisque as much as I did.

"I don't like it," Leonard pushed the soup away.

"You don't like the soup or the Supreme Court Decision?" I asked.

"Neither. I don't like the decision, I don't like the soup and I know that the wetlands have to be restored."

"June 23 will go down in our country as a day of infamy." Harry was scraping the bowl.

"You haven't told me about your tattoo," I said.

He looked at his tattoo and laughed. "You want to know about this foolish old man, do you?"

"Yes."

"I want to talk property rights!" Harry pounded his Waterford Colleen patterned red wine glass on the table and spilled merlot on my new cream-colored pants suit.

"You owe me," I said.

"I'll pay your cleaning bill," he said.

"Tell me about the tattoo. I don't need you to pay my cleaning bill."

Harry's wife had died of ovarian cancer. It hadn't been the best of all marriages but he was sorry to see her go.

After her death one woman after another brought him covered casseroles. The casseroles were tasty but the women weren't.

Harry missed the wife he hadn't liked much and began to frequent Tiki's, a bar on Main Street in downtown Westbruk.

Every night he'd sit on his stool and nurse one drink.

One night a beautiful woman with long black hair sat next to him. She was young enough to have been his daughter. He didn't talk to her. She didn't talk to him. They both sat on the stools, nursing their drinks, one drink each, till closing time.

The next night she was there again.

"I'm Harry," he told her.

"I'm Lunafour," she said.

That was the end of the conversation.

She drank a pineapple daiquiri.

He drank a scotch and soda.

The third night Harry told Lunafour how he felt about property rights.

The fourth night Harry took Lunafour to dinner.

She wore a low cut black lace blouse that revealed her breasts almost to her nipples. Harry was uncomfortable and had a difficult time eating his well-done steak.

"Do you want to sleep with me?" she asked.

Harry nodded.

"You'll have to do something for me first," she said.

Harry was so crazy for Lunafour he would have done anything. I'll buy her a car, he thought.

"I need you to be tattooed," Lunafour said.

"I'll buy you a car," Harry blurted. He was on his third scotch and soda.

"The tattoo is all that's necessary," she said.

"That's how I got the tattoo," Harry told me as we sipped our cappuccinos laced with amaretto.

"What happened to Lunafour?" I asked.

"She disappeared with my car, the night I asked her to marry me. But, I had a good three and a half weeks."

"Why did she want you to get a tattoo?" I asked. "You were willing to buy her a car."

"I don't know," he said.

28.

Dear Dessa Dreams,
I was going to marry Handsome Holden until I found out Ugly Glenn is rich. I say cute is temporary; money is forever. Where can I get a plastic surgeon for Glenn?
Decided in Denver.

Dear Decided,

I dreamt about a man who was old and wrinkled and opted for plastic surgery. He went to the hospital and just before he went under the Anesthesiologist asked him if he had been informed of all his choices.

"What are my choices?" the man asked.

"You can have or not have the surgery," the Anesthesiologist said.

"What would I do if I didn't have it?" the patient asked. "I have too many wrinkles. Nobody likes an old man with wrinkles."

"Depends on the old man's attitude," the Anesthesiologist said.

The patient said, "I'll have to think about this some more."

"Okay," said the Anesthesiologist.

The patient got up and left the hospital.

The Plastic Surgeon came in to the operating room. "Where is my patient?" he said to the Anesthesiologist. "I've had a bad night and I don't have time to dilly-dally around."

"You always have bad nights. You never have time to dilly-dally around."

"You're right," said the Plastic Surgeon. "Cancel the surgery!"

The Plastic Surgeon was friendly to everybody he passed that day. When he reached home, he dilly-dallied with his wife. Nine months later they had a baby.

The patient went to the library and took out some "how to improve" books. He read the books, followed the instructions and nine months later, after joining five different social clubs, three charities, one book discussion group and a senior citizen basketball team, the man had more friends than he ever had when he was young and wrinkle free.

Go to the library. Take out as many books as you can find on Values, Philosophy and Ethics. Read them. Follow their advice. Find yourself before you get married. This way you won't have to look for a plastic surgeon. But if you do look for a plastic surgeon when you're old, I won't hold it against you. In fact, I'm thinking about finding one.

Sincerely, Dessa Dreams.

I was thinking about plastic surgery. I had too many wrinkles and didn't know how they got there.

"Does your mouth hurt?" I asked Monney.

"The Novocain's still working."

The Novocain worked most of that spring day in 1996. Instead of driving Monney home after her root canal, we went to Charlene Silverman's house to stuff envelopes for the Friends of the Library.

When Charlene did something, even stuffing envelopes, she did it with style. She provided the envelope stuffers with tea served in Spode Fleur de Lys cups, sandwiches, scones, clotted cream, raspberry preserves, and freshly baked tiny cookies. We wiped our fingers on Charlene's ironed and starched white napkins before we stuffed envelopes.

"I don't like to go there anymore," Charlene said. Her manicured hands were fast. The lady knew how to stuff her envelopes.

"Go where?" I asked.

"New York," she said.

"I love New York." I'd been there twice and couldn't wait to go again. I'd read great reviews about "Titanic" and "The Last Night of Ballyhoo," new Broadway plays, and was dying to see them.

"Not Manhattan," Charlene said. "Upstate New York."

Monney didn't look up. Charlene was fast. Monney was methodical. Her stuffing was neat. "What do you have against upstate New York?" Monney asked.

"Big flies," Charlene said. "You have no idea. There aren't any swarms of big flies in California."

"Nuke 'em," Dorothy Tepler said. Dorothy was the Friends of the Library membership vice president and drove me nuts because she kept the member list on index cards. She was the only one who knew where those 577 cards were.

"Put the names on the library computer," I'd once suggested.

"Would you like to enter the 577 names, Dessa?" she'd said. "I don't know how to use a computer."

I never brought up the subject again.

"Nuke them! Stamp them out! There's gotta be a spray! Maybe DDT." Dorothy was still enjoying the cookies and hadn't started stuffing.

"Get some bats." Monney's slow but sure method afforded the largest pile of stuffed envelopes.

Charlene laughed. "What would I do with bats?"

"Bats eat flies," Monney said.

"The cures sound worse than the illness." I said, meaning both the DDT and the bats.

"There you go again, Dessa," Monney said. "Bad mouthing bats."

What is wrong with her? I'd never badmouthed bats before. And even if I had, which I hadn't, what was wrong with badmouthing bats?

"I don't want bats or flies. If Charles insists on going to New York, he can go without me." Charlene was stuffing as fast as she could. I could tell that she wanted her pile to be higher than Monney's.

"If people would just let nature take care of what it's supposed to take care of, the world would be a better place." Monney's pile of envelopes was so high it hid her face.

In the late afternoon Monney's Novocain was still working so we hiked a new trail on the Wetlands to work off Charlene's goodies. We traipsed over the berm, around the strawberry field, past the bunker, and up a hill to a stable we'd never seen before.

"Wow!" I said. "This place doesn't seem that big but we're always finding something new."

Monney nodded. She looked pale. Was the Novocain wearing down? We were pretty far from any help and if there were people working at the stables, I didn't see them. "Are you ready to turn around?" I asked her.

"We can go a little bit further."

"Why did you put me down?" I asked Monney as we walked away from the stable toward a grove of eucalyptus trees that housed some blue heron nests. "About bad mouthing bats?"

"I wasn't putting you down," she said. "But I do want people to realize that there are many ways to handle problems that won't kill off our planet."

I guess I would have asked Monney what she meant, but just then I spotted Luna coming out from a white tent next to the eucalyptus trees. She was brushing her long black hair that was wet and hung limp down her back. She wore dark blue jeans and a short sleeved, white silk tailored blouse. A cog stone tattoo was on her right arm above her elbow. "Luna, is that you?" I asked when I got closer.

"I'm not Luna." The beautiful young woman wasn't old enough to be Luna.

"Sorry," I said. "You remind me of somebody I met once."

"You have a good memory," she said. "I can't remember anybody I meet just once."

"I can't either," Monney said, looking pained.

"Is your tooth hurting?" I asked.

Monney shook her head. But I could tell she was suffering.

"Do you know Luna?" The girl that looked like Luna asked.

"Do you?" I asked. The conversation was getting creepy.

"You belong to one of the Westbruk Wetlands clubs," she said, looking directly at me.

"I belong to the Westbruk Wetlands Land Trust and the Amigos." (Monney now belonged to two Wetlands support groups.) Her cheek was swollen. Her eyes seemed glazed by pain.

"My people have always lived here," the girl said.

We were at least forty-five minutes in walking time from Monney's house. How would I get her home? Would she faint?

"My jeep's over there," the young girl said. A 1975 Ford Bronco was parked on the other side of the tent.

The Luna look-alike drove us to Monney's house and didn't say a word. Not even when I thanked her.

Three days later, when Monney was fully recovered, we walked the Wetlands to the area near the stables again. The white tent and Ford Bronco were gone.

On July 3, that year (1996) Monney called me on the phone. "I need you to do something," she said.

"What?"

"Something fun," she said.

I was at Monney's house before eight, on the morning of July 4th, dressed in tennis whites, shorts and a t-shirt, which I wore often, even though I didn't play tennis.

"Have you eaten?" Monney asked when she opened the door.

"I can't get anywhere on time in the morning if I eat."

"Good," she said.

Was she going to feed me? I hoped so.

"Take off your t-shirt," she said.

Monney's husband was sitting in his big fat chair reading the Westbruk Bulletin Gazette. His face was hidden but I could tell he was laughing.

A cartoon of a Blue Heron sporting sunglasses standing on the elongated neck of an electric guitar decorated the tee shirt she handed me. The caption below the Heron read, "Cool Blue."

"This is what we're all going to wear," Monney said as she put her t-shirt on top of the shirt she was already wearing.

"Don't step in the shit!"
Monney's husband told us when he
dropped us off at the place we were
supposed to meet the other members
of the Westbruk Wetlands Land
Trust who were going to march with
us in the Westbruk Fourth of July
Parade.

We found the Land Trust float
two blocks away. The flatbed truck
had two boards nailed together to
form a triangular pyramid. An
unrealistic depiction of the Wetlands,
painted with cartoon like birds in
blue skies over looking green
gardens, decorated the boards.

"It could look like that," Monney
said.

"Yeah, sure." I didn't care what
the painting looked like. I was
hungry.

That morning, after eating the
refreshments provided by the
Westbruk Land Trust, I found out
that ingesting coffee and doughnuts
on an empty stomach made me giddy
and light headed. I'm not going to
faint I told myself as I sat on the curb
with my head between my knees
waiting for the parade to start.

We walked in front of the Land Trust float and behind golden palominos ridden by riders costumed to look like California Rancheros.

"Clap your hands," Monney ordered.

I clapped. Ten minutes into the march we started our mantra. "Save the Wetlands! Save the Wetlands! Save the Westbruk Wetlands!"

The morning fog was gone and the sun was straight over our heads. The giddy stomach caused by the coffee and doughnut breakfast marched along with me until the people standing and sitting on the sidewalks along the parade route started to clap and cheer for us. Some of them joined in our litany, "Save the Wetlands! Save the Wetlands! Save the Westbruk Wetlands!"

"Save the Wetlands! Oh shit!" The Palomino directly in front of us gave no warning before it dumped. Both Monney and I stepped into its crap.

29.

Dear Dessa Dreams,

I've been staying with my mother while my wife is in Chicago taking care of her sick daddy. My mother cooks and cleans better than my wife. She darns socks and doesn't lose them in the wash. Mother doesn't argue with me. She says that I'm wonderful. I don't miss my wife one bit. What's the best way to kill a wife?
Looking for a woman just like Mom, in Missoula, Montana.

Dear Looking,

Stop looking and don't kill your wife!

I dreamt about a married couple. The husband went to Detroit to see his mother. He asked himself, why can't my wife be as good as my mother? Why can't my wife make a cherry cream pie like my mother makes? Why can't my wife sew on my buttons? I have a lot of missing buttons. Why doesn't my wife laugh at my jokes the way my mother does?

I better ditch my wife and find a new woman.

The wife went to New York to see her father. When the wife spoke, her father listened. When the wife wore a new dress, her father told her how pretty she looked. When the wife cooked, her father said the food was delicious. The wife said, "I better ditch my husband and find a man just like my father."

So the husband looked around. And the wife looked around. The husband couldn't find a woman as good as his mother. The wife couldn't find a man as good as her father.

"What should I do?" the man asked his mother.

"Go home and be good to your wife," his mother said.

"What should I do?" the wife asked her father.

"Go home and be good to your husband," her father said.

The husband and the wife got back together. They decided to remodel their house and got divorced over the stress it caused.

Be nice to your wife and don't remodel your house.

440

Sincerely, Dessa Dreams.

"Do you still want an ocean
view?" Leonard asked me one
morning before he took off to work.

I nodded at the man who didn't
hold my hand anymore.

"If we build a room over the
garage--," he said as if I could finish
the sentence for him.

I could finish it. If we built a
room over the garage we would have
an ocean view. Of course, the
configuration would mean knocking
down walls and getting rid of our
sons' bedrooms.

"They don't need the bedrooms,"
Leonard said. "They're not coming
home again."

Arthur was 36. Eli was 33. They
were both married. Neither had
children.

"I don't want them to come home
again," I said. What did I want?

"I thought you always wanted an
ocean view," Leonard said.

I looked at him. My sixty-two
year old husband didn't have a
wrinkle on his face. He ran at least
six miles four times a week. He still

carried his golf bag when he walked around the golf course. But his curly hair was thinning. His eyebrows were turning gray.

"People get divorced when they remodel," I said.

Two members of the Friends of the Library board had divorced after they remodeled.

"No matter what I do or say, you won't be pleased," Leonard said. "I've never been able to do enough, have I?"

I stood there and didn't say anything. What was there to say? Leonard had had to compete with my dream Leo and had never measured up. I didn't think he cared.

Leonard shrugged his shoulders and left the house.

I shrugged my shoulders, walked upstairs, took off my clothes, put my red plaid flannel pajamas on, climbed into my yet unmade king sized bed and reached for my cog stone.

* * *

"What should I do, GOD?" I say. "Should we build the room over the garage? If we do, we'll have a view of the Wetlands and the ocean."

I'm in a new room. I can smell the newness. The paint is wet. Everything is very clean. A valuable Persian rug with a floral design in muted browns and reds covers the black walnut floor.

The fourth wall is one large sheet of glass that spans the wall from ceiling to floor.

I look out. Coyote smiles at me. Blue Heron waves. Peregrine Falcon whizzes by. "Does anything or anybody move faster than Peregrine Falcon?" I ask.

GOD laughs. "An airplane flies faster. A rocket ship is speedier."

"I guess," I say. "What a wonderful room!"

"It's a jail," Leo says. He stands naked in front of me. He can't be older than thirty. I'm sixty-one. How does he stay so young?

"It's not a jail. This is the best place in the world. You and GOD are here. What could be better?"

"Real life," Leo says.

He pulls me to him. I'm naked, too.

Real life isn't as good as this, I think. Leo kisses me, strokes me, then we make love on top of the Persian rug.

"Let's fly out of here and check out the Wetlands," I say after we pleasure each other three times.

"We can't fly out of here," Leo says. "We're stuck."

"No!" I argue. "We're not stuck!"

"We're trapped, Dessa!"

"No. No. We're not!" Why am I arguing with Leo? I only argue with Leonard.

"Come, I'll show you." I examine the bookcases looking for the exit and can't find it. "Where is the door?"

"There is no door," Leo says. He's dressed like an astronaut in a science fiction film.

"It's your choice, Dessa, GOD says.

"What?"

The phone rings.

* * *

I rolled over. Why was the phone on Leonard's side? "Hello," I said after I picked up the receiver. Whoever called had given up. If it were important, he or she would call back.

I stared at the acoustic tiled, dirty white ceiling. When we remodel, we'll have to scrape that junk I told myself. But if we scraped would the sounds in the house echo? There was so much to think about if you remodeled. So many changes to make if you start with only one change.

The phone rang again. "Hello," I said.

"Hello, Grandma," my son Arthur said.

"There's no grandmother here," I said. My heart was beating.

"Oh yeah! There is."

My heart enlarged. The beating went up to my throat and down to my stomach.

Eight pounds, two and a half ounces, Jacob (Jake or Jakey) David Lechmann was born on July 17, 1999. He was perfect. He still is. The two of us fell in love the minute we saw each other. "How high, Gamma?" he still asks me.

"Higher than the sky," I always answer.

"How much higher?" he asks.

"A million, billion, zillion, dillion."

"Me too," he always says. "I love you gamma that much. A million, billion, zillion, dillion." Then he throws himself into my arms and kisses my cheek.

"Oh Jake. You are the best thing that ever happened."

Leonard smiles when this occurs. Jake is the best thing that ever happened to him, too.

We didn't build the room on top of the garage. I guessed we weren't going to have a room with an ocean view. Leonard and I didn't discuss it any more. We didn't discuss much. Sometimes we talked about Jake but not enough to break through our barriers. We didn't even argue any more.

I did my thing. He did his. We were in our sixties and I observed that other people in their sixties lived like we did. Quiet lives, I thought. Quiet dull lives.

Some choice, I thought. Stuck in a room in a dream. Trapped in a life without a dream.

* * *

"GOD, I don't want to live this way."

"Then don't."

30.

Dear Dessa Dreams,

I do garbage. I jump out of the truck, pick up the garbage can, and dump it into the back of the truck. I do this over and over and over. All day long. Five days a week. I can't smell the garbage any more. I can't smell anything.

How do I recover my sense of smell?
Handicapped in Hanford.

Dear Handicapped,

I dreamt about a person who stopped hearing, feeling, seeing and smelling. "I don't want to hear that screeching soprano sing "Carmen" off tune," she said. So she missed the sound of her granddaughter saying "I love you." I don't want to feel the ache in my toe," she said

*and she missed the feel of her new
lover's kiss. "I don't want to look at
the beggars in India," she said. And
she missed seeing the Taj Mahal. "I
don't want to smell the skunk," she
said. And she missed smelling the
rose.*

*Go to a doctor that specializes in
olfactory recovery and get your
smeller restored.*
Sincerely, Dessa Dreams.

It took me a while to realize that
Handicapped in Hanford wasn't
handicapped. He was a man who
realized that even if you had to smell
garbage, the important thing was to
be able to smell.

On January 12, 2000, Leonard
put a borrowed yellow ladder next to
a "For Sale" sign on a weed-covered
vacant lot across the street from the
north mesa of the Westbruk
Wetlands. "Climb to the top, Dessa!"
he said.

"How tall is that ladder?"
"Fourteen feet."

"I'm not climbing," I said. There
are things you don't do when you're
sixty-two.

"If you climb the ladder, you'll
see the ocean," he said.

"If I drive to the beach, I'll see
the ocean," I said.

"If you climb the ladder, you'll
see the view we can have if we buy
this lot and build a house," he said.

"We're going to buy this lot?" I
asked.

"If you want us to," Leonard
said.

I looked at the ladder. Fourteen
feet looked awfully high.

"I'll hold the ladder," Leonard
said. "You won't fall."

I couldn't believe that I was
brave enough to scale the rungs. I
couldn't believe what I saw when I
got to the top. Buildings outlined the
skyline of Long Beach to the north.
White ripples danced a top the
Pacific Ocean between San Pedro
and Catalina Island. Palm Trees
grew at the edge of the mesa where,
in my dreams, the Gun Club stood.
This was my cog stone dream vista.
I threw my arms to the sky and
yelled, "Oh GOD!"

We bought the lot the following day.

"The living room, dining room, kitchen, office and bedroom will be upstairs," Leonard said. "That way we'll always have a view."

"Are you nuts?" I said. "I'm not going to lug groceries up stairs."

"We'll build an elevator," he said.

"An elevator," I said. "That's ostentatious."

"So? We'll be ostentatious."

"I don't want to be ostentatious."

"Too bad!" He wanted to be ostentatious.

"That's obnoxious," I said.

He had always wanted to be obnoxious as well as ostentatious.

"I hate you," I said.

He laughed.

Our architect, John Carris, designed freestanding, modern looking storefronts and strip malls. He didn't design houses. Leonard liked him, knew him through his commercial real estate dealings and said John would give us a good deal.

"The house will be gray with lots of windows," Leonard said.

"Chrome furniture. Glass tables. Easy to maintain."

"Ugly," I said.

John Carris looked at the rough sketch I'd made and lifted his gray bushy eyebrows. "You want all your living space up stairs?" he asked. "What do you plan for the first floor?"

"The garage," I said.

"You need a nine car garage?" John's gray bushy eyebrows lifted again.

"Nine cars?"

"You have room for nine cars," John said.

We sat at a granite table in John's office. One wall had cubbyholes stuffed with blue prints and shelves piled with office supplies. In the back there was a small room where his employees, two other architects, worked. A refrigerator housed the cold bottles of water John offered us when we walked in. There was a sink where he got water to make instant coffee in his microwave oven.

"Have you ever designed a house before?" I asked.

"I can do the job." John didn't look up from the drawing I'd sketched. "Where did you put the walls?

"There are no walls," I said.

John laughed. His gray bushy eyebrows wiggled.

I could tell I was going to hate him as much as I hated Leonard. "If we build walls we won't be able to see the ocean from the kitchen or the dining room."

"What's going to hold the house up?" John asked.

I don't want any walls," I said.

"Okay," John drew a large X through my drawing.

"What are you doing?" *Are we stuck with this guy?*

"I'm separating your great drawing into four triangles. I really want to focus in, Dessa."

Maybe he isn't so bad.

John stood up. He was very tall. "Let me mull on this a few days."

"Buying the lot is the craziest thing we've ever done," I told my dad on the phone.

"What are you making your husband for dinner?" my dad asked.

"Nothing," I said. "He doesn't deserve dinner."

"Shana made me pot roast," he said.

I liked my dad's new wife, Shana. Leonard, Arthur and Eli adored her. She knows how to talk to people, they said. She also knew how to look good. In her early eighties she dressed in expensive clothes that showed off her still perfect figure, didn't leave her condo without makeup or perfume and stood straight. My 89 year-old dad was crazy for her.

"Just the way I like it," my dad continued to talk about the pot roast. "All the pretty little vegetables. Really colorful."

"You don't eat vegetables," I said, wishing I was sitting in a comfortable chair instead of standing at the kitchen counter. I knew it was going to be a long conversation.

"I only ate the meat and potatoes," my dad said. "I didn't tell Shana I don't like vegetables. Why should I hurt her?"

Why hadn't he been more careful with my mother's feelings?

"I have some things to discuss with you, Dessa."

"Okay," I said. "What?"

"I want to tell you about some things I know."

"Like what?" I asked.

"Like good looking thin women keep their husbands."

"Dad, that is such crap."

"Nice women use nice language," he said.

I felt like spouting off every crummy word I'd ever heard but I didn't.

"Women should keep their houses clean," he said.

I looked at the dirty dishes piled in the sink.

"They should provide good food for their husbands."

I was providing tasty take out. If Leonard wanted something home cooked, he could cook it himself, I thought.

"People shouldn't argue," he said.

"I'm talking to the biggest arguer in the universe."

"You're talking to the man that used to be the biggest arguer in the universe. This is important, Dessa."

"I'm listening," I said.

"I learned this stuff when I was eighty-eight. You should learn faster."

"I'm listening," I repeated. I probably sounded impatient, but I really did want to hear what he had to say.

"If somebody said black, I used to say white," he said. "If somebody said north, I said south. Now if a person shows me a daffodil and says it's coffee-brown, I say, 'Isn't coffee-brown a great color?' If someone says vanilla ice cream reminds him of chili con carne, I say, 'Isn't that interesting?' I don't argue anymore."

The thought of him not arguing made me sad.

"There's another rule, Dessa."

"What?" I asked.

"Be kind," he said.

Bubby had told me to be kind just before she died. "I've heard that rule before," I said.

"It's the most important, Dessa."

Two days later my dad sat on the toilet, pushed down, closed off his carotid artery and died.

"I wanted to show him the house," I said.

"So did I." It was the first time I'd seen Leonard cry. Arthur and Eli cried, too.

At the funeral parlor, a thin man about eighty grabbed my arm before I could walk into the isolated, family chamber. "Your dad was a good man," he said.

"Thank you," I said and tried but failed to move away.

"When I lost my job, my wife Hilda was sick. Your father gave me a thousand dollars."

"My goodness!"

Before I walked into the room set aside for family bereavement, other old men told me their stories. My father had come in the middle of the night to drive one man's daughter to the hospital when her husband, the gonif, beat her.

"Your father paid for my mother's funeral," another old man said.

"When my wife was dying, your dad came to visit me every day."

To this day, I bawl in movies. I cry reading books. Tell me a story about the sadness of a stranger and

I'll sob as if you were telling me about my best friend. But I stood like a stone at my dad's graveside.

31.

Dear Dessa Dreams,

I hang out with downers. My boyfriend hasn't been in a good mood for seventeen Saturdays. (I only see him on Saturdays). My best girlfriend hasn't laughed for twenty-two weeks. How do I cheer them up? Don't wanna be sad, in San Diego.

Dear Don't Wanna,

I dreamt about a group of sad people. They lived in a place where it always rained. They said the dampness caused pains and aches.

Then their leader said, "Let's move. Let's go to a place where it doesn't rain."

Some of the people said, "Good idea. We'll pack in a minute and off we go."

And they packed in a minute and off they went.

The leader led them to a place where it didn't rain all the time. I think they moved to Southern California. And these people weren't sad any more. (I'm not trying to tell you that there are no sad people in Southern California. There are. I know some of them.)

Not all the people followed the leader. The people that didn't follow him said, "We're not leaving. We'd rather be miserable here than happy someplace else." So they stayed miserable.

I think you should tell your friends a good joke. If you can't find one, write again and I'll find one for you. If they don't laugh at the joke, introduce them to each other. Let them be miserable together and you find happy new friends.
Sincerely, Dessa Dreams.

I wanted two bedrooms. Leonard wanted three. Leonard said the house should have a modern feel. He liked chrome. I did some research. Modern houses that featured chrome didn't have much resale value. Leonard said "upside down houses" with living quarters up stairs didn't have much resale value either so what difference did it make? By the time the plans for the house were finished, we spoke to each other in short gruff sentences.

The first two contractors who saw John Carris's blue prints decided not to bid.

"It's too much," the first non-bidder told me.

"Too complicated," the second one said.

We couldn't afford the more than a million dollars the other three bidders asked.

"Do Plan B," John said.

Plan B was for us to be the owner contractors.

"We don't know how," I said.

"We can't," Leonard said.

"You'll hire a superintendent," John said. "I know just the guy."

Monday morning, September 10, 2001, Leonard and I stood on our lot.

"Gorgeous car," Leonard said as John parked his Midnight Blue, 2000 C-Class Mercedes Benz sedan at the curb in front of our lot.

"Architects must make a lot of money," I said.

"He deserves a lot of money," Leonard said. "He has to deal with you."

There has to be a rusty nail on the lot that I can arrange for Leonard to step on.

A tall man, about forty-five, dressed in beige denim slacks and a short sleeve yellow shirt got out from the passenger side of the car. He had dark curly hair and olive skin. He resembled Leonard and looked exactly like Leo of my cog stone induced dreams. "You look familiar," I said.

"I think I would remember if we met before," he said. "My name is Ishmael--."

"Ishmael Aron," I said.

"We've met?" he asked.

"I'm psychic," I said.

"No, you're not," Leonard said.

"Where did we meet?" Ishmael asked.

I wanted to say on a beach when you were eleven and I was ten. I wanted to say in my dreams. "What happened to the tattoo?" I asked. His cog stone tattoo wasn't on his arm any more.

"Where did we meet?"

"You came to the *Michael Malone* tryouts," I said. "I was the director."

"Of course, the Westbruk Playhouse," he said. "I used to act a lot."

I looked at the weed-covered ground while John and Ishmael recited the reasons Ishmael would make the perfect superintendent; the salary was discussed and negotiations were made.

That night Leonard and I sat at the dining room table, pencils in hand, subcontractor's bids in front of us, marking numbers on pages and pages of paper.

"Did you notice how much Ishmael looks like you?" I said.

Leonard looked up from his columns of numbers. "You're crazy."

"Ishmael looks more like you than our sons do," I said.

"We have to work on the numbers, Dessa."

"I'm too tired to go over the numbers again."

"I'll do the numbers," he said.

I went up the stairs, put on my yellow silk and lace nightgown, reached for my cog stone and went to sleep.

* * *

GOD says, "It is 1964.

I'm standing in front of the Gun Club. "Leo," I call, "where are you?"

"Hi! Dessa," he says, putting his hand on my cheek. He's dressed in the same outfit Ishmael wore at the building site, same beige denim slacks, same short sleeve yellow shirt.

I'm dressed 1964-appropriate in my pink Mary Quant mini dress. The hem is six inches above my knees. Why is Leo dressed in 2001-style?

"It doesn't matter what you wear to a fire," he says. Leo can read my mind.

"I need to find out something," I say. I want to know if he's related to Ishmael.

"Look! Dessa!"

Fire trucks speed toward us. They don't have sirens. They don't make noise. It's silent on the mesa. There is no bird song or insect hum.

The fire trucks stop in front of us. Their brakes don't screech. Firemen throw cans of gasoline at the Gun Club. Matches are lit and the fire starts. I can feel the heat. I should run, I think, but don't. Red orange flames jump to the sky and heat my bones. The flames swallow the Gun Club. The building implodes and it turns to ash. The firemen turn their hose on the ashes and remaining flames. "Great exercise," says the fireman nearest to me. How funny to hear his voice. I saw the fire but didn't hear it. No crackle, no booms. No rush of water putting it out. No noise.

"Did we time it?" says the fireman nearest to me.

"It went fast," another fireman answers.

"Leo, I have to ask you about Ishmael," I say.

He doesn't answer because thousands of bees are buzzing toward us. I take Leo's hand and try to run but I can't budge him. "Move!" I say.

"It's September 11th," he says.

* * *

I woke to an unfamiliar voice on the radio. "September eleventh, two thousand and one, everybody. People on the west coast are just waking up." The announcer's voice sounded high pitched, like he was nervous. Hearing a buzzing sound, I looked around. Bees were swarming around my bedroom!

"Oh no!" screamed the voice on the radio. "I can't look!"

I pressed the radio off button. Where were the bees coming from? "Leonard!" I yelled.

He came wet and naked from the shower.

I pulled my blankets to my nose. "Put something on. Open the windows!"

He opened the windows, knocking the screens outward.

"I told you to put on some clothes!" *What if the bees sting him?*

More bees flew in. And then they all flew out. What a creepy way to begin the day!

I took my shower, got dressed, came down the stairs and saw my husband shaking. He was watching NBC. Katie Couric looked so sad. What is wrong? "Oh!"

I called Arthur first. He was already watching TV. So was Eli.

I saw the twin towers implode in the same silence the Gun Club imploded in my dream. Leonard had pushed the mute button.

He was still shaking when he left to go to his office. I didn't shake. My tears didn't flow. I didn't believe what I was seeing. It must be some awful nightmare, I thought as I sat in front of the television and ate bananas.

In the afternoon I called Monney.

"I can't talk about New York," she said.

"Okay." I peeled another banana.

"How's the new house coming?" she asked.

"Do you know anything about the Gun Club?" I asked.

"Why?"

"What happened to it?" I bit into my banana. It was the perfect food for sitting in front of the television all day.

"The Westbruk fire department burned it down," she said. "It was an exercise."

"In 1964?"

465

"Yeah!" After a beat, she said, "We could have used the building for a museum or a nature center."

"True," I said.

"I want to watch television, Dessa."

"Okay," I said. "Monney, I think you're a good woman."

"So are you," she said.

On September 13, I stood on our vacant lot and decided it was too dangerous to build. There were oil wells on the wetlands to the south and a naval depot to the north. Some terrorist would probably want to bomb us.

"We're going to build, Dessa," Leonard said.

On Monday, January 14, 2002 we broke ground and I noticed there was a FOR SALE sign on my soon to be new neighbor's house. What did that guy know that we didn't?

The following Monday, Leonard told me, "Ishmael hired his daughter."

"I bet her name is Lunafive," I said.

"Lunalyn," Leonard said.

"I bet she's beautiful and has long, dark hair," I said.

"She's a looker," Leonard said.

"I bet she's trouble," I said.

"Why do you say that?" Leonard said.

"She's always been trouble."

"What?"

I didn't answer.

The steel enforced block walls that would house the elevator were erected the first day Lunalyn came to work. She wore jeans, a long sleeve chambray shirt, and sported a tool belt around her slim waist. She looked like the Luna who appeared in my cog stone induced dreams, like the girl who had stolen my sandals, like the model I had seen in the *HISTORY & GEOGRAPHY* magazine, like the woman who had been an extra in the *CABEL STURMSS* mini-series and like the teenager that Grandpa had killed when I was ten. "I remember you," I said after Ishmael introduced us.

"I don't remember you."

"You were camping," I said. "In a white tent. On the Wetlands north mesa. Near the stables."

"Oh, yeah," she said.

"You said that you weren't Luna," I said.

"I'm Lunalyn," she said.

"Get to work, girl," her father ordered.

"Talk to you later." Lunalyn winked at me.

In March the house next door sold and my house was framed.

In April my new neighbor moved in. I met him on a Sunday. "Hi!" I said to the good-looking hunk who smiled down at me.

"I'm just a country boy from Clay County, Arkansas. Came to California with a dollar in my pocket and a whole lot gumption," he said as he gave me a tour of his house. We were in a small closet of a room with bookshelves on three sides that would be used for his library, he said, as soon as he bought some books. Luke Levarose, my new neighbor, said he'd always wanted to read books. "Now I finally have the time."

"Oh," I said, wanting to know what made him too busy to read.

"I took my dollar and bought some chewing gum. Sold the

chewing gum and bought some candy. Sold the candy and bought some cigarettes."

"You sell cigarettes?" I felt queasy. Cigarettes killed.

"Nah!" he said. "I'm a consultant to stock brokers and financial planners."

"Consultant?"

"I give tips. You want to buy something. I know where you can get it."

What something? What is he talking about?

"I'm glad to meet you, Dessa. I am so honored to have you as my neighbor."

Wow! I thought. I liked Luke.

By July, I could walk on my second floor. In August, I walked up the stairs and found Luke, the country boy, lying on top of Lunalyn. He turned to look at me and didn't stop what he was doing. After a smile and a wink, he said, "I saw and I bought. This is how the country boy does what he does." He showed me a cog stone tattoo on his right wrist and I rushed down the stairs and told Leonard. Leonard told Ishmael. Ishmael told Lunalyn. Lunalyn told Luke.

A week later, Luke came to speak to me. "You have a big mouth, Dessa," he said.

"You have your own house," I said. "Why mine?"

"I was helping you, Dessa."

We were standing on the un-walled second floor and he was too close.

"I baptized your house for you," he said.

That afternoon Luke showed Leonard and me a surveyor's marker at the curb between our two houses. "I measured," he said.

"Measured what?" Leonard asked.

"You're trying to take over my property," Luke said.

"You're nuts!" Leonard walked away leaving me with Luke.

"I'm a country boy," Luke told me and smiled. "In the country we don't let an inch go without getting paid for the inch."

What is he talking about?

Later, Leonard told me not to pay attention. How was I not going to pay attention to a neighbor?

The following week Lunalyn married Luke in Las Vegas.

Two weeks later a representative from the gas company said the gas line couldn't be installed. A Lunalyn Levarose had called and reported that our gas line was on her property.

The Westbruk Building Inspector, Mr. Sloane, dropped by to tell us that Luke Levarose had called to report that our house was too close to his property line. We would have to pay a surveyor to determine the exact property line between the houses. Until then all work on the house would have to cease.

"What the hell is the matter with you two?" Leonard screamed at Lunalyn.

"You owe us!" Lunalyn screamed back.

Luke walked out of his house and stood behind his wife. "Don't fool with a country boy," he said in a slow drawl.

"Fire her!" Leonard told Ishmael.

"She's my daughter."

The next day, Mr. Sloane, the building inspector, was at our property again. Lunalyn was holding up page 16 of our blue prints. After a careful search of our plans, Lunalyn had ascertained that our house would be too high and she felt that she, being a good citizen, should point it out to the city.

Leonard had a surveyor out to the lot the next day. We didn't owe our neighbor an inch. The gas company agreed to go ahead. The Building Inspector, Mr. Sloane, a heavy set man with a graying moustache and a balding pate, decided against climbing to the top of the house to measure the height. And as the plans had been okayed by the city and it was obvious the plans were being closely adhered to, we could go on building.

"We're not done, city boy," Luke told Leonard.

"Fire her!" Leonard told Ishmael.

"She's my kid," Ishmael said. "If she goes, I go."

"Then you go," Leonard said.

Ishmael walked off our property, got into his black 95 Chevy pickup and drove off. Luke and Lunalyn walked into their house.

"What are we going to do? I asked Leonard when we got home.

He was slumped in a chair and looked so bad he scared me. "We can handle it, Dessa," he said.

Is he crazy? How were we going to build a house without somebody on the job who knew what to do?

Leonard called John, the architect. He agreed to take over Ishmael's job if I would stay at the site, watch things and phone him if I noticed something that needed tending to. What something? How would I know if anything was wrong? My throat hurt and my stomach ached.

When Leonard and I went to check for rain damage after a small down pour on November 9th, a police car was waiting at the curb and I spotted Luke and Lunalyn watching us from their front window.

"How can I help you?" Leonard asked the policeman.

"Your neighbors have reported that you harass them," the clean-shaven young man said.

Leonard bit his thumbnail then ran to the Levarose's house. When Luke opened the door before my

husband knocked, Leonard yelled,
"Are you crazy?"

The officer was behind Leonard
when Luke said, "I guess you can see
what I mean, Officer. Here I am as
peaceable as all get out."

"You're nuts!" my husband
screamed. He lifted his hand as if he
were going to hit Luke.

I grabbed his arm. Leonard
pulled away from me and walked
back to the building site.

"We'll never walk on their
property again," I told the policeman
as we stood at the curb in front of
our lot.

As soon as he drove off, Luke
came outside. "Goes to show you,"
he said, "you better not mess with
this country boy."

The run in with the policeman
and the fact that we were stuck with
the Levaroses as neighbors put
Leonard into doldrums he couldn't
seem to shake. I would have joined
him if I hadn't been so busy
watching men erect walls, lay floors
and nail ceilings. The roofers
installed red tiles. The plasterers
plastered walls while standing on
stilts. To the west I could see the

ocean, Catalina Island and San Pedro. To the south were the wetlands. To the east, the Saddle Back Mountains. I tried not to look north toward Luke and Lunalyn.

"Hi!" I said when the cell phone rang.

"You're not going to believe this, Dessa." Leonard sounded so agitated. He'd been in business for more than 40 years, he said. "And nobody's ever duped me like this."

I called Ishmael.

The next morning, Ishmael stood without saying a word while the plumber told me he hadn't put in the pipe that would connect water to the kitchen, the electrician said he hadn't connected electricity to any plug in the living room, and the painter said he had brought the wrong paint for the wine cellar.

"What can we do about it?" I asked each man.

"Well, it will involve this and that and more money," is how I heard the answers. The "more money" part was shouted, I thought.

When we finally sat at the top of the stairs, Ishmael said, "Why did you call me, Dessa? What do you want to say?"

I wanted to say a lot of things, like tell me what happened to your cog stone tattoo. Do you know a man named Leo? What can you tell me about Leo's Grandpa? These were the things I wanted to know. Instead I showed him the official looking envelope I had been carrying in my jeans pocket.

"What's that?" he said.

"It's a letter that says you owe child support," I said. "It's a letter that says Leonard and I were supposed to garnish part of your pay each week and send it to the County Attorney's office. It's a letter that says eighteen thousand dollars is owed to the county attorney. It's a letter that says that this is the tenth letter we've received on this subject." Somebody had been signing Leonard's name to all the letters that had come by registered mail. I was so mad at Ishmael.

He grabbed the envelope out of my hand and ran down the stairs to the Levarose house, knocked on the door and yelled, "Lunalyn! Get out here!" He kept yelling "Lunalyn!"

over and over again like Marlon Brando yelled "Stella" in *STREET CAR NAMED DESIRE.*

Luke opened the door, eyed Ishmael, and, then, walked past him to where I stood on the sidewalk. His long hair looked as if it hadn't been cut or combed for weeks. His face looked like it hadn't been shaved for days. He smelled of liquor and vomit. "She left me," he said.

Ishmael put his hand on Luke's shoulder.

"She's pregnant," Luke said. "She took off with this country boy's baby in her belly."

"Where did she go?" Ishmael asked.

Luke cried, "I think she went camping."

Camping? Ishmael looked so much like my cog stone induced dream Leo; I wanted to help him. But I steeled myself and said, "How are you going to pay off the eighteen thousand?"

He took a checkbook out of his back pocket, wrote a check for eighteen thousand, handed it to me, put his arm around Luke and walked with him into Luke's house.

When the check cleared, I drove to the end of Cabrillo Avenue, parked and walked on the dirt trail past where the stable used to be, to the area where Monney and I had first seen Lunalyn next to the white tent. The tent was there.

When I got back to the building site the painting contractor, a man of about 25, dressed in white overalls told me that I shouldn't have left the job. "We need somebody to coordinate," he said. "That bastard you hired to do the plumbing has held up my men for hours."

"I offered to pray about it," the plumber, another young man about twenty-five said. "I told him Jesus will help us."

I walked outside and called Ishmael's cell.

"Who do I remind you of?" he asked.

"Somebody called Leo."

"That's my father's name," he said.

"Could you tell me about your father?" I asked.

"I need to find my daughter," Ishmael said.

I told him where she was and said goodbye.

Then I pushed numbers on the phone again. "Hi, Celia," I said to my husband's secretary. "Can I speak to Leonard?" I didn't know how to deal with plumbers and painters. I wanted Leonard to come and help me.

"I think you should sit down, Dessa," Celia said. *What is she talking about?* She sounded so odd. "The paramedics are here."

"Huh?" My throat hurt. I could feel my heart beat.

"I think Leonard's had a stroke," she said. "I was just about to call you."

"Only relatives can see him," the nurse at the Larchwood Hospital said.

"I'm his wife." For better or worse, I thought. My throat and eyes hurt.

"Oh." The nurse handed me a nametag to paste on my t-shirt.

An IV was attached to Leonard's wrist. He was shivering. When I

walked across the room and hugged
him, he didn't stop shaking. Please.
Please. Please. I prayed. "Does it
help that I love you?" I asked. I did
love him. And it was the wrong time
for such an important epiphany. I
was too scared.

Leonard trembled. I hugged him
and held him as tight as I could,
tighter and tighter until I felt the
shaking stop. "Do you know what's
wrong?" I asked. I wanted to hear
his voice. I wanted to see if he could
pronounce the word stroke. Did
people with strokes shiver?

"Potassium," he said.

"Potassium?" *What kind of
disease is potassium*?

"You gotta take me home,
Dessa."

In the hall I phoned Doctor
Antonmer, my husband's doctor.
"When are you coming?" I asked.

"I can't come," he said.

"Is there something wrong with
you?" I asked.

"It's protocol," Doctor Antonmer
said. "Larchwood isn't my
hospital."

Protocol? What an ugly word!
"He wants to go home," I said.
"What is potassium?"

"He shouldn't go home till the
doctor on call gives the okay,"
Doctor Antonmer said. "He's
suffering from potassium depletion."

"What does that mean?" I asked.

"People can die from it," the
doctor said.

"He wants to go home," I
repeated.

"That would be too dangerous."

"You have to stay," I told
Leonard.

"No way, Dessa."

"Yes way," I said. "You can't
get potassium at home."

"You're bossy," Leonard said
and took my hand.

We hadn't held hands for a long
time. I could feel tears in my eyes
and willed myself not to cry.

Doctor Stevenson, a smiling
man, made his rounds in the early
evening. "I know you," he told my
husband.

"I remember you." Leonard
wasn't smiling.

"I have to wash my hands,"
Doctor Stevenson said.

"We gotta get outa here," my husband whispered.

"You have to be examined," I said.

"You want that quack to examine me?" Leonard got out of bed.

I pushed him back in. He got out again and was one handedly putting his clothes on while his left wrist was still attached to the potassium feeding IV.

I couldn't catch my breath.

"The guy's a quack," Leonard said, putting his feet into his brown loafers. "I ran a credit check on him."

"Why would you run a credit check on him?" I was pretending to be calm as my heart pulsed in my forehead.

"Lots of people have sued him for malpractice. You can't let him touch me, Dessa."

"What is this? Lie down and let the doctor examine you!"

"Have I ever lied to you?" Leonard ripped out the IV.

I turned on the cell phone that wasn't allowed in the hospital room, called Doctor Antonmel and shivered and stuttered as I reported the situation.

"Okay!" Doctor Antonmel said. "What's Stevenson's first name?"

"What's Stevenson's first name?" I asked Leo.

"Fred."

"Fred," I told the doctor.

We sat in Doctor Antonmel's office forty-five minutes later. Leonard was going to have to be monitored, eat potassium-enriched foods, and take potassium pills until his potassium count went up. He couldn't drive until it was up, the serious, gray haired doctor told us. The fourteen medical books on his large teak desk were all opened to "P" for potassium.

It was ten more days before I went back to the building site. My new house was almost finished. How had so much gotten done?

"Ishmael took over," the painting contractor said.

Why? I wondered.

The inspectors inspected. This needed fixing. That needed redoing. But if we did the fixing and redoing, the inspectors would come out in three weeks again. If they approved what they saw, we could move in.

"How do you feel?" I asked Leonard.

"Fine," he said.

"How is he doing?" I asked Doctor Antonmel.

"Not so good," the doctor said. "Those potassium numbers aren't going up."

"Why?" I asked.

"Blood pressure pills deplete potassium."

"Does he need blood pressure pills?"

"His blood pressure is too high," the doctor said. "Your new house has caused him a lot of stress, Dessa."

"Leonard, I love you."

"So what else is new?"

"I need you to stick around."

He kissed me. He still knew how.

Doctor Antonmel kept changing Leonard's blood pressure medicine until the second week in December when the potassium numbers began to make a slow upward climb.

By the end of January 2003 our house was finished, thanks to John Carris, our architect, and Ishmael Arons, the superintendent who had supposedly quit the job. Ishmael never walked on our property again but I was told that he stayed at Luke's house and shouted orders. John gave him a copy of our blue prints so when a sub had a question he walked next door and asked Ishmael.

The only thing left was a major architectural clean up.

On the morning of Tuesday, February 12, 2003, I went to meet the special architectural cleaner. It was pouring outside. Inside nothing leaked. We had hot water. The stove worked. Rain obscured my view, but I knew where the Wetlands and the Pacific Ocean were. It was too bad that Luke lived next door but, at least, Leonard was getting better.

The wet, skinny, special architectural cleaner moved his mops, pails and other supplies into the garage as I watched. Then the rain let up and I walked outside to examine my new purple and blue, lavender and rosemary garden. The fragrance after the rain smelled better than my most expensive perfume.

Luke and Lunalyn walked out of their house. So she's back, I thought. Luke looked the way he had when I last saw him, unkempt, unshaved and a little drunk. Lunalyn looked like Luna in my cog stone induced dreams except that she was very pregnant. She waddled into the street in front of my house and Luke wobbled after her. I couldn't make out what she said to him. He yelled, "Not to this country boy, you ain't!"

She said something else to him. He slapped her face. Luna fell forward into my lavender. I ran to help her. Luke socked her in the stomach before I got to her.

"She's pregnant!" I yelled.

He was trying to sock her again when an arrow shot through the air and pierced his back. His blood spurted like water in a fountain as he fell on top of Lunalyn. I stood still for a moment, too scared to move, then, I screamed and pushed him off her.

Lunalyn turned over, looked at Luke and shuddered before she took

my hand and let me pull her up. She
was heavy. My back and arms were
still aching from the exertion when
Ishmael's pickup turned the corner,
brakes squeaking. Lunalyn got in to
the truck and they sped away.

When the police came and
pronounced Luke dead, the skinny
cleaning man acted as witness. I was
too shaken to answer a question.

32.

Dear Dessa,

*Sometimes I feel that I met you in
a different lifetime. That's not
possible, is it? But you did know my
father's name was Leo. He and my
mother have been dead for a long
time and I still miss them.   My great
grandpa and his girlfriend Luna
raised my dad. Luna and my great
grandpa were movie extras, models
and thieves. All our relatives and
ancestors were outlaws. When they
had money they lived grand. When
they didn't they stole what they*

needed and lived in card board boxes on Cardboard Beach or hid in the mists on the Westbruk Wetlands. Great Grandpa was a remarkable archer. He used to pretend he was shooting Luna in the back, and she pretended to die. But, unlike me, Great Grandpa never killed anyone with his arrows. Even so, he was responsible for many deaths because he couldn't swim and was a paid lifeguard. When Great Grandpa got old my dad seduced Luna. She was my mother.

I hoped I wouldn't become an outlaw, but until I worked for you I always stole from my employers. I had my cog stone tattoo removed because I thought if I didn't have the tattoo, I'd change my ways.

All the women in my family ask the men in their lives to put a cog stone tattoo on their right or left arm in return for sexual favors. They figure if a man would submit to the pain, he'd treat them pretty well.

Men in my family tattooed themselves to remember who they were.

When I was seventeen, I got a girl pregnant. She died shortly after she birthed Lunalyn.

I first saw my daughter in Solly's Grocery Store. I was there to steal a can of beets. Lunalyn was sitting in her maternal grandmother's grocery cart. My baby was about nine months, dressed in pink and so beautiful, I gasped when I saw her. She looked like my mother, Luna.

Lunalyn's maternal grandmother reached for a can of artichoke hearts and all the cans on the shelf toppled. The noise startled Lunalyn and she started to cry. I picked her up and ran out of the store while her grandmother screamed, "Kidnapper! Kidnapper!" Over and over again.

I should have left Lunalyn with her maternal grandmother. I don't know how to be a father.

Lunalyn has three children. So she wouldn't have to do jail time for child abandonment, I promised to provide for the three tots. Lunalyn said she was sending the children the money. I didn't know she wasn't taking care of it.

I want to apologize for the problems my daughter and I have caused you. I know we contributed to your husband's illness and for that I'm truly sorry.

I'm tired, Dessa, and hope my time on earth ends soon. When the people in my family die, they get into the fetal position, turn east and put cog stones on their shoulders. I'll do the same or Lunalyn will it do it for me.

I wish you well.
Sincerely, Ishmael Aron

GOD, Leo is dead. He's actually dead! Grandpa didn't murder Luna. Please don't let them haunt me anymore.

* * *

I folded the letter, stuck it in its envelope, put it and my cog stone in my sweater drawer between the purple cashmere and yellow angora.

Then I glommed on to Leonard like a barnacle sticks to the bottom of a ship.

Arthur and Eli packed and arranged for the haulers when we moved to our new house. Leonard wasn't up to it and I was too busy hovering.

Once we were settled, I got up earlier than Leonard did. I went to sleep later. If he took a nap, I put my fingers under his nose to feel if he was breathing. Hating sports, I sat with Leonard in front of the TV and watched any event he chose. I also hate cooking, but took it up to make sure that he ate potassium rich foods. As soon as I found out that there is lots of potassium in bananas, cantaloupes and potassium fortified juices such as V8 and prune, I gave up cooking, but still stuck to my husband like rubber cement.

In September, Leonard said, "Leave me alone, Dessa. I'm fine."

"Oh."

I called Doctor Antonmel and said, "Leonard says he's fine. He doesn't want me to watch him all the time."

"He is fine, Dessa," the doctor said. "Healthy people don't need constant watching."

"Oh!"

I called Monney. "Monney," I said. "I need to talk."

"I don't have time," Monney
said. "Could you do me a favor?"
    "What?"
    Monney had become a Westbruk
Wetlands Land Trust Docent. She
wanted me to follow a class of third
graders around the Wetlands, making
sure no child veered from the trail.
Chasing after school kids didn't
sound like fun. But Monney could
sell me the Brooklyn Bridge and
Leonard wanted me out of his way,
so I went.

33.

Dear Dessa Dreams,
    Jenny used to be uglier than a
drunk skunk on Tuesday. Since she's
had a tummy tuck, nose job, breast
implants, her ears pinned back and
orthodontic work on her teeth she's
gorgeous and I'm in love. My best
friend John says if I didn't fall for
her when she was repulsive, why fall
now? What do you think?
Shallow in Boise, Idaho.

Dear Not So Shallow,

Tell John to nose out. The first time I saw one of my favorite places it was ugly and stank more than your drunk skunk on Wednesday. Jenny and the Westbruk Wetlands improved. I say jump on the improvers' bandwagon. That's the best place to be.
Sincerely, Dessa Dreams.

John Carris, the architect, called a few weeks ago. He said, "*HOUSE OF ARCHITECTURAL EXCELLENCE* wants to feature your house in their January issue."

"Wow!" I said, then, changed my mind. "I love this house but please, no, John."

"It could help publicize the Westbruk Wetlands," he said. "You could tell them why you love it so much."

"I'll think about it," I said.

I thought about it. Would it help John, my architect?

"No," he said when I called. "I'm never going to design another

house. Well, maybe my own
someday."

There was silence on the line and
I imagined his bushy eyebrows
wiggling.

"I thought it could help you," he
said. "I thought it would be good
publicity for the Wetlands."

I knew that people who read
*HOUSE OF ARCHITECTURAL
EXCELLENCE* wanted to look at
pictures of glorious houses and
probably wouldn't be interested in
the Wetlands.

But I had to tell somebody how
important the Wetlands are. The
information needed passing on. Who
would I tell?

And then I knew.

I'm now a history docent for the
Westbruk Wetlands Land Trust and
give my spiel to the most important
people.

Epilogue

I have fifteen minutes to talk to these third graders. Fifteen minutes to tell them how important this place is. I need to let them know that the Westbruk Wetlands are estuarial wetlands, a place where fresh water meets the ocean. I have to let them know that estuarial wetlands rival great prairies and rain forests in their life supporting properties. How do I communicate that we're lucky to be here? How do I convey that California Brown Pelicans, California Least Terns, Belding's Savannah Sparrows, American Peregrine Falcons, all endangered species, and one wrinkled old lady have been rejuvenated on these sacred grounds?

The students are quiet. They wait for me to say something. Maybe if I don't talk they'll get it just by being here. Would they sit in silence for fifteen minutes?

"Are you crazy?" the Western Fence Lizard says. He's doing pushups in front of me.

I take off my gray sweatshirt and tie the long sleeves around my waist. "Hello," I say.

"Hello," the children answer.

"My name is Dessa Halom Lechmann." I reach into my jeans pocket and pull out my cog stone, glad to have a use for it again. "This is a cog stone. Skeletons and cog stones have been unearthed, dug up, on this mesa where we are. The skeletons were in the fetal position facing east."

"What's a fetal position?" asks a child with bright red hair, glasses and freckles.

I scrunch down to demonstrate, my Jeans too tight for the maneuver. When did stiffness become a way of life? I wiggle around to pull myself up.

"The cog stones and skeletons have been carbon dated to show an age of more than 9000 years. Imagine!" I continue.

"I can't," says the red haired girl.

"I'll tell you about it," I say. "Thousands of years ago snow melted on top of the mountains and rushed with the river to meet the sea. So many birds and ducks flew in the sky; they almost eclipsed the sun. Animals roamed the land. Fish swam in the water. Plants with purple and yellow blossoms perfumed the ground. So did plants with edible red berries. The people that lived here were good to each other and the land." *Am I losing them?*

Great Blue Heron waves to me. "Tell them a story," it says. "Fraaahnk braak."

"What story?" I ask.

"Fraaahnk braak," Great Blue Heron answers. "You'll think of one."

And I do.

"Nine thousand years ago," I tell the children. "There was a woman who lived on this mesa and she looked like me."

"Was she old like you?"

Am I old? "She was the same age as I am," I say.

"How old is that?"

"She had exactly the same amount of wrinkles as I do," I say. "She was just as stiff."

"Did she have blonde hair?"

"No," I say. "My blonde hair comes out of a bottle. She had dark hair or maybe it was gray. And her two front teeth were missing. So I guess she didn't look exactly like me because I have my two front teeth."

"This woman," I continue, "was worried. She knew that the Westbruk Wetlands would be perfect as long as the people who lived there were kind to each other and good to the land. How am I going to get the people to keep being good and kind? she asked herself.

"That night the sky was dark and the moon was full. A star named Cog was extremely unhappy because other stars made fun of him. He wasn't shiny enough. He wasn't big enough. Sometimes, when Cog was tired; his light would dim. Sometimes his light went out.

"His mother told the other stars to let Cog alone. 'Some stars are weak,' she said.

"'Cog's just a child," his father said. 'He'll get stronger when he's older.'

"'And his grandmother said, 'Cog will be the most important star someday.'

"'Why do you say that?' Cog's mother asked.

"'Because Cog will be used to teach earthlings the most important things," the grandmother said. 'And when earthlings know the most important things, they will be able to save the universe.' Then the grandmother's starlight went out and she died. Cog was very sad.

"Other stars had heard what the Grandmother had said about Cog and they were jealous. 'Why should Cog be most important?' they asked.

"'He won't be,' said a shiny star. 'I'll be the most important.'

"Shiny Star shot through the sky. Other stars followed. They circled Cog and pushed and shoved.

"Cog, sad about his Grandmother's death and not very strong, didn't know how to defend himself. So he stayed where he was receiving hit after hit, bump after bump, until he fell from the sky to the north Mesa of the Westbruk Estuarial Wetlands. On ground impact Cog turned into a stone.

"In the morning when the sun came up pink from the east, the old woman with the missing front teeth found the stone and immediately knew it was special. 'You are here

to pass on information, aren't you?'
she said to Cog. 'If I can carve a
whole bunch of stones to look like
you, I can use them to teach people
what needs to be taught.'

"By afternoon the woman had
carved three cog stones. Before the
year was out she and her friends had
carved hundreds of stones that
looked like Cog.

"When the moon was full and the
stars were bright the carved stones
twinkled and people treated each
other and the Wetlands well.

"But then the cog stones
disappeared and people who lived
here thousands of years ago left the
area.

"New people came. They dug
irrigation ditches, erected a dike,
stopped the flow of the ocean into
the clear waters, and shot more birds
and ducks than they could eat.

"The ducks and birds that weren't
shot flew away. The fish died.
People got sick. Native plants
stopped growing. The whole place
stunk and the Wetlands were ruined.

"More new people came. Some
of these people found the lost cog
stones. The cog stones twinkled at

the people who found them. 'Are these stones trying to say something?" the people asked.

"One man said, 'I think we're supposed to save something.'

"A woman said, 'Westbruk Wetlands. Westbruk Wetlands. Save the Wetlands.'

"Some people planted plants that used to be native to the area. Some people excavated the dirt and let the ocean meet the clear water again. Pretty soon the birds and ducks flew back. The fish began to swim in the pools again. And I get to tell you how wonderful this place is. And you get to tell other people."

When the children leave, Rattlesnake slithers by. Great Egret waves its wing. Coyote winks at me.

I go home and kiss my husband.

"Are you all right, Dessa?" he asks.

"Yes," I say. "I am."

About Diane Schochet

Diane Schochet graduated from UCLA, majored in Theater Arts, has a real estate broker's license, taught school (4th grade, community college literature, English as a Second Language), directed, produced and acted in Community Theater productions, was a creative dramatics consultant for school districts, museums, and community theaters, took writing classes all over Southern California, including advanced novel workshops through the UCLA novel writing program, wrote two plays produced by a professional children's theater group. Her non-fiction profiles include: weddings, chili cook offs, old hockey players, elephant keepers, and other kooky stuff have been published in periodicals such as Career, Porthole, Active Times and 4H.